Praise for the Novels of Mindy Mejia

LEAVE NO TRACE

"Mindy Mejia's latest is riveting."

—*US Weekly*

"Mejia's thrilling tale works both as an engaging mystery and a haunting meditation on grief, abandonment, and the lost places within ourselves. Brutal, devastating, and utterly riveting."

—*Kirkus Reviews* (starred review)

"The author uses Lake Superior's violent storms and the Boundary Waters' forbidding wilderness to intensify the story's emotional impact and heighten its exploration into the unpredictability of half-buried secrets."

—*Booklist* (starred review)

"Atmospheric . . . arresting."

—*Publishers Weekly*

"Mejia's writing crosses back and forth between exquisite literary descriptions and thrilleresque escapes and acts of violence."

—*New York Journal of Books*

"With intensely complicated characters, a fast-paced plot, lots of twists and turns, and an impeccable ending, *Leave No Trace* is the type of book one finishes in one sitting, preferably with rain pattering on the window and a cup of coffee in hand."

—*Minnesota Monthly Magazine*

"Spellbinding. . . . Dark and atmospheric, with palpably vivid details and complex characters harboring plenty of secrets, *Leave No Trace* is the perfect combination of gorgeous prose and edge-of-your-seat storytelling. Clear your calendar, this is a book you'll want to swallow in one sitting. A stunner!"

—Kimberly Belle, internationally bestselling
author of *The Marriage Lie*

"A tense and gripping read that plumbs the depths of grief and longing, *Leave No Trace* is as thrilling as a whitewater rapid and as dark as the Minnesotan wilderness itself. Mejia has a gift for creating characters who feel like family, and by the end of this book I would have followed her gutsy speech-therapist heroine Maya to the ends of the earth. Through twist after twist, this riveting story will have you asking yourself just how far you would go to find out exactly where you came from."

—Amy Gentry, internationally bestselling
author of *Good as Gone*

"I fell in love with Mindy Mejia's *Everything You Want Me to Be*, and with *Leave No Trace* she solidifies her position as one of my go-to authors. . . . This novel deserves the top spot on your reading list!"

—Hannah Mary McKinnon, author of *The Neighbors*

"Set against the backdrop of Minnesota's Boundary Waters, Mindy Mejia continues to create characters that are both vulnerable and strong as they navigate the wild terrain through seemingly impossible relationships. *Leave No Trace* is a thrill ride of a novel that captures the ferocity of both nature and humankind."

—Karen Katchur, author of *River Bodies*

"Mindy Mejia's *Leave No Trace* leaves the reader breathless: Daring characters, a suspenseful story you will tear through, and the ticking clock of an approaching dark, cold Minnesota winter. Riveting."

—Lori Rader-Day, award-winning author of *The Black Hour*

"Riveting and beautifully rendered, *Leave No Trace* hooks you from the first page and never lets go. A must-read thriller."

—Laura McHugh, award-winning and
internationally bestselling author of
The Weight of Blood and *Arrowood*

"*Leave No Trace* is a masterful gem with that rare combination of provocative and magical descriptions, compelling characters, and a breathtaking, heart-pounding plot. . . . I haven't been this transported by a journey in the woods since reading Cheryl Strayed's *Wild*. This story will linger with readers long after the last page is turned."

—E. C. Diskin, author of the bestseller
Broken Grace

"This psychological thriller is a triumph."

—*Minneapolis Star-Tribune*

"If you couldn't tear yourself away from *Everything You Want Me to Be*, you definitely need to pick up this new book by Mindy Mejia."

—*Bustle*

"Mindy Mejia kicks things up a notch, delivering another nail-biting page-turner that grabs you early and never lets go."

—The Real Book Spy

"Excellent. . . . A strong sense of place infuses *Leave No Trace*, especially the expansive Boundary Waters—a place of wild beauty."

—*The Associated Press*

EVERYTHING YOU WANT ME TO BE

People's Best New Books Pick, *The Wall Street Journal*'s Best New Mysteries, 2017's Best Fiction Books

—*Bustle*

12 Books *Gone Girl* Fans Should Have on Their Wish List

—*BookBub*

"Fans of Gillian Flynn's *Gone Girl* will devour this fast-paced story."

—*InStyle*

"Ms. Mejia displays the enviable ability and assurance of such contemporaries as Megan Abbott and Laura Lippman in convincingly charting inter-generational passion and angst."

—The Wall Street Journal

"Readers drawn to this compelling psychological thriller because of its shared elements with Gillian Flynn's *Gone Girl* (2012) will be pleasantly surprised to discover that Mejia's confident storytelling pulls those themes into an altogether different exploration of manipulation and identity."

—Booklist (starred review)

"In the spirit of *The Lovely Bones* and *Everything I Never Told You* . . . compelling."

—Marie Claire

"A suspenseful and heart-wrenching thriller about ambition, obsession, and what happens when the lies we tell about ourselves become indistinguishable from the truth."

—Robin Wasserman, author of Girls on Fire

"For fans of *Gone Girl*, *The Girl on the Train*, and *Big Little Lies*."

—Book Riot

"An excellent book full of surprises, fans will be thrilled to find that this is one tale that falls into that very slim category of rare 'one-day' reads."

—Suspense Magazine

"Twisty . . . a page-turner, and compelling."

—Minneapolis Star-Tribune

ALSO BY MINDY MEJIA

Everything You Want Me to Be

The Dragon Keeper

LEAVE
NO TRACE

A Novel

MINDY MEJIA

EMILY BESTLER BOOKS
—
ATRIA
New York   London   Toronto   Sydney   New Delhi

EMILY
BESTLER
BOOKS

ATRIA

An Imprint of Simon & Schuster, Inc.
1230 Avenue of the Americas
New York, NY 10020

First Emily Bestler Books/Atria Paperback edition July 2019

EMILY BESTLER BOOKS / ATRIA PAPERBACK and colophon are trademarks of Simon & Schuster, Inc.

For information about special discounts for bulk purchases, please contact Simon & Schuster Special Sales at 1-866-506-1949 or business@simonandschuster.com.

The Simon & Schuster Speakers Bureau can bring authors to your live event. For more information, or to book an event, contact the Simon & Schuster Speakers Bureau at 1-866-248-3049 or visit our website at www.simonspeakers.com.

Interior design by Alexis Minieri

Manufactured in the United States of America

10 9 8 7 6 5 4 3 2 1

Library of Congress has cataloged the hardcover edition as follows:

Names: Mejia, Mindy, author.
Title: Leave no trace : a novel / by Mindy Mejia.
Description: First edition. | New York : Emily Bestler Books/Atria, 2018. | Identifiers: LCCN 2018012230 (print) | LCCN 2018013880 (ebook) | ISBN 9781501177385 (ebook) | ISBN 9781501177361 (hardcover) | ISBN 9781501177378 (paperback)
Subjects: | BISAC: FICTION / Suspense. | FICTION / Mystery & Detective / General. | FICTION / General. | GSAFD: Mystery fiction. | Suspense fiction.
Classification: LCC PS3613.E4443 (ebook) | LCC PS3613.E4443 L43 2018 (print) | DDC 813/.6—dc23
LC record available at https://lccn.loc.gov/2018012230

ISBN 978-1-5011-7736-1
ISBN 978-1-5011-7737-8 (pbk)
ISBN 978-1-5011-7738-5 (ebook)

*For my mom, who read to me every night
and taught me the power and pull of story.
She also almost died a lot.
If there's a better way to breed a writer,
I haven't found it yet.*

———————————

LEAVE
NO TRACE

1

———

B Y THE TIME the boy in ward four attacked me, I'd already
nicknamed him The Lost One in my head. He'd been admitted a week ago, transferred from police to orderlies while
dozens of reporters swarmed the entrance, overwhelming security
in their struggle to get a clear shot of our newest, involuntary patient. Inside, he'd put up such a fight that three men had to hold
him down while they administered sedatives and brought him
straight into isolation. The boy who came back from the dead, the
newscasters called him. The picture they flashed, the only one they'd
gotten before he'd become a violent blur, showed a sunburned, lean
face and dark hair pulled back in a ponytail. His eyes were a ghostly
blue, the kind of eyes songs get written about.

Ward four wasn't on my rotation so I didn't see him after that,
but I heard about him everywhere. Cashiers at the gas station
chewed on their theories. Newspaper editorialists speculated on

worst case scenarios, calling him a savage and a murderer. The fascination bled into the Internet, where social media accounts popped up overnight. A fake Twitter handle had already gotten ten thousand followers, someone on Snapchat made him a Bitmoji avatar, and countless people on Facebook filled his timeline with unanswered questions. The entire city of Duluth was obsessed with him; I could practically feel thousands of eyes gazing up the hill toward Congdon Psychiatric Facility, trying to peer inside these old, brick walls.

A few days after his admission Dr. Mehta called me into her office. I was the assistant speech therapist on staff, my shiny, new title after earning my graduate degree from the University of Minnesota and getting promoted from orderly. It still hadn't sunk in, even five months later. Every time I put a note on a patient's record, my signature line popped up, startling me, like I was impersonating someone whose comments mattered. Me, Maya Stark, the recalcitrant kid who was suspended from high school, a professional therapist? I looked like I belonged on the opposite side of the couch. I was the maroon-haired punk girl who ran her German shepherd along the lake walk, making all the tourists snatch their kids out of harm's way. Yet here I was. Twenty-three years old and called in by the head psychiatrist to work with the most famous patient we'd ever had.

"I can't tell if he understands us or not," Dr. Mehta said, pacing behind her desk in a swirl of sari fabric. For a shrink, she rarely sat down. She also lint-rolled herself a lot because her wife fostered cats, like an illegal amount of them. "Understands the diction, that is. He knows perfectly well we're trying to communicate with him and he wants nothing to do with us."

Dr. Mehta was young, at least for being the senior psychiatrist in charge of an entire mental health facility. She'd made a name for herself authoring papers and conducting studies on the harmful effects of physical restraints and isolation on patients. The key to recovery, she proposed, was enabling the patient's sense of autonomy within a group dynamic. Treating them like humans. Imagine that.

"Are flashcards okay?" I figured I'd start slow.

Dr. Mehta nodded and sighed, pausing to stare at the blanks in the record on her computer. "We're looking for any response at this point. Anything at all."

I waited until after the dinner rounds were finished, when stomachs were full and the wind murmured invitations against the dark windows. This was the loneliest time of day, when you let yourself wish there was someone to talk to.

A veteran orderly named Stan admitted me into the locked outer doors of ward four and walked me down the linoleum hallway lined with isolation rooms on either side. A few patients stared at us through the windows. One was banging his fist dully on the glass, but the rest sat on their beds or paced. I counted eight in total, eight patients who weighed more than they knew. All of them pressed on Dr. Mehta's conscience until she could get them safely reintegrated into the common wards.

"I don't think you're gonna have any luck with him," Stan said, keys jingling at his hip. "He's completely ignored everyone who's gone in there except Carol."

Carol Kelley was the seventy-year-old kitchen attendant who brought meals to all the isolation patients. She clipped herbs from her own garden to garnish the mush and served it like she was having Sunday dinner with friends around her kitchen table. Everybody loved Carol, even the sociopaths.

"What does he do?"

"Examines things—his clothes, the mattress. Feels the walls. Likes to drag the bed over to the window so he can see out. Stands there pressing the glass. Sometimes it looks like he's trying to break the whole damn thing."

"Does he eat?"

"Some."

"Any response to his name?"

"Huh. Like a wall, that one. You could call him Tarzan and he wouldn't care."

Lucas was his name. Lucas Blackthorn. He'd been arrested for breaking and entering at an outfitter's store, attempted robbery of the store, and two counts of aggravated assault on the owners who'd caught him in the act.

Stan paused outside the room. "I'll be right here at the window."

"I can take care of myself."

"That's why I'm standing outside the door, and not between you and Tarzan."

Some of the orderlies resented my promotion, my leap from a blue-collar hourly wage into the hallowed ranks of the salaried, but not Stan. He gave me a grin, unlocked the door with a metal creak, and waved me inside. I stepped in and waited for it to shut behind me before looking up.

The patient faced the back of the room with his hands on the cement block wall in a push-up position. From the way he stood with his shoulders tensed and legs braced it looked like he was trying to move the entire wall. I took a step closer and noticed his hospital shirt was torn at the bottom and he'd used the missing strip to tie his hair back.

"Hello, Lucas."

He remained still for a second, but then surprised me by turning his head. I saw his face in person for the first time.

He wasn't a boy.

My brain stuttered on that one thought for what felt like a stupidly long time as our eyes met and held. Why did all the media keep calling him a boy? Lucas Blackthorn looked at least as old as me and stood a foot taller. His cheeks were hollow and shaded with the beginning of a beard. His skin was a deep reddish tan, not the pasty white of most of our long-term patients, and his eyes conveyed things that no first session speech therapy could have drawn out: intelligence and caution mixed with undisguised curiosity.

Moving slowly and deliberately, I walked to the bare mattress between us. There was no table, so we'd have to start the flashcards on the bed. He watched my progress, studying my hair. The short, pixie-cut combined with its dyed color grabbed a lot of patients' attention. One of the men in ward two, a lifer named Big George with a traumatic brain injury, even liked to touch the ends of it that swished in front of my ears. I made sure he stuck to the left side so he didn't get distracted by the tiny silver hoop earrings along my right ear. Lucas noticed those, too. I watched him catalog every part of me, absorbing the appearance of this outsider to his room, like someone would analyze a newly discovered insect. His gaze paused on the blue fabric bag I carried, his expression unreadable now.

I put a hand on my chest and waited until his attention snapped back to my face.

"I'm Maya." Three syllables. Slow rate, distinct pronunciation. I didn't smile. I'd never trusted strangers who smiled at me—they always wanted something.

Patting the place where my pulse beat too fast, I nodded and said it again. "Maya."

He swiveled back toward the wall, dismissing the insect. I glanced behind me where Stan was shaking his head through the lead glass. Shrugging, I started to pull out the flashcards when suddenly Stan's face changed. His eyes widened and his mouth opened in a warning I couldn't hear.

I hesitated and before I could turn around, a giant force threw me into the wall and something was being looped around my neck. The metal door shrieked as Stan wrenched it open and I was pulled back, my body turned into a human shield. The thing around my neck tightened and I panicked, unable to breathe. Lucas had my arms locked behind me in an impossibly strong grip. I fought against it, desperate to free myself.

"Keys," he said in a hoarse voice. I bowed my body against his, trying to find some slack in the cord around my throat, but met only a column of unyielding muscle. If anything, the cord grew tighter.

My vision started to contract, black creeping in at the edges. I kicked viciously, striking his shins so hard they should have snapped in half, and used the rest of my oxygen in the process. The last thing I saw before everything went dark was Stan's hand, holding out his ring of keys.

I came to on the floor in a gasping, head-pounding mess. Stan lay next to the door, unconscious, and Lucas Blackthorn was gone.

"Agghhh." I grabbed my head and waited for the air to work its way back through my body. When I could get up, I crawled over to check Stan's pulse and saw blood trickling down from his hairline. He was alive.

A noise came from the hallway. Lots of noises, as my ears started registering them.

I peeked out and saw patients at their isolation windows, banging and shouting. Farther down the hall, it became obvious what they were excited about: Lucas Blackthorn, trying to find the right key to get through the second set of doors.

Without any conscious thought, I slipped Stan's baton from his belt and darted down the hallway with Lucas's back the only thing in focus, my progress muffled by the noise from the other patients. At Stan's station I tripped the emergency security button and lifted the baton. Lucas was only a few feet away now, punching key after key into the old locks, oblivious to the electronic security square mounted above.

I waited, willing myself to breathe quietly while eyeing his upper arms, his thighs, the major muscle groups I could aim for without causing unnecessary injury. He couldn't have more than twenty pounds on me. Thirty, tops. My fingers flexed over the baton while I mentally traced the route from the front desk to this ward, counting the seconds until backup arrived. Then he flipped the keys over and found the badge, Stan's security badge, which he stared at for a split second before pressing it to the door, making it beep and flash green. I didn't hesitate this time. As soon as I heard the locks disengage, I swung the baton into his leg.

He stumbled into the outer hallway, still on his feet, and started to run for the exit at the end of the corridor. I launched myself at him, jumping on his back and sending us both crashing into the wall and rolling to the floor.

He scrambled to get up and I didn't care how famous he was, I didn't care if he was lost; there was no way this guy was escaping on my watch. I hooked my legs around his and locked the baton across his chest, trying to pin his arms. Shaking my hold, he flipped us both to our backs, crushing me underneath him, and grabbed for the baton.

Voices and footfalls thundered toward us.

"A little help," I yelled and immediately regretted it. The words were like fire racing through my bruised throat, and I couldn't help the moan that followed them. At my sound of pain, he released his grip on the baton and fell inexplicably still. We both paused in that crazy position—like a piggy-back ride tipped on its back—before his weight disappeared, lifted off me by the cavalry of orderlies and security staff.

"Stan!" I waved some of them toward the ward entrance, before being seized by a fit of coughing.

Automatically I covered my throat with my hands, trying to stop the convulsions while the team clamored around, practically tripping over me to secure our wayward patient. Their boots braced and stomped inches from my head, sending vibrations through the linoleum and into my skull, which felt as fragile as an egg on concrete. No one offered to help me up. Their voices sounded far away, eclipsed by the pull and drag of air in my throat, the unsteady rise and fall of my chest. Only the tremor in the floor, the possibility of being trampled, made me turn my head to the side and that's when I saw him watching me.

They'd flipped him on his stomach and pulled his arms behind him. He was putting up no resistance and barely seemed aware of their efforts to subdue him. For a strange, endless moment, our stillness separated us from the rush of legs flooding the corridor, from the shouts and determination swarming above. We stared at each other, our faces both resting on the cold, flecked tiles less than three feet apart.

Then a needle flashed in the fluorescent lights, the men picked him up, and Lucas Blackthorn was gone.

2

SHOULD HAVE stayed on site to write up the incident report, but I figured a full body assault earned me a little sick time and the idea of writing it at my kitchen table sounded infinitely more appealing than the desk I shared with the exercise therapist. I almost made it out of the building before Nurse Valerie caught me and dragged me back to the medical ward. As soon as my butt hit the bed, two more nurses appeared, raptor style, and they started tearing into me about the boy who came back from the dead.

"He's not a boy," was all I could say as they rubbed ointment on my neck. It was hard to swallow.

"He doesn't look like a teenager, that's for sure," Valerie replied, trying to give me a pill that I repeatedly rejected. Painkillers and I didn't mix. "He must have had to grow up fast out there in the woods, but they only show pictures of him as an adorable kid on the news."

"How do you think he survived all those years?" another asked and they started tossing out theories from the media. Reporters were falling all over themselves to cover every known moment of Lucas Blackthorn's life and mysterious reappearance. Hikers gave interviews about stories that had only been campfire yarns before, tales of strange sightings in the wilderness, noises and shadows that had sparked Bigfoot rumors, and every conversation ended with the same question: Where was his father?

Josiah Blackthorn had taken his son camping in the Boundary Waters ten years earlier and neither had been seen since, not until now, when Lucas had emerged from the wild—violent, uncommunicative, and alone. I'd wondered about the Blackthorns, too. Right now, though, the only thing that interested me was the distance between my head and my pillow. As they traded tidbits various journalists had dug up, I slipped my backpack over my shoulder and slunk away.

It was dark as I coasted down the hill from Congdon toward the giant shadow of Lake Superior. The entire city of Duluth, Minnesota, clung to the side of an ancient basalt ridge, fighting the slope toward the water, and you knew you were getting close to my neighborhood when the pavement started buckling like waves on a high wind. Paint peeled off crooked porches where old couches and lawn chairs faced the giant warehouses lining the docks. Lincoln Park was a hop, skip, and a world away from Canal Park, where tourists snapped pictures of the lift bridge, took their sightseeing cruises, and ate their fennel and watermelon salads. We didn't get a lot of fennel south of Piedmont.

When I pulled up in front of the house, I was surprised to see the lights on and Jasper out in the yard.

"How's my boy?" I opened the gate and a battering ram of slobbery muscle knocked into my legs.

Jasper barked and nosed into me, demanding attention.

"I could've used you today, Jazz." I bent down and he immediately flipped over to present his belly. For a German shepherd who prided himself on guarding our house from the dangers of everything from thieves to seagulls, belly scratches turned him into a grateful pile of ooze.

I obliged him for a while and let my bag slide to the ground. Even though the nights were still warm—practically mid-October and I couldn't even see my breath—I wasn't up for our usual evening walk today. Extra petting would have to suffice.

"Dr. Mehta—you remember her? She smelled like cats? Anyway, she asked me to go see a new patient."

Lucas Blackthorn's face swam in front of my gaze with that enigmatic expression that seemed oblivious to being pressed to the floor by a half dozen guards and orderlies. He'd been focused only on me and he seemed . . . stunned. Maybe he'd been upset that a girl had thwarted his escape. Maybe he'd been slapped by a moment of lucidity. It was hard to see an expression like that and avoid judgment or assigning meaning where there might be none, or at least none that readily translated outside the labyrinth of a patient's mind. I shook my head, forcing the image away.

"Look." I tugged down the collar of my hoodie. "Look at my neck."

Jasper obediently smelled my throat, licked the skin, and then snorted abruptly. Apparently the nurse's ointment wasn't tasty.

Laughing, I let us inside the house. As soon as the door opened, Jasper flattened me against the jamb, raced through the entryway, and sent up a torrent of barks from the kitchen. I followed in time to see him prancing in front of the table, tail wagging, as a man jumped up and backed around the wall, half behind my father.

They could've been brothers, the two men both wide-jawed, sun baked, and too big to fit comfortably on the kitchen chairs, but even with one look you knew who was in charge.

"For Christ sake, Butch. He can't lick you to death," Dad said, picking up his beer for another swig.

"Come here, Jasper." I called the dog to me and patted his neck before telling him to go lie down.

"How many times do I have to come here before he leaves me alone?" Butch Nelson crossed his menacing, tattoo covered arms, the tough guy pose at odds with the boyish rose of his perpetually wind-burned cheeks. As the first mate on my dad's salvage tug, he wasn't easily disturbed, but he'd been attacked by a stray when he was a kid and refused to see the point of any canine life since. He sat back down, careful to face the kitchen door where the dog waited with hopeful eyes.

"Jasper became anxiously-attached as a puppy. He has confidence issues." Dropping my backpack near the table, I glanced at the depth map covering the spot where I'd planned to write up my incident report with a ramen noodle and Oreo cookie dinner and the house to myself. Today was obviously not the day for plans. "What are you guys up to? I thought you were heading to Thunder Bay."

"Grant money came through." Butch grinned.

"You got it?"

Dad glanced up from the table, nodding, and I adjusted the hoodie to make sure it covered my neck. A hint of a smile passed over his face, but the logistics of the trip were already crowding it out. He was planning, navigating, submerged in the details.

"So which ship is it? The *Madeira*? The *Vienna*? The *Fitzgerald*?"

"The *Bannockburn*."

Our eyes met before he turned back to the map, leaving a sudden silence in his wake.

The *Bannockburn*. The ghost ship. I moved to the kitchen on autopilot and started looking through the cupboards, not sure at all if I had the stomach to eat.

My dad had spent most of his life on the water. His boat provided tugging and towing services in the summer and icebreaking in the winter, plowing the way for the thousand-foot lakers that lumbered in and out of the Duluth and Superior harbors, which—contrary to Minnesota's seemingly landlocked geography—was the largest freshwater port in the world. No matter how many ships he guided to safety, though, it was what lay underneath the surface that called to him. No one knew exactly how many ships Superior had taken. Most of the official crashes had been documented in the last hundred years, but add in the unregistered boats, the rum-runners during Prohibition, and all the countless vessels sailing before modern navigation or lighthouses and you might as well be looking at something the size of a mass grave and guessing how many bodies it could hold. Dad was just a kid when his father explained to him about the cold temperature of Superior, how the icy water pulled bodies down and kept them there, and he'd been fascinated by the cemetery at the bottom of the lake ever since. Salvage work came rarely because there wasn't any money in it, so Dad and Butch recently started applying for grants based on the historical and cultural value of the lost ships. Someone must have agreed, giving them a chance to steal back what Superior had swallowed.

They began murmuring, drawing routes and pointing out hazards while I found a brick of ramen noodles and popped it in the microwave. I watched the bowl spin until Dad's voice cut through my reverie. He'd gotten up for another beer and caught a glimpse of my neck.

"What the hell happened to you?"

I tugged the zipper on the hoodie higher, trying to cover as much skin as possible. If it looked half as bad as it felt, my neck must have been one solid bruise. "It's nothing."

"Maya." A two-syllable warning that wasn't going to tolerate any bullshit.

I sighed. "A patient tried to escape tonight. I was in his way."

"He strangled you?" Butch craned his head to try to see the evidence.

Refusing to make eye contact with either of them, I relayed the fight briefly in the most generic terms possible.

Butch started to ask another question, but I waved him off, telling him I couldn't discuss a patient's case. Dad's eyes shifted from my neck to the depth map, and he took a long drink.

"We're not going anywhere. We'll shelve the trip until spring." He cut off Butch's objections. "It'll give us more time to plan."

"Dad, no."

Ignoring the beep of the microwave, I followed him and planted my hands on the table when he would have folded up the map. "You're going."

"Look at your neck, Maya. That's unacceptable. I'm going to talk to Dr. Mehta—"

"No, you're not. I'm twenty-three years old and this is what I do. I got the job done tonight, and I'm going back to work tomorrow, and the day after that. Dr. Mehta knows what I'm capable of."

"She's—"

"We talked about this when I agreed to stay here," I reminded him.

My fingers spread over the shoals and dug into the dark basins. All their notes and arcs of possible routes had turned the lake into a biology class dissection of something still alive. "Dad, it's the *Bannockburn*. I wouldn't even be here if it wasn't for the *Bannockburn*."

He drew back. We hadn't talked about her in years and even then it had been about endings, not beginnings. His hand dropped to the western edge of the lake and brushed over the cliffs and towering pine forests where he'd met my mother.

She'd told me the story, one of the few she shared. A geology student at UMD, she'd been studying how ice formed in the cracks of the North Shore's basalt face and caused rock slides over time. It was why the world's largest lake was getting even larger; it ate the land around it. She needed to document the cliffs from the water and hired Brian Stark, a young salvage tug captain, to pilot her along the shore. He asked her out every time they sailed, as determined as the lake breaking against the rocks, but she didn't agree until he told her the story of the *Bannockburn*.

In 1902, a young crew set out on Lake Superior in the S.S. *Bannockburn* with 85,000 bushels of wheat in her hold. They didn't know the gales were coming, or maybe they did, but they didn't know enough to be afraid. Every November the lake turned gray, the water churned and raged against the coming winter, and hurricane-force winds whipped the waves into forty-foot crests. The lake became hungry.

The *Bannockburn* was downbound that day and spotted by two other ships also fighting their way through the storm. Then she vanished. A single life jacket printed with the boat's name washed up onshore three weeks later. A few other clues surfaced, fragments here and there, but the lake didn't give up any secrets. Countless ships had disappeared on Superior, but the *Bannockburn* was the only one sighted after she was lost. Tales of glimpsing the *Bannock-burn*'s profile on the horizon of the water spread through the Great Lakes. It sailed as a ghost ship on the waves, warning other boats of impending danger before disappearing into the wind.

Something about that had appealed to my mother, something my dad couldn't have predicted at the time, but it got him a date and—a few years later—a marriage and baby, too. My earliest memories were on Dad's tugboat, squealing at the empty horizon and claiming I'd seen a phantom ship as we sped into the endless blue. The *Bannockburn* was one of the great mysteries of Superior, and now Dad and Butch were going to chase it down.

"Don't worry about me." Ignoring the discomfort in my throat, I smiled at Butch. "I'll have Jasper for company."

Butch gave the dog a dirty look and grunted.

"And I still have the bathroom to finish. I was thinking about new hardware, because I don't like how—"

"Maya," Dad scanned me up and down, still searching for hidden wounds. "Someone just tried to kill you."

"He wasn't trying to kill me." And then, before I could stop it. "Trust me, I know the difference."

Pain glanced over Dad's face and suddenly neither of us knew what to say. There were too many ghosts in the room, and none of them had sunk with the *Bannockburn*. After a minute I mumbled goodnight, slung the backpack over my shoulder, and left the kitchen, forgetting my noodles in the microwave until I found them the next morning, a cold, tightly coiled lump that had lost any chance for salvage.

Jasper followed me into the bathroom, where I splashed water on my face and avoided looking at the angry, red line bisecting my neck, instead staring glassy-eyed at the handles of the knotty pine cabinet I'd installed last year. Nickel. Maybe brushed nickel. My throat ached and my head began to pound, but it wasn't until Jasper nudged me that I flipped the light off and crawled under my duvet.

He curled up at my feet, facing the door and the voices that drifted down the hallway, while I booted up the computer and began outlining my incident report. Hours later, long after Butch's truck had fired up in the driveway and Dad shuffled off to bed, after even Jasper's vigilance had faded to huffs and doggie snores, I was still awake with the ghosts.

3

THE NEXT DAY, after helping Dad load the pickup and promising to text every day and use the radio to hail him for emergencies, I clocked in at Congdon and went to make my rounds. I always walked the wards before my sessions; it let everyone know I was there and that today was a speech therapy day. Nobody liked surprises in a psychiatric facility.

During my rounds, I stopped and chatted with any patients open to it. Some saw my bright maroon hair coming and hit the decks. Others seemed starved for attention and followed me from one end of their ward to the other. Today's hot topic was the angry red bruise circling my neck. Eliza, a teenage cutter with some cleft palate issues, kept trying to touch the mark like it was a holy relic.

"Did it hurt?" she whispered.

"It sucked, Eliza. I don't recommend it."

She just stared at my throat.

"Are you working on your presentation for later?" Eliza was part of my advanced group being prepped for discharge. I'd assigned them all the task of speaking about their stay at Congdon, what had brought them here, and what they'd learned about themselves. There was no time requirement, no formal structure or underlying assessment, but it was probably the most important speech they'd ever have to make. If they could articulate their thoughts, find words big enough, true enough, they might find a way to own their stories.

"I've thought about it. I didn't write anything down yet like you asked us to." She dropped her head on the *s*'s, forcing the words out past the slight nasal emission.

"No problem, you've still got a few hours. Grab your journal and see what happens."

She glanced back up and met my eyes this time, hesitantly making that connection. It had taken months for her to become confident enough to do that. I acknowledged her progress with a smile and pointed to her room. "Go."

"I was about to say the same thing to you," said a voice behind me.

Swiveling, I found Dr. Mehta arching a perfectly plucked eyebrow.

"What are you doing here?" she asked.

"Working. Am I supposed to be at a meeting?" I panicked, pulling my phone out to double-check the schedule.

"I assumed you'd be taking some sick time, not submitting incident reports at three in the morning and preparing for your sessions the next day like nothing happened. Come on."

She nodded toward the exit and we headed to the opposite side of the building, where the medical ward and the administrative offices were located.

"How are you feeling?"

Wary of the direction we were taking, I shrugged. "Fine."

"I'll be sure to note your expressiveness in my comments. *Speech therapist ironically unable to communicate in more than monosyllables.*"

We both laughed and then she got serious again.

"I'm terribly sorry about what happened."

"Really, I'm fine. I don't need rest or medical attention. And hey, you said you were looking for any response, right? So that assignment should be listed with full credit in my next review."

"The assignment isn't over yet."

"What?" I stopped walking and Dr. Mehta paused a few paces ahead of me, waiting for me to catch up, until it became obvious I wasn't going to move. Finally, she gave in and turned around.

"He's still unresponsive. Every staff psychologist has attempted communication this morning and they get nothing. You're the only person in this building he's had any reaction to."

"So, I get to be his personal punching bag?"

"In the version I heard, *he* was *your* punching bag the last time you two met."

"That's not the point. I didn't think you promoted me to the position of brawler."

Dr. Mehta paced back in her tirelessly calm way. "You said you didn't need any rest. Now was that true or are you trying to overcompensate for a self-perceived but nonexistent weakness?"

Sometimes it was irritating having a psychiatrist for a boss. I shook my head, trapped. "I'm good."

Dr. Mehta smiled and swept an arm toward the medical ward doors in front of us. "Let's do a little experiment, shall we? He's fully restrained."

I took a deep breath to center myself and followed Dr. Mehta into the ward and all the way down the corridor to a private, high security room with an orderly posted outside.

Straps held Lucas to a hospital bed in the center of the room and handcuffs encased his wrists and ankles. He faced away from the door. There were no pictures in the room, no color, and no windows, just the smell of antiseptic and the sound of another patient moaning down the hallway. I drew closer to the bed where his leg was elevated in a sling. An ice pack covered most of his thigh, but the rest of his leg was exposed, revealing a network of scars.

"Hello again, Lucas." Dr. Mehta crossed the room to stand in his line of sight. "I've brought another visitor, this time an old friend of yours."

There was no movement from the patient, so I walked around and stood next to Dr. Mehta. From this angle I could see his face and was surprised by a fresh cut along the outside of his temple. Had he hit his head, too? Without thinking, I took a step closer. His eyes flickered up to mine and held.

No one in the room spoke. We stared at each other, unblinking, without expression. This look was nothing like the connection Eliza made with me earlier and a moment passed in which I had the unreasonable feeling that Lucas Blackthorn knew me, that he could've found my neck among hundreds of exposed throats. I lifted my chin, refusing to look away. Finally, he dropped his eyes and a flush of something crossed his features.

He opened his mouth experimentally and then spoke in a low, hoarse voice clearly unused to dialogue.

"Does your neck hurt?"

"Yes." I set my jaw.

He considered me, as if memorizing the exact shade of red on my skin before making his next effort at speech. "Sorry."

I nodded toward the cut on his face. "What happened to your head?"

He didn't answer and eventually Dr. Mehta spoke up.

"Lucas resisted his transfer to the medical ward and unfortunately hit his head on a door." Then she drew closer to the foot of the bed, glancing at the web of scars on his calf. There were long, paper-thin marks and fat, blunt scrapes in all stages of healing, the darker browns layered over faded patches like new saplings taking over an old growth forest. "The injuries to your legs, Lucas, remain a mystery."

"That's an easy one." I lifted the blanket up, revealing identical markings along the inside of his other leg, and met Lucas's stare. "You've been climbing trees. Right?"

He nodded almost imperceptibly, his eyes locked on mine, but when Dr. Mehta donned her glasses and moved in for a closer look, he kicked his good leg and lashed a foot at her face. The handcuffs cracked against the bed rail as she jerked back and I threw an arm in front of her, moving us both out of his range. Murmuring an apology, Dr. Mehta led me back into the corridor and shut the door.

"Are you all right?"

She clasped her hands under her chin and beamed. "Did you hear that? Two separate exchanges and he even initiated the first on his own. He's verbal and quite responsive when he chooses to be."

"Yeah, hurray. Did you just get kicked in the face?"

"I'm fine." She waved, already marching toward the ward entrance. "If he remains this lucid, we might even be able to facilitate some interviews with the Ely police."

My stomach clenched. "That's great. I'm glad I could help."

"You understand this is your primary case now."

"What? No." It came out louder than I intended and I lowered my voice, checking to see if anyone was in earshot. "You were there. You heard him. Perfect enunciation. Appropriate grammar, inflection, and word choice. He doesn't need speech therapy. He needs behavioral therapy."

It was absurd to diagnose that after maybe six words, tops, but she didn't even argue the point. "And you don't think you have a unique vantage point to help him?"

"I'm not a psychologist."

"Indeed, because you majored in speech pathology, focusing your attention on the outward projection of constructed, premeditated messages. One might wonder if you intentionally avoided the messy inner realities of psychology."

"Don't shrink me right now, doc."

"Impossible at any time." Her eyes still gleamed with the victory of Lucas's breakthrough.

"I'm not qualified for this. I wouldn't know what to do."

"I'll assist you at every stage."

"And my rotation is full. I'm busy helping Greta work on her *r*'s so someday she can pronounce her own name. And Big George, with his—"

"You were also a patient here once, Maya."

Her simple statement, voiced intentionally low so only I could hear it, killed the rest of the excuses in my throat.

In the four years I'd worked at Congdon, she'd never once brought up that fact. She'd treated me like any other employee, worse even—assigning me to the most aggressive patients, the foulest messes, the hardest shifts—and I'd always been grateful for that veneer of indifference. Now the reminder lay like an exposed nerve between us. We faced each other silently, boss and employee, doctor and patient. For a second, I forgot which one I was supposed to be.

She looked the same now as she had the first day we met—composed, sober, and impossibly invested in all the crap swirling around her. She'd walked into my room wearing a bright yellow tunic and extended a hand to me, palm up, with skin like warmed earth. I hadn't known what to do with that hand. From anyone else it would have meant, *Gimme your wallet.* On Dr. Mehta, though, the tiniest shift of a thumb or curl of her wrist changed everything about the gesture, like the slightest change in inflection gave ordinary words entirely new meaning when she spoke them. *You don't think you have a unique vantage point?* Like I was one of those gulls living in the cracks of the seawall, finding refuge in the fissures, peering into the depths.

After a moment, Dr. Mehta offered that same hand in the space between us, waiting for me to respond. I swallowed.

"But . . . Ely. If you want him to talk to the Ely police, I don't think—I can't . . ."

"You won't have to. We can use our liaison, Officer Miller, as an intermediary."

Reluctantly, I placed my hand in hers and she clasped it, acknowledging my agreement.

"I'll send you his file right away. Read it thoroughly." She turned her attention back to the far end of the ward and nodded. "You might be Lucas Blackthorn's best chance to reclaim his life."

With that, she badged the door open and left the medical ward.

I stood there alone until a nurse pushing a patient in a wheelchair needed to get by, then numbly held the door open, glancing down the corridor to where the orderly stood guard.

When Dr. Mehta first mentioned this job at our last outpatient therapy session before I turned eighteen, I thought she was kidding. Then it felt like she was trying to recommit me and I ran fast and hard in the other direction. I refused to even look up the hill at Congdon as I drove to and from the university each day. A semester passed where I pretended I was a normal girl, someone whose mother hadn't abandoned her, who'd never covered herself in blood, or been handcuffed to a bed like Lucas was handcuffed right now. My pretending didn't work very well. I realized I had nothing to say to the normal girls; I didn't even speak their language.

Then Dr. Mehta sent me a Christmas card and made the offer again. Would I like to work part-time at the hospital to help other patients find their voice? I could start as an orderly and work my way up after I graduated. Before I even finished reading I knew my answer. Maybe I wasn't the most qualified person for the job—I needed two degrees in order to become a certified speech therapist—but desperate, hopeless, crazy? Those were languages I spoke fluently.

Swallowing, I paced back down the hallway into Lucas's room and around the bed. His eyes opened and fixed on me. I took a deep breath and spoke softly.

"Do you want to get out of here?"

Emotion flooded his face and he started nodding almost before I'd finished. "Yes. I have to."

The urgency in his voice stirred something deep inside me. A recognition. Damn Dr. Mehta for always being right.

I sighed. "Okay. But you'll have to talk to me, though. They want to know things and they won't let you leave until we've told them what they want to hear. Do you understand?"

His eyes widened and he shook his head slightly.

"I didn't, either, at first. Don't worry. I'll help you."

I started to leave but turned when he said my name.

"Maya." He pronounced it again, slowly, as if suspicious of the vowels. "Thank you."

I didn't trust my voice, so I just nodded and left, wondering what the hell I'd gotten myself into.

4

ROBERT AND MONICA Anderson owned a camping outfitter store in the tiny border town of Ely, Minnesota. According to their website, they stocked Kevlar canoes, state of the art rain gear, powdered guacamole, and anything else a Boundary Waters voyager could dream of needing for a trek into the wilderness. At 12:26 a.m. on October 5, long past the busy summer season and even the smaller burst of travelers who wanted to see the fall colors from the bow of a canoe, Monica was watching Netflix in their apartment above the store when the sound of smashing glass surprised her. She called 911 and crept downstairs with a utility knife and her phone.

Expecting to find the same kids who'd vandalized a house down the street, Monica was shocked to see a hunched figure behind the store counter, pulling open drawers, rifling through the contents, and shutting them again. Before she could report more than that to the 911 operator, a scream and a series of crashes cut off the rest of the phone call.

Robert, startled awake, grabbed the hunting rifle he kept in their bedroom closet and rushed downstairs to see a dark figure wielding a knife. He aimed into the shadows and fired, but the cry that followed the blast was too high, too familiar. He ran forward as his wife's body was shoved at him and caught her before she hit the ground. Someone pulled the gun out of his hands and threw it across the store to the sound of more shattering glass. Sobbing on the floor, he cradled Monica and looked desperately around for a phone, a weapon, anything. When the intruder tried to dart past them, Robert lunged for his feet, tripping him. The person responded by flipping over and kicking Robert in the head until he lost consciousness.

The police took Robert's statement from the hospital, hours before his wife slipped into a coma and died. The intruder, who'd been chased down by responding officers, had to be physically restrained during his mugshot and fingerprinting, which eventually revealed him to be a lost child from the missing persons list. Even in the cryptic language of police reports, it was obvious they hadn't known what to do next. At nineteen, he was too old for social services to get involved and the most they could charge him with was B&E, attempted robbery, and assault. The Ely police transferred him to Duluth—complaining about extensive damage to the jail cell—and if he was anyone else the judge would have sent him to prison for a few years, but the boy who came back from the dead got a commitment order and a ticket to Congdon.

And now, after two weeks of silent violence and disregard for every human around him, he'd decided to talk. To me.

I read his entire file three times. His mother, Sarah Mason, had died of a brain aneurysm when Lucas was five. Besides his father, Josiah, his only other known relative was a maternal grandfather currently living in an Alzheimer's unit outside Chicago. He'd attended a series of elementary schools around the Midwest before his disappearance. Good grades—better than mine, like that was a challenge. His therapy notes were less inspiring. The Congdon psychologists had tried communicating with him a dozen different ways: They'd showed him pictures of the Northwoods and of his father, played music popular from the year he went missing, demonstrated games he might have enjoyed as a child, even played the video for all entering campers about how to leave no trace of themselves when they journeyed into the wilderness. I found it on YouTube, all the rules for burying fish entrails, collecting firewood, hauling every scrap of trash back out of the woods, and saw how ridiculous it would look to someone who'd been a ghost for the last ten years, who had probably watched those campers light their choking pine needle fires and dig their shallow fish graves.

After exhausting everything in the file I left Jasper curled up in bed and went to the bathroom, the one room I'd remodeled in an attempt to breathe the Northwoods into our house. I'd refinished the knotty pine cabinets, found the driftwood that was displayed on the back of the toilet, and even convinced Dad to pay for the slate tile floor. He and Butch had been impressed by the results and wanted me to do other rooms, too—the kitchen, the living room—but I kept changing my mind about the paint color and hardware, unable to get it exactly right. Now, though, I didn't frown at the olive-toned walls. I didn't cringe at the drawer handles. All I could see was the contrast between my world and everything Lucas had known. This bathroom was as close to the Northwoods as Dr. Mehta was to being committed. Pacing the house while Jasper snored, I wracked my brain for a connection, some pathway into Lucas Blackthorn's head, and by dawn I'd scribbled a list of the few things I knew for sure.

One, something or someone had driven Lucas out of the Boundary Waters.

Two, he didn't find what he was looking for at the outfitter's store. The police confiscated nothing from him except a few sharp rocks.

Three, he wanted to escape Congdon, and I'd bet anything he was trying to get back to the glacial waters and shadowed forests that called him home.

———

The next morning I wrote my first patient transfer order and brought Lucas back to the isolation ward, this time to a room with a desk and two chairs bolted to the floor. I wasn't allowed to bring any pens or pencils, wear belts or shoes with laces, and I had to remove all the hoops from my ear.

When Stan let me into the room for our first session—take two—Lucas was limping along the far wall and rubbing his wrists. As soon as he saw me he turned, impatiently, like I was late for an appointment. Then his eyes narrowed when an orderly followed me in and took a post at the wall.

"Hello, Lucas."

His focus shifted back to me, but he didn't respond.

I tilted my head. "It's customary to greet people by saying Hi or Hello, followed by their name."

Lucas nodded slightly and humor played across his features,

like he was warming up to a particularly silly game. He took a long breath and tested his voice. "Hello, Maya."

"This is Bryce." I flapped a hand behind me. "He's here to protect me. Do you understand why?"

No answer.

"Do you remember what happened the last time we met in one of these rooms?"

"You gave me this." He pointed to his leg and took a slow, uneven step.

"I don't think you"—each word out of his mouth was deliberate, as if he was tasting them first—"need anyone to protect you."

I repressed a smile and met his gaze squarely. "It's important you understand how the institution works. Your behavior can earn you trust, and the privileges that go with that trust. Bryce or someone like him will be here until you can prove you aren't a danger to me or anyone else. At that point you may be able to move into another ward, where you can move freely in common areas and interact with other patients and staff. You can earn grounds privileges—"

He looked confused.

"The ability to go outside," I elaborated and noticed his flare of interest. "Walk around the yard and get some fresh air. You might also earn day trip privileges, where you go out into the town with one of us on staff."

"*You* would take me into the town?"

"Maybe me and Jasper."

He returned my grin with a questioning look, but I didn't explain.

I gestured to the table and we both walked carefully toward it, watching each other's progress, and lowered ourselves into the seats as if choreographed. I placed my hands on top of the table, palms down, and he mirrored me. So far, he was responsive, taking cues both verbally and nonverbally, and showing no hint of aggression. I didn't hear any palate issues, no stuttering, stammering, or signs of more serious communication issues like aphasia. It was tempting, oh so tempting, to dive right into the deep end of the pool. You could see the lucidity in his eyes, the intelligence, but that's how every cop and therapist had gotten nowhere with this patient. Instead I glanced at Bryce—who already looked bored—and gave Lucas the opportunity to direct the conversation, the kind of tiny power no one outside these walls would even notice. Inside, it was a major currency.

"Is there anything you want to ask me before we get started?"

He leaned forward. "Why am I here?"

I exhaled and debated the answer. Did I go into the incident? Monica Anderson's death? Robert Anderson's fractured skull? We'd have to deal with those things eventually, but there were minefields everywhere and I didn't know which step would make him explode. Slowly. I had to go slow. "You don't remember what happened?"

His brow wrinkled and I couldn't tell if he was blocking it out or he just didn't like my reply. Whichever it was, he avoided my question, too.

"When can I leave?"

That one was easier. "They don't put a timeline on it."

"They?"

"The doctors, and primarily Dr. Mehta. She'll discharge you whenever she feels you're ready to rejoin society."

He was quiet for a moment, processing that. At close range, his eyes looked bluer, colder. Then, so quietly I almost missed it, "What do I have to do?"

The million-dollar question. I took a breath and weighed my

answer carefully. "The first and most important thing is to demonstrate you're not a danger to others or yourself."

He glanced at Bryce, hulking in the corner, and then slowly rolled his hands palm up on the table. *See?* Showing me his uncuffed wrists, the inner skin as white as a flag, he challenged me to deny his cooperation.

I gave him a moment, taking in his posture, my silent acknowledgment of what he wasn't saying, then set a blue cloth bag on the table—the surprise bag covered with emojis that I brought to all my sessions—and started pulling tiny objects out and setting them in a careful line between us.

They were rocks, all different colors and textures, each no bigger than a quarter. Dr. Mehta had cleared me to bring them; we both knew it took a much bigger rock to bash someone's head in.

"This is greenstone." I pointed to the first one and waited until he picked it up. "It's been weathered down for the last two billion years. Do you know what a glacier is?" I didn't question his nod or how he might have received the knowledge. I didn't look at him at all as I told the story of the ancient volcano that erupted pillows of basalt into the land that would become the Boundary Waters. How all the softer stone had been carved out by ice sheets, and the basalt itself transformed into greenstone before the ice melted into hundreds of lakes. Handing him the greenstone, I picked up the next rock and told the story of the Knife Lake slate, before moving on to the granite, and then the milky ball of quartz, as pure and unforgiving as January ice.

I'd pried the stones out of the frozen rock garden in the corner of our yard this morning. My mother, the geologist, hadn't grown vegetables or flowers. She'd planted rocks and told me their history as if it was her own. I could almost hear her voice as I repeated it to Lucas now.

He touched them all, holding each specimen as I explained how they'd formed the home he'd known for most of his life, but the longer I spoke the more I sensed he was looking at me instead of the collection. He let me tell him about the rugged terrain, the life of the oldest exposed rock in the world, while silently studying me. I couldn't tell if he was absorbing any of this, if he was even interested, until I finished describing the last one and began gathering them up to put them back in the bag.

Without warning he reached out and stopped my hand, taking hold of my wrist. Bryce, who'd been falling asleep in the corner, pushed himself off the wall and rushed over but not before I'd jerked Lucas's wrist up and twisted it, forcing his arm down and crumpling his shoulder into the table. Half crouched over the top of him, I held Bryce off and locked eyes with Lucas.

He didn't put up a fight. There was no struggle in him beyond the surprised rise and fall of his chest, the widened eyes racing over every inch of my face as if searching for something that had just skittered away. Immediately I perceived I'd overreacted, but the strange look on his face froze my grip in place. Before I could regroup, his jaw moved.

"I know you."

It was a whisper, the words leaked out in a rush of breath I barely heard over the thud of my own heart.

Then Bryce moved in, sinking his meaty fingers into the hospital gown around Lucas's shoulders and finding purchase. "All right, man. Let her go."

In slow motion Lucas unwrapped his fingers from my wrist, I released my hold, and we both returned to our choreographed sitting positions. Bryce withdrew a short step, hovering behind Lucas's chair.

"What did you say?" I asked even though I could still feel his whisper rippling in the air. *I know you.*

"Nothing." Less than ten seconds later, his face had changed completely. He looked worried, not making eye contact, and somehow I knew it didn't have anything to do with the giant orderly breathing down his neck. He was . . . scared. Like he'd suddenly found whatever he'd been searching for in me and regretted looking.

Being careful not to startle him, I gathered up the rocks and dropped them into my bag. When I stood up, Lucas did, too, retreating from the table until his back touched the wall and leaning against it as if trying to will himself through the concrete.

"How did you know all that?"

I didn't answer right away. I watched Bryce text Stan to let him know we were done and thought about the summers I'd spent paddling the Boundary Waters with my mother. I remembered her expression as the sheer rock faces came into view, how she inhaled the Precambrian balm of those cliffs. *I know you.*

It took an immense effort not to lie. I met his eyes as the door unlocked behind me, sensing the current of fear still running high. "I used to know a geologist. She said rocks are the language of the Earth."

Then, turning away, "See you tomorrow."

5

OVER THE NEXT few days, my life fell into a new routine. I woke up and walked Jasper, then came home and prepped for sessions with Lucas. A lot of my other appointments got rearranged or handed off, which made both the patients and staff irritable, but I was racing against a deadline. Get him out of isolation by the end of the week, Dr. Mehta had ordered, which meant I had less than five days to make Lucas Blackthorn play nice with others.

I changed up the security I brought to our sessions, dragging along all genders and races. No one on support staff was smaller than me, but I found a petite, sweet-looking nurse to come one day, who agreed on the condition that I let her smuggle a can of pepper spray in her bra. Lucas looked each and every one of them up and down when they came into his room, as if scanning for weaknesses, but never took a step in their direction. I asked Carol the kitchen attendant to chat with him while he ate his meals, which she probably would have done anyway. After lunch, I took him to the men's group physical therapy in the gym. When we walked in the first time, with Bryce and me shouldering him on either side and a security guard posted outside the door, he stopped short and surveyed the room. Twenty-odd patients, representing a spectrum of psychological disorders, were all doing yoga. Or the Congdon version of yoga. Three or four actually followed the instructor's poses, while the rest either stayed in seated meditation or flowed it their own way. Big George was trying to balance on his head and shoulder with one arm reaching for the ceiling. A few stared at the walls, rocking back and forth.

"What's wrong with them?" Lucas asked.

"No more than what's wrong with you." I shot back without thinking, then cringed, but Lucas actually cracked a grin. It was the first time I'd seen him smile and it made him appear like the teenager he was.

"I look like that?" He nodded at Big George, who was waving gleefully at me. I waved back.

"We have patients with a variety of abilities. There are a dozen cognitive disorders in this room right now, but that's not who these men are. It doesn't define them." I bumped his shoulder with mine, a deliberately friendly contact that he received without any defensive reaction. "Come on. Let's vinyasa."

On the days group exercise went into the grounds, he had to stay in isolation. I couldn't take him outside, not only because he'd run but also because I'd begun noticing something strange when I drove into work. People lingered outside the gates every morning when I arrived, staring into my car, pointing their phones at the building's facade. I didn't know who they were, but I knew instinctively who they were watching for. No one had stood outside Congdon before Lucas's arrival. They'd never thought about the people living here except to be grateful for the fence, for the line of demarcation that separated us from them.

Since I couldn't bring him out, I brought the outside in: a handful of acorns that he built into a tower, a cup of powdery sand from Park Point beach, a scattering of fallen leaves, their brilliant colors leeching to brittle brown. I didn't interrogate him and I asked him nothing about his past, keeping my questions light. Did he like the food here? *No.* Did he know how to read? *Yes.* I brought him books from the Congdon library, first *The Lorax*, then *The Swiss Family Robinson*, and read him passages from it. He listened without comment, always glancing at the orderly, the locked door, the bars encasing the window, crushing the leaves between his fingertips until they turned to dust on the table.

There were things that made sense about Lucas. He hated loud noises and tended to cover his ears when another resident began screaming. During group exercise, he flinched away from sudden bursts of laughter and stayed at the fringes of the room, gravitating toward the quiet misery of the dementia patients. He made absolutely no sound when he walked and I found myself studying his footfalls, how he hit the floor with the ball of his foot, placing each step with the sureness of a lynx on a rocky slope. And as much as I tried to draw him out, as sure as I was that he had absolutely no speech disorders, he spoke as little as possible. He gave one-word answers, shrugs, refusing to elaborate on any subject, his expression the definition of involuntary.

It was the other things, the stuff that didn't make sense, that kept popping up at three in the morning when I should have been at least resting if not sleeping, but rest seemed impossible around

Lucas, like his tension was contagious. I hadn't brought up his comment from the first day—*I know you*—because it was wrong. All the time I'd spent in the Boundary Waters ended years before he and his father had gone missing. I hadn't met Lucas Blackthorn outside these walls. I would've remembered those ridiculous blue eyes, how they became sharper, eerier, the longer they stared at you. And he did. He studied me from the minute I walked into his room until the door closed between us. He watched my face, my hands, my shifting postures, once I even caught him staring at my breasts and it would have been so much easier to say I was simply the first girl he'd ever met. Was there anything more fascinating to hetero teenage boys than breasts? But I couldn't make myself believe it. There was something more in his face, a caged fear that made me certain he wanted to snatch back those three whispered words. He knew me, and it made him afraid.

I consulted with Dr. Mehta every afternoon, sharing my session notes and my frustration. She had a stocked inventory of rational explanations; I might remind him of someone from his early childhood; I represented an institution he didn't understand or trust; he'd probably spent years in silence and solitude and could be dealing with a form of social anxiety. She coached me, soothed me, gave me fresh ideas and insight, and on the night before my last shift of the week she told me there was a bed open in ward two.

"If he can maintain his self-control through your session tomorrow, we'll transfer him to the common men's ward and see how he does." Her eyes narrowed. "Challenge him. I believe he's ready for it."

––––––

The next day when I went to Lucas's room, I went alone.

He was waiting for me in what had become his usual spot, cross-legged at the end of the bed with *The Swiss Family Robinson* dog-eared on the mattress next to him, twirling one of the acorns I'd brought by the stem.

When he realized no one was coming in behind me, his eyebrows lifted.

"Congratulations," I said, moving to the table. "You've been upgraded to a lower risk status."

Lucas followed me and sat down, carefully setting his hands palm down on the table like always, a study in restraint.

"No more bouncers," I said, without knowing whether Stan was watching us through the door. "And after today you could be moving to a different floor."

"A different floor." He repeated it and the tendons in his hands clenched. "Not out?"

"Not yet. We'll have to talk about other things, when you're ready." I held his gaze and waited a beat, then two, as the silence built between us.

It bubbled up again, that tremor of fear. No matter how much Dr. Mehta tried to explain it away, the fact was he didn't react this way to any of the other staff. Just me. As if he thought I alone knew something about him, something damning. Watching for any sudden movements, I pulled a large sheet of paper out of the surprise bag and unfolded it on the table. Lucas blinked at the map and, after a moment's hesitation, leaned in to study it more closely.

"This is Duluth." I pointed out Congdon's location on the summit of the hill, overlooking the entire city, then showed him some of the main areas and landmarks. After watching my finger trace roads and parks for a while, he asked where I lived, so I pointed to my neighborhood and talked about it. To my surprise, he started asking questions. How long had I lived in Duluth? Could I see the water from my house? Did I like watching the ships? Did I live alone? He processed everything I said before asking the next thing, and the next thing, and by the time I looked at my watch the entire hour had almost elapsed.

My heart kicked up as I reached into the bag for the other map and carefully unfolded it over the top of Duluth. This map was a wash of blues and greens, charting over a million acres that stretched along the Canadian border for almost a hundred and fifty miles. The lakes squiggled over the page, pouring into each other in rapids and waterfalls, creating endless waterways dotted with islands and hugged by fat peninsulas. The land was a sea of pine, fir, and spruce towering over the water, an evergreen empire built on less than one foot of topsoil before their roots hit solid granite. I knew those shorelines and shadows, could hear the loons calling each other, and feel the razor gaze of the eagles soaring overhead. No matter how long you stayed away, the Boundary Waters never left you.

Lucas recognized it immediately, I could tell, but instead of leaning closer and engaging as he'd done with Duluth, he braced himself against the back of the chair.

"It's your turn." I spread the map out, trying to make my voice as smooth as the paper. "Tell me about your home."

He was frozen for a moment, then he sprung out of his chair and began pacing along the back wall, his shoulders tensed, hands fisted. My mind raced, wanting the answers only he knew but afraid to push him too far and risk an episode that would keep him locked in isolation. I took a deep breath and spoke as calmly as I could.

"How long did you live in the Boundary Waters?" I parroted his question to me back at him.

He spun away and started tracing the wall, as if searching for fault lines. I waited, holding my breath. Then, just when I thought he'd gone nonverbal again, he spoke.

"Ten years."

Two words, and they opened up a hundred questions in my mind. How did he know it was that long? Did someone tell him when he'd arrived at Congdon or had he used some kind of calendar? Maybe he'd counted, winter by bone shuddering winter. Ignoring the impulse to press further, I moved to the next question he'd asked me.

"Could you see the water from your home?"

He turned and, registering my small smile, caught on to the game we were playing. I waited, while he decided how he was going to handle round two. After a flickering glance at the map, he nodded.

Which lake? I wanted to know. There were hundreds, water in every direction; water was the highway of the Boundary Waters. But again, I repressed the bubbling questions.

"Did you like watching the canoes?"

Another nod, and this one didn't surprise me. Some of the reporters had speculated on whether he'd been lost, painting melodramatic pictures of a boy trapped in the wilderness, desperate and alone, and maybe it could have been true for the space of one winter when campers were few and far between. In the summer, though, someone was always paddling quietly through the pristine woods. For a boy with the endurance to survive, help would have been easy to find. He hadn't reached out—he hadn't been lost. The Bigfoot stories, the wild man in the woods, were probably born of glimpses of Lucas skirting the edges of the campsites, watching the parade of humans from a comfortable distance.

Then, the question we both knew was coming next.

"Did you live alone?"

I stood up and moved around the table, closing the distance between us. Lucas backed into the wall and something dark flashed across his face.

"Ten years ago your father, Josiah Blackthorn, took you camping in the Boundary Waters. You were nine years old. He was thirty-six. No one saw either of you again. Your campsite was found ravaged by what looked like a large predator, maybe a bear, and even though you've both been on the missing persons list all this time, everyone assumed you were dead."

I thought of the photo they kept posting on the news, a half-lit shot of the dark-haired man and boy sitting on a dock. As a boy, Lucas had been slender and bright-eyed, leaning into his father's side and grinning at the camera while the man stared past the lens toward the lake. The picture had been taken at a park in Iowa, three months before they disappeared.

"Do you remember your father?"

He let out a gunshot of a laugh, void of any humor, and his jaw trembled. There were memories—vicious, raging memories.

"How long was he with you? When did you last see him?"

He locked his eyes on mine, exhaled unsteadily and spoke.

"Fifteen days ago."

I took another step forward, my mouth dropping open.

"You've been together all these years? He's alive?"

His head dropped and his voice came low and clipped. "I don't know."

"Where is he?"

"Why are you asking?" His arms flew up, shoving me away, and I stumbled into the table before catching my balance.

Agitation. Focused aggression. Instead of trying to calm him and de-escalate the situation, I put my finger on the wound and pressed. "If he's sick or hurt, he needs help."

"Like you're helping me?" He raged, pacing the perimeter again, but I put myself in his path, blocking his way. He tried to push me aside but I grabbed his hand, not really holding it so much as arm wrestling in midair. We struggled for a minute. When he finally gave up, he jerked back against the wall and glared at me. I lowered our hands, keeping an awkward grip around his knuckles.

"I promised I'd help get you out, didn't I?"

He shook his head and stared at the locked door, his eyes filling with tears that he furiously blinked away. "Not that way. I'm not turning him over, not even if I have to rot in here."

"Turn him over?" I repeated, my mind scrambling to catch up.

He pulled his hand free and scrubbed at his face. I watched his chest rise and fall as he worked to bury the emotion. When he finally spoke, it was with a horrible, quiet certainty.

"No one can help us. That's why we disappeared."

6

KARP LYKOV WAS a man who had to disappear. In 1936, he lived in a remote village in Siberia and was working in the fields when a Communist patrol shot his brother at his side. The Bolshevik government had made it their mission to systematically eradicate religion from the country, seizing church property, harassing believers, reeducating children, and executing priests and the devout like the Lykovs. In the wake of his brother's murder, Karp gathered his wife and children and fled to the only place the Communists couldn't follow: the taiga, three million square miles of unforgiving wilderness. They lived for over forty years in total isolation, using only a few pots, a spinning wheel, and a loom for tools. The family built their log cabin by hand and planted crops on a mountainside, surviving famine and endless winters without any contact with the outside world, that is, until 1978 when a group of prospecting geologists happened upon them.

By that time Russia had changed. Instead of ordering executions, the government sent religious people to mental hospitals and diagnosed them with "philosophical intoxication." Psychiatry had become a political weapon, but one that couldn't touch the Lykovs. They refused to leave their wilderness home. They accepted few gifts from the geologists and those only grudgingly, as though the pleasures of salt, forks, and paper were inherently sinful. Ultimately it wasn't the spices or tools that struck the Lykovs down, but a series of illnesses due to their harsh existence. One by one, the entire family died in the 1980s except the youngest daughter, Agafia. Concerned, the geologists tried to convince her to return to civilization with them, but she refused. Standing sentinel near her family's graves, she urged the geologists to leave and waved them on when they hesitated.

In her seventies now, Agafia Lykov still lives in the taiga, the place where she was born and where someday she's determined herself to die.

―――――――

"Josiah Blackthorn is alive."

Dr. Mehta spooned spices from various pots into her pestle and began grinding them with the mortar. Her office filled with the familiar pungent fragrance, making the air heavy and sharp. It took ten minutes to prepare a traditional chai, five minutes to let it cool, and another fifteen for her to drain the entire pot while I pretended to sip my single cup. That was a half an hour, measured in blisteringly bitter tea, for our monthly "check-in" sessions.

"That's why Lucas keeps trying to escape. It's not just leaving Congdon, it's not just the Boundary Waters: He's trying to get back to his father."

"Believe me, Maya," she poured the spices into an electric tea kettle and set a timer, "no one is more gratified than me to hear Lucas has trusted you with this information. The U.S. Forest Service is making renewed efforts to locate Josiah and any information from his son will help. They've canvassed the western area closest to Ely by both water and air, trying to find any trace of him but so far have turned up nothing."

"What about Quetico?" The rangers wouldn't have any authority to search the Canadian reserve, which extended the wilderness by almost another two thousand square miles.

"To my understanding, they're working in tandem with the Canadian authorities and"—she cut over my attempt to ask another question—"we'll go over this in detail, I assure you, but right now we're here to discuss Maya Stark, not Josiah Blackthorn."

I dropped into my usual spot in one of her overstuffed chairs and stared at the moss-eaten trunk of an old oak outside the window. Dead leaves circled the ground around it and its branches curled naked into the sky. "There's not much to say. My boss trusted me with a challenging assignment and it's taking over my life."

"What did you do this weekend?"

I'd spent most of it replaying my last conversation with Lucas over and over to the beat of Jasper's paws hitting the boards of the lake walk, but she didn't want to hear that.

"I went to the hardware store. The nickel handles I put in the bathroom are all wrong. Copper would be perfect with the wood tones and the floor, but then I'd have to get new fixtures, too."

"Is it possible," she ruminated while pulling out two squatty brown cups, "that your fixation on this bathroom allows you to avoid other areas of your life?"

"Like remodeling the kitchen?"

"Like making friends. Socializing. Pushing yourself out of your avoidant attachment style and opening up, building relationships and trust. It all starts through meaningful interaction with someone outside of Congdon."

"I signed up for three different social media accounts in the last week. My phone's been going crazy." The notification buzzes had made my pocket vibrate all morning. I pulled the phone out and she came over, donning her glasses to examine the screen.

" 'Stephanie posted to Lucas Blackthorn's timeline?' 'Lake Superior and 5K others liked @therealblackthorn's tweet?' " She handed it back. "The *lake* liked it?"

"It's got an account, too."

"Of course it does." Dr. Mehta perched in the chair across from me. Behind her head hung a framed quote that had been in this office for as long as I'd known her. It read, *What lies behind us and what lies before us are tiny matters compared to what lies within us.* Dr. Mehta had spent eight years and counting trying to counsel what lay within me.

"I said meaningful interaction, Maya. I don't imagine you're contributing to these conversations, as it would violate HIPAA confidentiality."

"No, but some of these people are obsessed. And I'm talking the clinical definition." I pulled up one of the apps and scrolled through the comments. "They're reposting all the photos of Lucas, turning them into memes and artwork."

I showed her a picture of Lucas's face—captured when they were transferring him to Congdon—superimposed over a forest. Another version showed him half in shadows with the bottom of the frame bleeding into red. Someone posted one last night of Josiah

54

fractured into a broken tile mosaic of greens and blacks, and the amount of detail and painstaking nuance must have taken hours, even days.

"They've divided into camps, people sympathetic to Lucas who are outraged that he's here, and the others who want him to rot in prison for what he did to the Andersons. They think he killed his father and buried him somewhere in the Boundary Waters."

The timer beeped and Dr. Mehta returned to the tea, stirring in milk and sugar with unhurried strokes.

"Haven't you noticed the people outside?" I peered beyond the oak branches toward the entrance. Something moved near the guardhouse. It was too far away to identify, but the lurkers were out there. I'd seen evidence of them online: pictures of the front entrance and even blurry shots of patients walking through the grounds, which prompted rabid speculation on whether any of them could be Lucas.

"Yes, the guards are aware of the issue. We've temporarily doubled security at the gate. Lucas has accumulated a large amount of fan mail—and some hate mail—as well."

"What?" My spine straightened.

"Which is all the more reason"—she brought two mugs over and handed one to me—"to get him to talk. The sooner the better. We need him to tell the authorities his story before the public superimposes their own. Eventually Lucas will be rejoining this society and we want him to be positioned to successfully engage with it, not recoil into a protective shell and redo his bathroom for the rest of his life."

I swallowed the tea without tasting it, but the astringency still puckered my tongue. "Someday you have to teach me that trick where people think you're nice."

"Happily." Smiling, she inhaled the steam from her cup. "How about the day when you don't try to divert attention to someone else during your therapy sessions?"

When I didn't reply, she took a sip and settled more comfortably into her chair. "Now, shall we discuss your progress in letting yourself form attachments? Or would you rather talk about your fears of the Ely police?"

Shifting, I took another bracing mouthful of tea.

Twenty minutes later the "check-in" was over and Dr. Mehta kept her promise to tell me the details of the search for Josiah. The police wanted to talk to Lucas as soon as possible. Once winter came, the lakes would freeze over and any search parties would be fighting subzero temperatures on snowshoe or by dogsled, and without Lucas's help they'd be searching blind.

I'd been shaking my head long before she finished. "He won't talk to them. He said he'd rot in here before turning his father over. Doesn't that sound like his father committed a crime?"

"The police haven't mentioned any outstanding warrants."

"What else could he mean?"

Dr. Mehta set aside her cup and laid a hand on my arm.

"You're doing a wonderful job with him, Maya—and I know this is frustrating—but you have to focus on reaching Lucas. His health is our priority. Work on gaining his trust, acclimating him, and hopefully we can get him to speak with the police soon." She turned back to the window. "It seems the path to the father is through the son."

I left her office, my stomach suddenly calm as I understood what I had to do. If I was going to get Lucas to talk, I needed to uncover what drove them into the Boundary Waters, trace their steps back to that first leap, which brought me to a catch-22. The path to the father might be through the son, but the path to the son was indisputably through the father. To reach Lucas, I needed to know Josiah.

In the following days I didn't press Lucas to say anything further about his father or the Boundary Waters, which was good because adjusting to his transfer proved difficult. Ward two, the high security common men's ward, was exclusively used for forensic patients, the ones who'd been sent here by the courts rather than those who sought care of their own free will. Most of their crimes were the logical result of impulse and lack of control—theft, creating a disturbance, resisting arrest, assault—with a few more serious offenses sprinkled in. One man had driven a car into a bus full of children with a homemade bomb that didn't explode. Another had hacked up his neighbors on Christmas Eve. That guy, a schizophrenic recluse who some of the nurses called the Grinch behind his back, responded well to his meds and had been transferred here from the state security hospital after ten years of perfect behavior. Sometimes he asked me to play Scrabble after I finished up with other sessions. He beat me every time.

Ward two was laid out over one long wing for continuous sight lines. The staff station was encased in glass and always had at least two nurses dispensing medication, herding patients to their scheduled activities, and buzzing them between the common areas and the sleeping areas. The open living room boasted couches bolted to the floor and squishy chairs that didn't cause major injuries when thrown. Classical music piped in after lunch and dinner and the walls were painted in soft grays and blues, like a cloudy day that might be clearing. I don't know if the window dressing made much of a difference with this crowd, though. To most forensic patients, Congdon was a prison and they were serving a sentence with no release date.

When security cleared me through on Monday morning for my first session with Lucas in the new ward, there was a scuffle going on in front of the TV and I helped the orderlies break up what turned out to be a disagreement over a channel change. Lucas wasn't anywhere in the living room or adjoining dining area. I finally found him in a classroom next to the nurse's station, the room where different therapists taught social skills, life skills, art, even cooking. Lucas sat on the floor behind the rows of benches, visible to the wall of windows connecting it to the nurse's station but hidden from the group of men still arguing over the TV. One of them began shouting again, and I walked into the room in time to see Lucas burying his head in his arms and rocking on the floor.

"There you are."

His head shot up at my voice and relief swamped his face, startling me.

I closed the door to the classroom, blocking some of the noise and set up our session on one of the benches. He sat closer to me than I expected and didn't even seem to consider whether he could use the felt tip pen I produced as a weapon. I gave him some loose-leaf paper and asked him to start a journal.

He frowned. "Is that going to get me out of here?"

I uncapped the pen and put it in his hand. "It's another step. Journaling can help synthesize experience." I explained how the act of writing engaged both hemispheres of the brain equally, making it a uniquely suited tool for processing and learning. Then he wanted to know about brain hemispheres and we spent twenty minutes talking about cognitive function, the nervous system, and right-vs. left-brained people. When the session was over, he touched the chipped silver polish on my fingernails and asked when I would be back, then watched from the safety of his classroom cave until I left the ward.

He wrote halting paragraphs over the next few days—poorly spelled and sometimes hardly legible—commenting on how awful the food tasted, how loud his roommates snored, how many times he could hear an alarm shrieking through the echoing old walls of the building, nothing that even hinted at his father or his life before Congdon. From what I could tell, he stayed as far away from the other patients as possible. He didn't socialize, he didn't speak when spoken to. He obeyed the staff directions on the second or third time given and sat through group classes staring out the window. One of his OCD roommates started monitoring Lucas and gave me a full report every time I appeared. *Lucas gave his breakfast to Big George today he went to the bathroom twice and stayed in the second time for sixteen minutes he's over there behind the second couch.* And then, when Lucas saw me, he would immediately rise and follow me to the classroom. He began starting our conversations, asking questions or bringing up points that he seemed to save up over the course of the day, although if Dr. Mehta stopped by or anyone else entered the room he would fall into characteristic sullen silence.

I played the part of his breezy friend, a warm and casual acquaintance happy to chitchat while correcting his spelling and grammatical errors. I brought him brochures for GED programs and colleges, which he didn't even glance at, a book of Sudoku puzzles, which he devoured with a rabid obsession, and Oreo cookies, which he spit out into a napkin after chewing one bite, making me question his entire capacity for judgment. The less I prepped for each session, the more he gravitated toward me. I didn't have time to wonder about his change of heart, though; I was too busy researching his father.

The Internet, for all its wastelands and perversions, was sometimes a beautiful thing. I searched for Josiah in a people finder database and got two hits, one of which was a ninety-two-year-old man living in New Hampshire. I ordered a full background check on the other one, Josiah Blackthorn, age forty-six, aka J Blackthorn, aka Joe Blackthorn, with a birth certificate registered in Detroit and previous addresses scattered all over the upper Midwest. There were no marriage certificates. He hadn't owned much property—a few trucks registered in his name every ten years or so, no houses or anything that would've fixed him in one place for any length of time. He'd received an associate degree in automotive technology in Illinois. Known relatives: two dead foster parents and one child, listed missing. I might have spent fifty bucks only to find out Josiah Blackthorn had been a drifter, except for the arrest records.

1992. DWI.

1995. Disorderly conduct.

1996. Public Intoxication. Disturbing the peace.

1996. Open container. Attempted assault.

And then nothing until a week before his disappearance when he'd been arrested for obstruction of justice in Ely, Minnesota, the same town where his son was taken into custody a decade later. Ely, the town I'd avoided for all of my adult life. There was no conviction or even a court record following that arrest, and no further information given. I stared at the bland paragraph, circled it, tried to google it and got no results. All the other arrests added up to a violent drunk, someone with a pattern of aggression who'd abruptly gone straight and kept his record clean. But obstruction of justice, after so many years of living quietly? Justice for what, or whom?

After Lucas's emergence none of the news stories mentioned that arrest, but the media had found a few other tidbits on Josiah. A couple of old coworkers gave interviews describing him as a solitary guy who packed his son up to go hiking every weekend and camping for weeks at a time. One of Lucas's teachers remembered the two as being startlingly similar. *Inquisitive, you know. Both asking follow-up questions, always wanting to know the why's and reasons for things. And of course they looked . . . they looked a lot alike.* The fluster, well camouflaged, but still there a dozen years later and it wasn't hard to see why. I printed out the picture of Josiah and Lucas on the dock together and taped it to the refrigerator, staring at it every time I felt hungry. If Lucas had been a beautiful child, Josiah was the rugged, brooding, startlingly handsome father. I didn't blush like the teacher, though; I looked closer.

Next to the Blackthorns' picture I'd taped another one, a shot of the Lykovs taken by the geologists who'd discovered them. There was nothing pretty about the Lykov family, not on an aesthetic scale, but something in their expressions made me pause as I stood in front of the refrigerator eating lo mein out of the carton. Joy emanated from their faces, a basic and consuming happiness. One of the rangers who visited Agafia in her later years told a documentary crew that the taiga purified people. Bad people couldn't survive in those subarctic forests; the deadly ravines and icy bogs would swallow them whole. Taiga, he said, cleanses your soul.

The Boundary Waters had the same power. I'd heard it in my mother's breath as she stared up at glacier-scarred cliffs, I'd seen it as we passed other campers portaging their canoes and gear, their entire lives distilled into sweat-stained backpacks with no room for abstractions like justice or its obstruction. They possessed a peace, I realized as the cold noodles slithered down my throat, that Josiah Blackthorn's face was screaming for.

There were no outstanding warrants, Dr. Mehta had said, but that final arrest stuck in my head. What was it that Josiah had needed to cleanse from his soul?

7

The woods are lovely, dark and deep,
But I have promises to keep,
and miles to go before I sleep.
—*Robert Frost*

JOSIAH

For as long as he could remember, Josiah Blackthorn hated roofs. When he was a child, ice dams had formed on the eaves of his foster parents' house and melted through the ceiling, dripping into the cupboards so all the food had to be stored in cardboard boxes while his foster dad spent the rest of the winter in a pissing match with the claims adjustor. They were ugly things, ceilings. His social worker's office was covered with pockmarked, foam tiles, the grocery store lived under dusty metal crossbeams, and he'd spent countless hours staring at the bug carcasses littering the fluorescent light fixtures at his school. There was always one shadow still moving, hurling itself against the plastic molding in frenetic arcs, but in all the time Josiah watched them he never saw a single bug escape.

All roofs came with a price. His foster mother showed them the gas and electricity bills every month. She did the same thing with grocery receipts and the register slips from Goodwill when they went clothes shopping. "If you get something for free," she told all her foster children, "that just means you don't know what it's going to cost yet." She wasn't an unkind woman, just mean with a dollar. She rubbed Calendula on their cuts instead of buying Band-Aids and made teas out of mullein leaves for their colds. As soon as the first spring rains came, she sent the boys into the woods behind their house, showing them how to find mushrooms, fiddlehead ferns, and dandelion greens. Josiah turned out to be a natural forager, instinctively memorizing the landscape, working his way farther into the shadows and hills where sometimes he would find a break in the trees and roll out an old sleeping bag so he could count the stars and hear his breath mingle with the scrapes and chirps of fellow night explorers. It was worlds better than sleeping under a stained ceiling with whichever foster boy was spoiling for a fight that week and as long as he came home with a basket full of morels, no one minded his absence.

The only thing he liked over his head, his foster dad joked as he grew up, was the hood of a car. Engines intrigued Josiah at the same level as the woods; they were a mechanical ecosystem and every part contributed to the function of the whole. He was the only kid in school who checked out books on cars and botany together. Eventually his foster parents helped him get a job doing tune-ups and let him tinker with their rusting Chevys until he saved up enough money to buy one of his own. When the foster subsidies ran out on the day he turned eighteen, they gave him a secondhand tent, wished him luck, and sent him on his way.

Josiah saw a lot of roofs over the next years and sometimes he wondered if he was the only person who noticed them. Every garage he worked at had a mechanic who'd been there for decades, with skin so stained they practically disappeared into the oil-splattered walls and telling stories that always ended with "Just you wait . . ." Josiah didn't wait. He worked as long as he could before the ceilings started to close in and the alcohol—which numbed much better than his foster mother's aloe vera—led to fights, cops, jails, and the inevitable firings. Camping until he ran out of money, he moved to the next town, which started the cycle all over again. He fantasized about leaving it all behind, building a little cabin somewhere so remote he could never find a way back, when he met a kayaking hippie named Sarah Mason.

———

The girl caught Josiah's eye the second she stepped out of her tent. She had dirty blond ringlets spilling out of a bandanna and tattoos peeking out of her tank top. Her nose was burnt watermelon pink and she seemed to be alone, too, their tents pitched on adjoining campsites along Lake Macbride in the tumbling hills of eastern Iowa. He leaned back in his camp chair as she tugged her boat down to the water.

"Can I help?" he asked.

"I doubt it." Flashing a smile, she set the boat in the lake without a backward glance. It was a two-person kayak and she used the second seat to prop up her bare feet as she paddled away.

It was the Fourth of July in a year no different from a half dozen before it. Josiah was between jobs again. He had a full cooler of beer, a week's worth of food, and every intention of not speaking to another living soul for as long as he could avoid it, yet all that mattered to him in that moment was watching the girl lift her face to the sun. She stroked leisurely across the lake, a solar powered creature he'd never encountered in nature before.

Every morning after that he asked if he could join her, feeling more perverse each time she turned him down. She left the campsite in the morning and wouldn't return until dusk. He offered her a beer and the only chair at his fire when she walked by at night, which she politely declined as she zipped herself into the glow of her tent. Josiah wasn't used to rejection, at least not the sexual kind. Generally, when he walked into the first bar in a new town, mascara-smeared eyes lit up. He was a drifter, an outsider, and his otherness offered what they craved, what—by definition—they couldn't have in their everyday lives. The less he said, the more they wanted him and he understood it. Women sought him the same way he sought the wild. This girl, though, had already found her wilderness.

Hiking through the park during the day, he tried to answer the perpetual question that framed his life: where to head next. He'd been contemplating Canada lately, a good place for a man to be alone, but suddenly solitude had lost its appeal. He found himself hiking further into the park, circling the lake, trying to catch a glimpse of his elusive neighbor. She wasn't beautiful, she might not even be interesting, yet there was something always dancing behind her eyes and he wanted to see what it did when it was set free.

At the end of the week when kids ran screaming through the campground with sparklers and someone lit illegal fireworks off on the other side of the lake, she was nowhere to be found. Her tent was dark and she wasn't milling around with the other campers near the grills and playground. He wandered down to the beach and lay on the sand, watching the nation's birthday saluted with the traditional spectacle of exploding gunpowder.

"A patriot, huh?"

Out of nowhere she appeared, easing down on her back next to him, and he was surprised by the force of the leap in his chest.

"More of a stargazer. I'm waiting for the smoke to clear."

"Astronomy." She shrugged her shoulders deeper into the sand, making a nest. "Let's see who can name more constellations."

That was the night he learned her name, that she was a graduate student from Iowa City, and that despite years of staring up at them he could only pick out one constellation in the entire sky—because Orion and Orion's belt didn't count as two. The next day Sarah let him kayak with her and the week after that he packed up his tent and drove to Iowa City, looking for a job.

He stopped drinking. Not right away, not cold turkey, but he didn't hate every room so much he needed to make them spin anymore and he didn't want to waste another night trapped in a jail cell, either. He pursued Sarah and leveraged her every swooning friend in his campaign to get her to date him without any concept of how dating actually worked. He was awkwardly honest, willing to describe every sexual misdeed, every rancid night behind bars. She laughed at each story, infusing them with a lightness he couldn't have imagined before meeting her, like sliding into a mineral spring and experiencing that first buoyant heat.

He learned her likes and dislikes and the meaning of every tattoo on her body, but the most important discovery he made about Sarah Mason, one night when he walked her home after class, was that she also hated roofs. Her sister had locked her in a toy box when she was three and she'd been claustrophobic ever since. Lecture halls were tolerable if they had windows, but she couldn't bear small waiting rooms, and the only time she'd tried boarding an airplane, she began hyperventilating and then screaming as soon as the cabin doors closed. So instead of asking to come in to her apartment, he found a bench overlooking the river and they talked all night, and when the sun rose, she kissed him until he forgot whether they were inside or out.

They went camping together, voyaging farther and farther into parks across the country with one tent and two kayaks, because Sarah liked having space to stretch out. He taught her to forage, how to distinguish the edibles and the medicinals from the indigestible and the poisonous. When they moved in together, tiny miracles began happening every day. She asked where he was going when he left in the morning; it mattered where he was, and whether he was sick or angry or thirsty or cold. Her love was a gift that asked for nothing in return. At night he gathered her close and talked about their cabin in the woods, because he couldn't see himself anywhere now without her. You're my sky, my everything, he whispered in the dark and he was right—until the day his son was born.

Lucas meant "illumination," "light-giving," and there was nothing more clear than the first time Josiah held his son and stared into his own eyes. Only a few moments in life have the power to unmake a man, and cradling that raw, barely formed human was Josiah's first. He fell in love, and it was terrifying.

The next years were the happiest and the hardest. Josiah worked as much as he could, stockpiling money for some vague future debt whose shadow seemed to loom infinitely larger every month. They learned about car seats and that back is best, breast is best, the five s's, and all the other hundreds of slogans and campaigns thrust into their lives by American baby culture. Ignoring as much of it as they could, they bought an infant life vest instead of a crib monitor and took Lucas down his first river at three months old. And Lucas *was* light-giving. He played games with his own shadow, entertained himself with bugs for hours, and scaled out of his crib to squirm his way in between his parents every morning before dawn so they could watch the sunrise together. Still, they couldn't entirely escape the tedium and the rules. At Lucas's first kindergarten conference they were admonished by the teacher that he should have been more socialized; Lucas looked at the other children like they were aliens and refused to stand quietly in line. Josiah laughed off her shaming, but it ate at Sarah the whole way home from the conference. She tucked Lucas into bed and stalked back to their living room, raging at the teacher with the assembly-line attitude, ripping up the conference papers, and when she whirled to hurl them at the trashcan—a blazing tornado of ringleted fury—an aneurysm burst in the frontal lobe of her brain and she fell backward, eyes open and staring at the cracked plaster of their ceiling.

That was the other moment. The worst moment. It was a strange thing to be thirty-two years old and know beyond all doubt you'd already experienced the highest and lowest points of your life.

When Josiah looked back on it later, from the lonely mouth of a forgotten river, he understood the price of Sarah's love. His foster mother had warned him, but he hadn't grasped at the time, with her penny-pinching ways, that cost meant more than money. Sometimes cost meant being carved down with grief. It meant fighting with the hospital to release Sarah's remains to him because he wasn't a legal relative and when they finally did, it meant lying awake at night wondering if she'd wanted to get married, if he'd made her sacrifice any portion of her infuriatingly finite happiness. Cost meant leaving Iowa City because he couldn't face playing with Lucas in the parks or walking the pedestrian mall without Sarah. Her love weighed down the air, made it almost impossible to push in and out of his lungs, so they moved. And for the rest of his life, Josiah never kayaked again.

Nothing in this world is free, his foster mother said. You just haven't found out what it's gonna cost yet.

Lucas was his last, greatest gift and he was prepared to pay anything, to forfeit the entire world and everything in it to keep his son safe. They drifted from town to town, staying in one place for the school year but packing up as soon as the last day let out in June and disappearing into the wild. Zion, Yosemite, the Sawtooth mountains, the Grand Canyon. All his savings made sense now, they paid for the summers spent gazing at sunsets and exploring the craters of ancient volcanoes. Josiah taught him survival; it was all for Lucas now, everything he'd ever learned for this one giggling, scampering reason. Lucas could build a fire at eight years old and fillet his own fish to cook over it. He hoarded maps and began campaigning for their summer destinations as soon as Christmas was over, which they usually spent in a snow-packed tent somewhere near the latest rental. When they were camping, Lucas didn't wake in a cold sweat crying for his mother. They talked about her over the campfire, Josiah grafting his memories onto Lucas's fading ones, and always found sites near the water where she would've wanted to be.

There were women, a whole new breed who saw "single father" as another asset in an already impressive list of attributes. They slipped their phone numbers to him with restaurant bills and at the laundromat, their eyes smug with intent. He hated them almost as much as he hated himself for being tempted. For wanting to betray Sarah's love. One woman asked him to come look at her Honda and, when he came to her house, slid her hand up his arm and inquired how much more he charged for extra services. He ripped the radiator hose out of her car and left her screaming in her driveway.

After a summer spent in the Badlands they drove all the way up to Ely, a weathered cluster of stores and houses where the road ended at the edge of Minnesota. The town was surrounded by green—national forests, state parks, and a place called the Boundary Waters Canoe Area Wilderness that intrigued by its very name. The Boundary Waters, a boundary between countries, between worlds, dividing the life he'd had with Sarah and the one that had called to him from dark horizons since he was a child.

He found an advertisement in the Ely paper to sublet half of a duplex and drove their truck full of camping supplies and tools to a house with peeling paint and a patchy, dandelion-strewn lawn. The woman who answered the door was bone-thin with crocodile teeth and sharp, hungry eyes.

"Yes?" Her glance measured up Josiah, Lucas, and the truck behind them, loaded with everything they owned in the world.

"We called about the apartment."

"Right. It's your lucky day." The rusting hinges shrieked as Heather Price opened the door wider. "There's a special right now—first month free."

8

———

NOW THAT WAS a half an hour well spent."

As Officer Keisha Miller and I badged out, most of the eyes in ward two followed our every move. The normal fights over the TV had stopped, hands twitched, and several heads had sunk behind the protective barrier of the couches.

"It wasn't my idea." I'd advised Dr. Mehta that Lucas wouldn't talk to the police, but pressure from the Duluth PD and the U.S. Forest Service had become intense, so we agreed to facilitate "an interview" with Lucas. Officer Miller, our liaison police officer, had asked question after question while Lucas clenched his fists and stared out the window. "He's not ready to talk to the authorities."

I inched her toward the stairs as she methodically folded up the Boundary Waters maps and shook her head. "Got a giant F.U. plastered to his forehead, if you ask me."

"He's a forensic mental health patient." Three more of them were peering through the door of the ward, tracking the receding flash of the officer's tie clip and badge.

"I just recorded thirty minutes of me talking to a wall. The chief said they're desperate for leads and what am I going to give him? The most I've done today is chase two groupies off the property."

"They got inside the gate?"

"Don't ask me how. Both of them were carrying 'Free Lucas Blackthorn' signs, which is the first time I've seen that. We've gone from interest to protest and now I'm clocking more time cruising the perimeter of this place than actually inside it." Officer Miller's shoes echoed in the stairwell as we descended to the first floor. Next to her, my tread was almost silent. We badged into the main hall and toward the front entrance, where shards of sunlight sliced the walls.

"I need a favor."

"There were more of them this morning." She nodded past the doors into the parking lot and beyond. "He wants out and they want in."

"I'm trying to piece together the Blackthorns' last days before they disappeared and I need to find a copy of a police report. Josiah Blackthorn was arrested, no charges filed, in northern Minnesota."

She paused near the security desk, putting her hat on. "That'd be public record. You know how to fill out forms, right?"

"It's urgent. And there might be a related case, but I don't know the details. I wouldn't know what to request."

The men in ward two had exhibited acute stress response symptoms at the sight of Officer Miller's uniform. Paleness. Dilated pupils. Shaking. I kept my hands still and waited while she looked me up and down. "You're his speech therapist. Your job is just to help him talk, right?"

"Maybe it'll give us something to talk about."

After a beat she nodded, slipped her sunglasses on, and told me to email her the details of the arrest.

———————

Officer Miller and I had gone through the Congdon orientation together along with a roomful of other new hires and volunteers, back when I'd first started as an orderly and she was rotating in as our liaison to the Duluth police force. For two full days we watched outdated videos and reviewed policies while she compulsively checked her phone like she was praying for a domestic disturbance to save her from the PowerPoint. I assumed she'd drawn the short straw for this gig until the end of the orientation, when Dr. Mehta joined us and invited the group to share any experiences that had compelled us to work at Congdon. A moment of silence suffocated the room before, one by one, everyone started telling their stories. Someone had a bipolar friend. Another person's father was diagnosed with an antisocial personality disorder. One of the volunteers suffered from bulimia for most of her childhood until realizing she needed help. Every person in the room spoke up except the two of us, but then—after the tissues had been passed and all the bolstering smiles began to fade—Officer Miller cleared her throat.

"I had a brother who was off, always low, never wanted to get help, never even wanted anyone to look at him. But I saw him. I saw him right up to the first morning of his junior year when he slit his wrists in the bathtub." Her eyes shimmered with deep pools of tears. I'd never seen an eye hold on to that much water, refusing to let it go.

That was my cue. I should have reached out for Officer Miller's hand or touched her forearm and told them how every night when my mother tucked me into bed I could see fault lines of pain cracking through her body, how the tighter I hugged her the more she crumbled away, as if the density of my love was too much to withstand, until one night she broke completely. She left a note on my nightstand, went to the bathroom, and ate two bottles of aspirin.

Everyone at Congdon had a story. Some of us had more than one.

"I used to be a patient here," I murmured and picked at a chipped spot on the table until human resources started handing out badges and explaining the building's layers of security.

What makes someone disappear?

After my mom's suicide attempt, we all tried to pretend things were fine. Mom cleaned the house and lingered in the shadows outside my school, waiting to walk me home. She showed me how to make grilled cheese and ramen noodles and how to tell the difference between gabbro and basalt. We built a rock garden in a corner of the yard and I memorized every mineral, their Mohs scale hardness, whether they were igneous, sedimentary, or meta-morphic, knowledge that seemed more vital than anything I was learning at school. Dad spent hours analyzing the composition of the lake bed, the shoals, all the underwater hazards that had wrecked countless ships like the *Bannockburn*. Maybe he thought it was something they could share, the intersection of rock and water, but we both saw how her eyes drifted off the map to places we couldn't follow.

During Dad's busy season in the summer, she took me up to her family cabin near the Boundary Waters, just her and me, and that's where she seemed the strongest. We paddled through lake after lake, silent amid the towering pines that surrounded us like a cathedral, our feet baptized on the shores of every portage. When we returned to Duluth in the fall everything seemed dirtier, harder. She stopped waiting for me after school. Then one day she accepted a job conducting a copper study on the Iron Range—Minnesota's mining belt that had once turned Duluth into a boomtown—packed a bag and left us a note saying she might not be back. Two months later she quit the job and began sending me rocks in the mail: a hunk of granite at the first snowfall, a nugget of amethyst for spring, carefully polished agates gleaming like birthday candles. I kept a rock and mineral field guide by my bed and studied them, trying to interpret whether a white hue meant purity or sorrow. Could I dissect her state of mind from an intricate banding pattern? There were never any return addresses on the boxes and the postmarks came from further and further away—North Dakota, Wyoming. I tried googling the towns, searching for her in newspaper photos and company directories, but the rocks were the only evidence she existed until one day even they stopped coming. She disappeared without a physical or digital trace. It was a gradual abandonment, like inching slowly into deeper, more frigid water until the bottom gives way. Was that better than Officer Miller's brother, two swift cuts and a last cascade spilled neatly into the tub's drain? They were both gone, leaving no path for anyone to follow.

If Josiah had left a path, I was going to find it.

While I waited for Officer Miller to find the arrest records, I began hunting, looking for other families who'd turned away from society. There had to be a precedent, a pattern. As the gales started battering the house, I curled up with my laptop and searched. The first and most famous case was the Lykov family of Siberia, and after I read everything I could find about them I discovered another story, this time in a different generation on a new tilt of the globe.

Ho Van Thanh had lived a quiet life until the Vietnam War spilled into his village and he watched his family die in an explosion. Some accounts said a mine blew up, others that the village came under siege by American bombers, and even the identity of the family members who died varied depending on who was telling the story, but they all agreed on what happened next. Thanh scooped up his infant son, Lang, and fled into the jungle. Eventually the war ended and life got back to normal, but Ho Van Thanh never returned. He raised Lang in a handmade treehouse where they ate corn and fruit. They caught animals in traps, made their clothes from tree bark, and every time the nearby villages grew and expanded, Thanh led his son further into the jungle, retreating almost to the top of a mountain in order to stay hidden from the world outside.

Forty years passed and Lang became the caregiver as Thanh aged and sickened. They didn't know the war had ever ended until nearby villagers heard rumors of the men in the jungle and made contact with them. When Thanh's condition became known, a team of people were sent to "rescue" them. Thanh was forcibly carried off the mountain and Lang met the world for the first time, wide-eyed and silent. Both father and son fell into a clinical depression in the months that followed and all the viruses

Lang had never encountered made him as sick as his father. It took them a year to recover and eventually they moved to a small house near their jungle. Lang adjusted to life in the village, but Thanh never did. His main ambition at eighty-seven years old was to return to the wilderness. When a reporter asked to see the place they'd lived for so many decades, Lang also jumped at the opportunity to go back and set off into the jungle without a second's pause.

I found other stories—Timothy "the Grizzly Man" Treadwell, Christopher McCandless of Alaska, and Christopher Knight, the Maine woods hermit, all loners who saw the open land as more pure and untainted by human civilization—but the Lykovs and Ho Vans were different. They were families, people bonded by love. The sacrifices they made were for each other.

I taped up pictures of the Ho Vans next to the others, my refrigerator transforming into a giant milk carton of the missing, and then stood back, squinting my eyes, letting the lines between them blur. The Lykovs and the Ho Vans were driven into the wilderness by tragedy and murder, by the ugliness of worlds they might not have survived. Something galvanized them, something they couldn't fight or ignore.

What had galvanized Josiah? He wasn't fleeing from religious persecution or escaping a war, but something made his son shake with fear ten years later. *I won't turn him over.* I needed him to talk to me, to trust me, to tell me something more substantial than how disgusting the food was today. I was done being his breezy friend.

Agafia. Lang. Lucas. I stared at their pictures on the fridge, the children of world-abandoning decisions. They hadn't chosen to disappear, yet they stayed. They'd remained in the wilderness for reasons beyond fear, beyond danger, because something in their environment fed them. Most children grew up hungering to see more of the world, but they had been satiated.

And just like that, I knew what to do.

Congdon wasn't only a building; the facility boasted sprawling grounds enclosed by a ten-foot wrought-iron, spiked fence. The entrance and parking lot took up the west side, the flower and vegetable therapy gardens were shriveled with their last gourd vines in the south, and the north and east sides boasted wooded, leaf-covered trails. Grass crunched under our feet as Bryce and I walked Lucas around the building, dressed in an oversized hooded coat. I glanced at the fence every few seconds and didn't breathe easier until we reached the evergreen cover of Congdon's own private forest.

"Wait here. Keep an eye out," I told Bryce, who shrugged and dropped onto a bench, pulling out his phone.

I led Lucas through the trees, winding our way back to a corridor of evergreens where it was darker and colder. Outside the grove the trees looked like they grew straight into the air but from within they loomed toward an invisible center point, blocking out the sun and dimming even the memory of brilliance. There were no paths in here, only layers of wet needles that infused the air with pungent decay. None of the patients who had grounds privileges came here on their walks; it was too quiet, too confined.

I stopped when the shadows engulfed us, when I couldn't see anything beyond the trees. The sounds of traffic and a distant airplane still intruded, but at least we were hidden from any of the protesters who might be prowling the edges of the property. It was the closest thing to the Boundary Waters I could give him.

He walked a few paces further, reaching a hand out to brush a low hanging branch. Then he squatted down, both feet planted firmly in the needles, and closed his eyes. His chest rose and fell, and no one in yoga class had every looked more at one with their universe.

"Thank you." The words were barely audible.

I sat cross-legged nearby and picked up a pinecone, rolling it back and forth in my hands, waiting for him to breathe his fill. Long minutes passed, but I wasn't impatient. He wasn't the only one who found solace in the shadows.

Eventually he moved, exploring the dank oasis—needles, dead branches, the hard-packed ground—and then crept over to examine me, as if I was a castoff of the trees, too. He pulled on a few strands of my hair and frowned, asking what color it was supposed to be.

"Brown."

His eyes narrowed and then a ghost of a smile played over his face. "That's ten points."

The Grinch had been teaching him Scrabble.

"Only if you don't land on a bonus tile." I kept my hands loose in my lap. "And you should really start stacking your words. Do you know what 'oe' is?"

He shook his head.

"The Scrabble dictionary calls it a westerly wind. You have no chance without oe."

He grinned, but the smile died as soon as he looked at my hair again. "Was it ever long?"

"Yes."

He drew back, as if long, brown hair frightened him. As I stared at his head, trying to figure out what was churning inside, he reached out again and picked up one of my hands, turning it over and tracing the lines of purple veins like a map he'd finally gotten permission to inspect. I let him, remaining silent until he began pressing on the pad of my thumb and watching the skin turn white before the blood flooded back into the tissue.

"We talked last week about your father."

No reaction, except an increase of pressure on my thumb.

"You said no one could help you and that's why you disappeared."

Again, nothing. His head stayed stubbornly down.

"Lucas." I tugged on my trapped hand. "What did you need help for?"

The pressure on my thumb was almost bruising now. He squeezed bone and tendon together as the red rushed in and out underneath the skin.

"You don't know?" he asked my hand.

I wrenched it out of his grip, pulling him forward so he had to catch himself before landing in my lap, his face inches from mine. His pupils were almost completely dilated, his breath unsteady.

"I wouldn't ask you if I did."

He drew back and began inching away, but I followed, not allowing him the avoidance. As we edged over the beds of needles, his back started to tremble.

"I don't know what to believe. It could be a trap. Look at you." He shoved a handful of dead needles in my direction. "I thought you were her and that's why they sent you. To trick me into talking. But she's not you because you're fine. You're right here and you're fine and she wasn't. She wasn't fine."

He backed up all the way to the base of a pine, pressing himself against the trunk and burying his head in his arms. I crept underneath the sharp branches, heart pounding.

"Who, Lucas? Who are you talking about?"

He raised his head. "Santa's bag. She was draped over his shoulder, all wrapped up like a bag of toys."

"Who?"

Lucas stared into the branches with unfocused eyes and a tremor rocked him back and forth before he swallowed and said in a plain, low voice.

"The body."

I saw it in a flash, a woman's lifeless form thrown over a shoulder, her long brown hair swinging toward the ground. Obstruction of justice and an escape from the world, to a place where justice didn't exist.

"Lucas, tell me about her. Did you know who she was?" I grabbed his arm and the contact yanked him from his memories and sent him reeling back, hitting his head against the pine.

"I don't know where she is."

"Lucas." I made my voice as calm as possible, inching closer. "Stay with me here. It's okay. I'm the last person in the world who would—"

Without warning he pulled my feet out from underneath me. My spine hit the ground and a rock grazed my head. The white noise of crunching needles made me roll over to see Lucas sprinting out of the trees.

Shouting for Bryce, I scrambled through the underbrush. When I broke into the clearing near the fence Lucas had already climbed three fourths of the way to the top.

"Don't do this, Lucas!" I jumped for his leg, but he kicked me off and I stumbled back. "This isn't the way."

He chanted as he climbed, hoisting one foot in between the spikes, and it was only when he turned back to look at me that I caught what he was saying.

"I'm sorry I'm sorry I'm sorry."

"Don't. Be. Sorry." I grunted as I hauled myself up an iron post and locked a hand over his trailing ankle. "Be. Better."

He tried to lift his body over the spikes, but I let go of the bar with my other hand and wrapped both around his foot. If he was going to escape, he'd have to haul me out with him.

A bang sounded right behind my head. I couldn't look. "Bryce?" More scrambling, scraping, a heavy breath, and just as Lucas pulled me up another foot, hoisting his torso over the top of the spikes with a Herculean effort, an arm shoved its way over my body and connected with Lucas's shin. I don't remember the actual contact. I saw the arm, thick and blotchy, and something clutched in the hand. A round black device, like a flashlight, but I knew it wasn't a flashlight. Before I could let go of Lucas's ankle, the current hit me and an overpowering clicking noise pounded the walls of my brain. Everything seized. My body turned into one solid contraction—muscles, tendons, and nerves all fused together. I was frozen, glued to Lucas's foot except there was no foot, there wasn't anything except a giant master power switch that had been flipped on inside my body and the relentless click, click, clicks that shot lightning from my head. An eternity passed before someone turned off the switch and all my muscles gave out.

The dull smack of the ground was a relief. I lay on the dead leaves with my legs twisted underneath me as my senses blinked back into focus, brain foggy but blissfully quiet. Someone ran through the leaves, crunching a frantic trail away from me and a voice began shouting in the distance. I rolled over and forced my arms, which felt like I'd been carrying my weight in granite, to brace me up. When I looked toward the fence, I saw what the yelling was for.

Lucas's body lay on the sidewalk through the bars and a spreading line of red snaked out from underneath his skull.

9

"LUCAS!"

I crawled to the fence and reached through the bars to shake his arm, but he was too far away. His body was crumpled toward the street and the thick gray coat prevented me from even seeing if his chest was rising. I kept repeating his name, telling him to stay with me as I worked to pull the phone out of my jeans pocket. It seemed impossible to extract. Every muscle in my body felt weak. Just as I finally worked it free a thundering of feet sounded from the sidewalk outside the fence and two security guards and Bryce descended on Lucas's still-as-death form.

Bryce felt his throat—"He's alive!"—and then started to push him to his back.

"Don't move him!"

"I'm not!" Bryce drew back and glanced at the security guard who paced the sidewalk and checked each direction of the street every two seconds. The other one clutched a phone to his head, muttering answers to the person on the line while he stared at the blood trailing along the sidewalk. I was on the wrong side of the fence, trapped. I wanted to run to the entrance and double back along the street, except one—I didn't dare leave Lucas alone with these guys, and two—I honestly didn't know if my legs worked properly yet.

"What the hell were you thinking, tasing him ten feet off the ground? You could have killed him."

"What was I supposed to do?" Bryce fired back. "You nearly let him escape. Awesome plan, Maya. They teach you that in therapy school?"

Arguing with morons was like kicking a boulder; your feet would bleed before you found a fissure, but anger with Bryce was the only thing keeping the terror at bay. Bloody feet were all I had.

"I had his foot. You could've called security, or didn't they teach you how to ask for help in kindergarten?"

We traded insults for another minute until one of the security guards stopped pacing and waved his arms in wild circles. An ambulance sped to a halt in front of us right as Nurse Valerie jogged down the sidewalk with two of Lucas's fans right behind her. The medics and Valerie examined Lucas while the security guards fought to push back the fans who were arguing about the right to peaceful assembly and holding their phones up, trying to catch as much as they could on camera. I struggled to hear the medical team's comments. Broken shoulder. Laceration near the temple. Multiple contusions. And then—making me release a giant breath I hadn't known I was holding—pulse stable.

As they loaded Lucas into the ambulance I stood up and immediately fell into the iron bars. The tingling ache in my body raced into my left ankle, concentrating itself into a massive throb.

"Are you okay, miss?" A medic appeared on the other side of the fence.

"I'm fine." I batted him off and took a lurching step sideways to prove it. "Go."

"She's the other tase," Bryce said, like his only responsibility for this situation was standing off to the side making up bullshit words.

"Follow us to St. Mary's," the medic ordered before climbing in the back and shutting the doors. The ambulance took off, lights and siren blaring.

"You shouldn't walk on that, Maya," Valerie was saying, but I'd already turned and begun limp-running to the building.

I ducked through the pines, putting as little weight on my left side as possible but every step felt like shoving my foot into a raging bonfire. Tears were streaming down my face by the time I retrieved my bag out of my locker, limped back to the parking lot, and got to my car. I fumbled the keys out, thanking God and Buddha and Henry Ford for designing cars with all the pedals on the right. As Nurse Valerie ran after me with an ACE bandage, I waved her off and gunned the car out of the lot and into the residential streets, zigzagging my way down the hill to St. Mary's hospital while my hands shook on the steering wheel. My only thought, as my phone buzzed incessantly from somewhere at the end of a long tunnel, was getting to Lucas.

———

A brace, four hours, and five refusals of ibuprofen later, I sat in Lucas's hospital room waiting for him to wake up. Dr. Mehta didn't look much better than me when she arrived. She'd been presenting at a conference in Rochester when she got the call and drove straight to Duluth, only stopping to pick up her luggage at the hotel. As I filled her in with what I knew, the attending doctor stopped by to check on Lucas.

"He's incredibly lucky to be alive. The fall could have been fatal, but he's going to walk away with only minor fractures to the skull and shoulder, and likely a concussion, although we had some difficulty assessing that."

Lucas stirred behind us, clanking his handcuffs against the bars of the hospital bed and groaning softly. I watched him until he quieted back down, half listening to the two of them discuss his test results, expected recovery time, and eventual transfer back to Congdon. My phone hadn't stopped buzzing since I'd left Congdon and I reluctantly checked the sites, already knowing what I would find.

The video was posted to the Facebook fan page, a forty-five second clip of the medics hovering over Lucas, trying to zoom in on his face, and then panning over to me laying behind the fence and Bryce hulking in the background. Three hundred people had already commented and, scrolling through the noise, I caught Bryce's name being mentioned and at least one of the guards. Swallowing, I felt a hand touch my shoulder.

"You've been here the whole time?"

The attending doctor had returned to his rounds, leaving the two of us alone next to Lucas's bed.

"Look at this." I tilted the phone. "It'll be on the evening news."

"Yes, I was talking to the board on the way here, discussing the best way to handle the publicity."

The sound of metal on metal came again. Even in sleep Lucas was restless. They said he was awake for the CAT scan but refused to answer any of their assessment questions about concussion symptoms, and the IV of pain medication had sent him back to la-la land before I gained access to see him.

"I'm curious about your decision to take Lucas outside, given his case history," Dr. Mehta asked.

I turned to the window. Only a sliver of Superior was visible above the old brick Victorians of downtown and the water looked gray, like a storm was coming in. "I thought he would feel more comfortable surrounded by trees instead of walls."

"And did he?"

"Yes, at first. We talked about Scrabble and then he told me a bit about his childhood." Dr. Mehta's gaze followed me as I sat down. Her reading glasses were still balanced on the end of her nose from when she'd been looking over the chart and I felt like a specimen in a petri dish, another lab result she could trust for answers. My skin felt too tight and a sickness began contracting my stomach.

"Did he give you any more details about his father?"

"No," I lied.

"I know you've had a traumatic day yourself, but can you pinpoint any correlation between your discussion and what made him attempt to escape again?"

The body. A body with long, brown hair. The sack of toys that wasn't worth turning his father over.

I glanced at the bed and pretended to think as I searched Lucas's face where dark bruises began to ring his eye sockets. My stomached pitched. Then I shook my head, meeting the hope and expectation in Dr. Mehta's face.

"Nothing obvious. His childhood memories were pleasant—I guess they had a dog at one point—so unless he's triggered by Scrabble, he must have been waiting for an opportunity. I'm sorry. I shouldn't have attempted it."

Dr. Mehta shook her head and motioned for me to come with her. "It was a good instinct. I see why you tried it."

She opened the door and held my arm to help me down the hall. Her touch, the warm, dry comfort of it, was hard to accept.

"If you remember anything else about the session, something that may have upset him . . ."

I nodded, seeing only the bright red exit sign at the end of the hall. "I know what to do."

The next morning I got a frantic text from Dad with a link to the video of Lucas, which had aired on all four local news stations and who knew how many more across the state and country. I spent fifteen minutes calming him down and telling him not to cut the *Bannockburn* expedition short, and I arrived late for my shift at Congdon to find Officer Miller waiting for me. She sized up the brace on my ankle, but didn't comment on it, handing me a thick manila envelope instead.

"That was fast." I unfastened it and peeked inside at the fat stack of paper.

"I looked the stuff over to see if it might help with the search but didn't see anything useful." She crossed her arms. "Arresting officer's information is on the top, in case you need anything else, and don't feed me any crap like you don't know how to make a phone call. I checked on you, too."

I didn't know what to say. It was impossible to lie or play it off, but I couldn't talk about my time in Ely, no more than I could've called their police station to request this case file myself. Silently, I re-clasped the envelope and hugged it to my chest.

When it became clear I wasn't going to offer any explanations, Officer Miller sighed and straightened her hat, nodding once before leaving. "Happy reading."

There was no time to go through it before my shift started. I stored the envelope in my locker and thought about nothing else during my morning sessions. Every hour dragged. I barely heard the jokes about how "shocking" my ankle looked or whether I was going to be the Bride of Frankenstein for Halloween. Even one of my aphasia patients, Greta, had to throw flashcards at me to get my attention. When it was finally noon, followed by what was supposed to be an hour-long session with Lucas, I grabbed the envelope and hobbled to my car, driving to the hospital without a word to anyone.

The nurses' station let me into Lucas's room and gave me an update. He'd been awake all night as the nurses—accompanied by security guards—administered drips, drew blood, and checked his vitals while he watched with a "creepy intensity" that made most of them hand the next round off to someone else. When I arrived he'd finally fallen asleep; he seemed to be dreaming, mumbling and shifting restlessly in bed. I helped myself to the pudding, roll, and juice on his untouched lunch tray, ignoring the meat-product that smelled identical to what we fed our patients, while pulling out the contents of the manila envelope on the other, unoccupied bed. As I chewed and read, the pieces slowly came together.

Heather Price, a twice divorced dental receptionist in Ely, was reported missing after she didn't show up for work for two days. Her duplex was empty, but the police found clothes belonging to a man and boy in the side she rented out—my heart rate picked up—when they conducted their search. According to neighbors, she lived alone. While they were searching the home, the police encountered Josiah Blackthorn, who'd just returned from a camping trip in the Boundary Waters. When asked about Ms. Price, Josiah lied. He claimed he hadn't seen her since he'd last paid rent, a story that was disproved by two neighbors who'd witnessed them fighting. Believing he was somehow connected to the woman's disappearance, the police arrested Josiah for obstruction of justice.

And Lucas? I flipped through pages, skimming for any mention of the boy's location while his father was locked up, but there was nothing. A scared nine-year-old had no place in a criminal report.

Two days after the arrest Heather's body was found. She'd died behind a house in the nearby town of Virginia and the medical examiner put her date of death within the time frame Josiah's camping permit said he was in the Boundary Waters. Heroin was found in her body, the death was ruled an accidental overdose, and within a week the Blackthorns disappeared.

At the bottom of the pile of papers were a series of photographs, mostly shots of the corpse and the townhouse, but the last one looked like a print of an ID badge from her job. The woman smiled at the camera with gaunt cheekbones and too-white teeth, her face framed by perfectly styled, flowing brown hair.

I stared at the picture and then jumped when a nurse and the security guard strode into the room. She glanced at the empty food containers on top of my stacks of papers and raised an eyebrow as she adjusted monitors and changed the IV drip.

"Has he woken up since you've been here?" she asked.

"No, just a lot of that." I motioned to his twitching hands as he unconsciously pulled against the restraints.

"You could try talking to him, but I'd stay on that side of the room if I were you. Chocolate pudding isn't worth an assault."

"Depends on the pudding."

"Not that pudding." After tucking the sheet in and recording his vitals, the two of them left me staring at Lucas's form, wishing I could take her advice.

I needed to talk to someone and I wished—for maybe the first time since I'd been committed—that I had a friend, someone I could trust. The street kids I ran with before Congdon had all heard what happened and avoided me like the plague after I got out. I started taking college classes in high school, with no time for pep rallies or clubs, and by the time I officially started at the university I was already a sophomore. Then it was all about getting accepted into the speech pathology Master's program, and the few friends I made there were largely study partners. We bonded over anatomy and assistive technology, and we hugged each other goodbye after graduation. Dr. Mehta called my lack of social support an attachment disorder. I never really cared about it until now.

Lucas's head lolled toward me on his pillow. A dusting of beard colored his cheeks, which looked more sunken than yesterday. His wrists were raw from unconscious fights with the handcuffs. Grabbing a bottle from a side table, I picked up his hand and carefully rubbed some lotion over the red welts, feeling his pulse thrum in time to the blips on the monitor. As I finished one side, his fingers twitched and closed over mine.

"Lucas?" I leaned closer. "Can you hear me?"

His head flopped away, but his fingers tightened.

"I need you to wake up. Do you know the name Heather Price?" I said it again, studying his face for any reaction. Another head jerk and a few mumbled words. Nothing I could decipher. I moved to his other wrist, trying to figure out why I was playing nursemaid to an unconscious, difficult patient who only gave me injuries and riddles. His wrists were warm, though, and for a second I tried to remember the last time I'd reached out and voluntarily touched another person outside of work. No memory came to mind. I glanced at the door to make sure we were alone before carefully closing my hand around his and drawing it to my coat.

"I'm here, see? I'm right here, but you've got to wake your lazy ass up." Then I dropped my voice even further and admitted what I would never say to anyone conscious. The reason I was standing here with lotion-covered hands.

"I miss talking to you."

My time was up; I had to get back to Congdon before the afternoon sessions began. Capping the bottle, I limped over to scoop up the police papers and stuff them away, then—on an impulse—I left the picture of Heather Price on Lucas's bedside table, writing a note on top of it in thick black marker.

Her?
—Maya

Eight hours later I pulled up to the house and forced myself to get out of the car. In my first afternoon session one of the female patients stomped on my ankle, laying me out flat and all I could think as I gasped and clutched it was that I should have known better than to wear the brace; some people looked at Achilles and only saw a heel. I used a crutch from Nurse Valerie for the rest of the day, refused the ibuprofen she tried to give me, and spent the drive home counting the number of incident reports I'd had to file in the last two weeks. My phone buzzed with an incoming call from Dr. Mehta, but I let it go to voicemail and pulled up in front of the house. At least the day was over. All I had to do now was get myself from the car to my bed. No problem.

I kept up the silent pep talk as I hobbled through the gate toward the house, where Jasper barked with manic excitement. As soon as I opened the door he shot out to pee without even a sniff or a lick hello.

"Sorry, Jazz. I know it was a long day." Guilt wormed its way through the pain as I waited for him to take care of business, until a voice too close to me said—

"Long, but interesting."

I whipped around, peering through the shadows to see Lucas standing by my front steps.

10

WHAT THE—" was all I got out before Jasper flew across the lawn.

Lucas sprang backward and almost cleared the fence, but Jasper caught him by the foot and held on fast. Kicking, Lucas tried to shake the dog while straddling precariously on top of the chain link.

"Jasper! Heel!"

He dropped Lucas's foot immediately and ran across the yard to stand guard between me and our trespasser, a low growl still trembling in his throat.

"Good boy." I scratched behind his ears.

"Good boy?" Lucas echoed, squatting on the other side of the fence, holding his foot. Jasper barked.

I stared at his huddled form, trying to wrap my head around the fact that he was somehow here and not unconscious in his hospital bed. How did he get out? How could he have walked all this way without being spotted by his "Free Lucas Blackthorn" fans? Three of them were stationed outside Congdon right now, holding signs as I'd driven through the gate. Smoothing Jasper's fur, I checked both directions, finding no signs of life on the cracked pavement or behind the drawn shades lining either side of the street. Maybe it was the throb in my ankle, or the darkness, or the nervous rumbles vibrating under my hand, but long seconds passed where everything felt like I'd crossed into some alternate world in which cause and effect had simply drifted away from each other, disappearing as effortlessly as balloons in the night. I gave up. Turning in slow motion, I pulled Jasper inside.

I took him to his kennel and paused to nuzzle the warmth of his bristly neck, to breathe in his earthiness until I felt grounded again. When I latched the door shut and turned around, Lucas was standing inside the front door watching me.

He wore a long, tan coat with one sleeve hanging loose because of the sling couching his fractured shoulder. His face looked even more drawn than when he'd been sleeping, shadowed with beard and eclipsed by those blue eyes. They followed me now as I slowly rose and faced him.

I opened my mouth, torn between a dozen burning questions, before finally settling on a simple demand.

"Explain."

"Okay," he agreed but said nothing else, instead peering inside the kitchen doorway. Then he moved along the hallway and looked in each room as if he'd never seen a house before. I supposed he hadn't, at least not in the last ten years. He disappeared into my room and I limped down the hall to find him staring at the bed. He startled when he heard me and ran a hand along the wall, stopping at a bookshelf full of rock guides and speech pathology textbooks.

"This is where you sleep."

"Yes."

He frowned at the dark blue walls and took a few halting steps into the room before edging back around me, so close I could smell alcohol swabs and the bleached cotton of his hospital scrubs. "And the other door?"

"Where my father sleeps, when he's not on the boat."

As he turned on Dad's bedroom light and surveyed the room, I flexed my foot, testing it, putting weight on it. If it came down to my sprained ankle vs. his broken shoulder, my ankle would win. Lucas barely seemed aware of my presence, though, instead inspecting the minutia of the bedroom—an end table cluttered with work gloves, drill bits, and creased maps, rows of weatherproof jackets in various stages of succumbing to the weather, hanging in the closet, and a dark wood jewelry box, set back in the corner away from everything else.

"What are you doing?"

Skirting past me again, he opened the linen closet and then went into the bathroom. When I followed he was standing next to the toilet, staring at the piece of driftwood I'd found on the shore last summer. I'd cleaned, sealed, and mounted the gnarled branch on one of the leftover slate tiles, and when Dad first saw it his mouth had dropped open. *It's beautiful, Maya*, he said. *I can't believe you took garbage and made it into this.* Running a hand over the wood, Lucas turned, shaking his head at the space I'd worked so hard to transform.

"Lucas." I squared off, blocking the door.

"I don't know this house." His wrists were still raw from the handcuffs he'd somehow escaped.

I took a step forward and braced my weight. "Of course you don't. You've never been here before."

"I remember . . ." He swiveled around, searching the walls. "I remember a mountain of salt."

A mountain of salt? I shook my head, trying to make sense of what he was saying. There were giant sand and taconite piles in the commercial zones near the harbor, but salt? Where would he have seen something that looked like a mountain of salt?

"I only have a little salt shaker here. Do you want to see it?"

He didn't reply, sinking instead into a crouch on the floor and holding his head. The doctor had warned about a possible concussion. Then I noticed one of his slippers—the kind they gave patients to use the bathroom or go to the cafeteria—was turning red.

"Come on. You're bleeding."

I helped him back to his feet and checked his pupils, which looked normal, then grabbed a first aid kit out of the cabinet. Jasper whined when we passed through the living room.

"So this was your grand plan?" I couldn't help the dazed laugh that bubbled out of my mouth when we got to the kitchen. "You wanted to escape Congdon to visit my house? I should have just bought some cookies and gone home instead of killing myself trying to stop you."

He frowned at his foot, looking calmer now. "Maybe you could've locked up your dog, too."

"I think whoever trespasses in a yard with a sign that says, ATTACK DOG ON SITE. ENTER AT YOUR OWN RISK. deserves whatever they get."

"Why do you have an attack dog?"

I dropped into a chair, exhaling gratefully at the relief of pressure on my ankle. "My dad got him as sort of a welcome home present after I'd been gone once. He's a sailor, so he lives on the lake for a good part of the year, and he worries. He thinks . . . he thinks I need protection."

Now it was Lucas's turn to laugh and I couldn't help grinning. "I know, right? Dad trained him as a guard dog, but he's a big softie underneath and it's nice to have the company. The nights can get pretty long in the winter."

"Yes, they can." His smile faded. After a moment he seemed to forget about Jasper and dropped into a chair, studying the kitchen as if looking for something he'd misplaced. I watched him carefully, trying to gauge his mental state and how to approach whatever came next.

"What about your mom?" he asked after an awkward pause.

I shrugged, dousing some cotton balls in iodine. "She didn't stick around. Take off your slipper and put your foot on the table."

He did, letting me examine it. There were two shallow scrapes from Jasper's incisors with some abrasions on either side. I swabbed the worst of it, ignoring his hiss of pain. The longer I wiped the blood off and applied bandages, the more surreal the situation became. Lucas Blackthorn was sitting at my kitchen table like he'd just dropped by to hang out. I should have called Congdon the minute I saw him. Or I should've let Jasper hold him while I phoned the police. As if it knew what I was thinking, my cell phone bleeped to tell me I had another message from Dr. Mehta and it finally occurred to me why she'd been calling.

"There's probably a manhunt out for you now."

"Why?"

"You tend to attack people, haven't you noticed?"

"So does your dog. Why isn't he chased down and locked up?"

Raising an eyebrow, I swung a hand toward the living room where Jasper could clearly be heard scratching at the kennel door.

Lucas smiled with chagrin. "Are you going to turn me in?"

"Any minute now." I stuffed the bloody slipper back on his foot, trying not to think about why I was postponing the inevitable. He'd assaulted the couple who'd found him robbing the outfitter store; he'd choked, fought, and shoved me; and his file at Congdon clearly labeled him dangerous. But he was also injured and there was something different about him in the dull light of my kitchen, the way he was still inspecting the house even now, drinking in the details of the spice rack and coffeepot with an intrusiveness that was almost endearing, a boy who'd never learned manners, who'd never been told not to stare.

"How's your shoulder?"

He ran a hand over the coat. "It aches a little. Not bad."

So, the pain meds were still working. He hadn't been loose long.

"Did you strangle anyone to get out this time?"

"Didn't need to." His face split into an unexpected grin and he began chatting freely. "I pretended to be sleeping until they took my handcuffs off to change my clothes. When they left to get something, I slipped out the window, took a jacket from an unlocked truck, and headed toward the lake. From there it was easy to find your house."

I grabbed an ice pack from the freezer, remembering how I'd showed him my street on the map of Duluth. It was a mistake real psychiatrists wouldn't make, giving personal information to their patients.

As I came back to sit at the table Lucas described the people he'd seen roaming the streets: the homeless, the packs of college kids, the drunken tourists, and the older couples bundled in their peacoats for a dinner on the town. I waited for him to finish, then casually asked if anyone had noticed *him*. As far as I knew, he was totally unaware of his fame or the controversy his reappearance had created. He said he'd stuck to the shadows, no one had spoken to him. I nodded, glancing into the darkness outside the window.

"Why?" The question slipped out before I could find a more professional frame for it. "Why are you here?"

His gaze lingered on me. Slowly he drew my hand across the table, taking the ice pack from me and setting it down.

"A couple reasons. The first is that I missed talking to you, too."

Too? I pulled back in surprise as it registered. "You were awake?"

"Sort of. I was surfacing when you were there and by the time I woke up, you'd left."

"I would have come back tomorrow."

He shrugged. "That wasn't soon enough."

The way he said it made heat flood my cheeks and, embarrassed, I ducked my head and started to remove my boot, but he lifted my foot onto his lap.

"What are you doing?"

"You fixed my foot. I'll fix yours." He pulled off the boot and sock to reveal the swollen, wrapped ankle. "I saw you limping when you got out of the car. What happened?"

"Gymnastics injury." I nodded to the ice pack, which he applied to the swelling,

His hands closed around my calf and beneath my foot I could feel his whole body tightening. He seemed to be searching for something in me, a sign, and I didn't know what to do besides return his turbulent stare and wait.

Finally, he took a deep breath and decided.

"We never talked about it, my dad and I. Sometimes I even

thought I dreamed the whole thing." He paused, and his gaze turned inward, seeing things I couldn't.

"He only told me one thing about the world outside—that they would take me away from him. They would separate us and we would lose each other, maybe forever. He promised he would never let that happen, but now it's happened anyway, because of me."

He leaned in until I could see my own reflection in his eyes, tiny and paralyzed.

"That's the second reason I'm here—to ask for your help. It's why I'm going to tell you." He paused, faltering.

"Tell me what?"

"Why we had to hide."

I made some noodles, the nice udon ones instead of ramen, and foraged the kitchen for mushrooms, onion, and shreds of leftover chicken to stir into a simmering soup that could warm the coldest of Duluth stomachs. Lucas stared at the pictures on the refrigerator while I cooked, the Blackthorns, Lykovs, and Ho Vans all lined up like members of the same social experiment performed every forty years across the globe. The boy Lucas was the only one smiling, beaming out at us, unaware of his fate, while adult Lucas swallowed and quickly moved on to examine the appliance itself, tracing the lines of the doors, the hardware, practically getting his head caught between the fridge and the wall in order to see how the wiring worked. When the soup was done, I set one of the bowls in front of his chair and put mine on the opposite side of the table.

"You have to slurp these. It's polite." I showed him how to grab the noodles with the chopsticks and suck them out of the broth.

He mirrored my every move as carefully as he'd done during those first tense therapy sessions. Mastering the chopsticks without an issue but slurping too quickly, he whiplashed one of the noodles and ended up with broth all over his face. Laughing, I handed him a napkin.

"We didn't eat food like this—my dad and I." Lucas commented after a while, swirling his noodles with the chopsticks and smiling at the merry-go-round it created in his bowl. "We had a lot of rice and fish, dried fruit, dried vegetables. Once we had a huge container of oatmeal, and we added blueberries and spices. It was way better than the stuff Carol at Congdon calls oatmeal. Are there different kinds?"

"Institution meals aren't the best of Minnesota cuisine."

"And this is?" He took another bite, slurping respectably loud enough.

I shot him a dirty, noodle-chewing look.

"It isn't terrible," he offered.

"Thank you for sharing your delicious food, Maya," I prompted, dabbing my mouth with a napkin.

"Thank you for sharing your food, Maya." He replied pointedly, grinning.

We finished the udon with only the occasional whine from Jasper interrupting the silence, looking at each other, then away. He'd taken off the stolen jacket and it was hard not to notice the line of muscle in his arms as he lifted the bowl and drank his broth, arms that had easily overpowered me the first time we'd met, that had practically scaled ten feet of fence before I'd caught up with him. He said he needed my help, but if I understood anything about Lucas it was that he was unpredictable. Even with one limb in a sling, I didn't know what those arms were going to do next.

I collected the bowls and rinsed them out, then limped to the living room and let Jasper out of his kennel, murmuring to him to behave. Lucas stepped into the edge of the room and waited. After a moment's hesitation Jasper trotted over, sniffed his legs and feet, snorted disdainfully, and went to his dog bed to lounge.

Lucas lifted an eyebrow. "So I'm okay now?"

"As long as I like you, he likes you." I dropped into the faded blue armchair next to the dog bed and absently scratched his ears. "I told you he's a big softie."

Lucas walked to the window, moving more stiffly than before we ate, which meant the meds were probably wearing off. With only the kitchen light to illuminate him, he looked tall and somehow lonely.

"I lived in a house like this when my mother was alive. Now the memory of it is mixed up with my memory of her. I remember warmth, soft lights, her legs folded into a rocking chair. There was a box with a bright orange fish that she fed and afterward her hands smelled like the lake in a morning fog. Sometimes I just sat on the shore and inhaled, years later, thinking of her."

He turned toward where I sat in the shadows.

"She died when I was in kindergarten. Aneurysm."

"I know. I read your file." I couldn't tell him I was sorry. At least he'd had a mother who'd loved him, whose departure hadn't been by choice.

"Did my . . . *file*"—he spoke hesitantly, obviously not having used filing systems in the middle of the forest—"tell you what my father did?"

"He was a mechanic."

"No, I mean what he did after she died." Slowly, he dug into the pocket of his scrubs with the hand that wasn't trapped in the sling. A piece of paper crackled as he pressed it against his stomach, flattening it out, then held it up to catch the meager light.

It was the picture of Heather Price with my writing scrawled at the top.

I half rose, but my ankle throbbed and pushed me back in the chair. "You remember."

"What do you know about her?"

I told him the little I'd read about Heather Price's life and death, careful to omit any mention of his father. Each detail seemed new to him, adding color and depth to the image I'd left on his bedside table. He began swaying slightly and stared at the face long after I'd finished. Then he crumpled the paper, driving the heel of his hand into his temple.

"She used to watch him. She smoked cigarettes and stared out the window while he mowed the lawn, but she wouldn't come out of the house. Dad always said that buildings smothered people and I remember thinking she was suffocating in there. I can still see her hazy face in the window."

His swaying got worse until I made myself get up and hobble over to him. "Come on, lie down."

I brought him to the couch, checked his pupils, and gingerly felt along his shoulder to see how swollen it was. He gave one tight nod, looking a little pale, so I retrieved the ice pack and wished for the first time since my mom had overdosed that we kept some aspirin in the house.

He relaxed into the couch cushions as I held the ice to his shoulder and while the condensation dripped over my hand he began telling me about his childhood. The memories were fragments, scattered over a dozen different houses, apartments, and RVs in the wake of his mother's death. He hadn't made many friends at any of the schools he'd rotated through, although he liked the science and gym classes. They'd visited a sour smelling building full of old people where a man in a wheelchair faced the wall. And the woods. He had countless memories of camping, canoeing, hiking, learning about all the plants and life cycles teeming around them. Lucas loved the woods best in the summer, but his father preferred winter, the silent, white days insulated from fair-weather nature lovers.

I stared at the ice pack, afraid to look up, afraid that if I made eye contact he'd stop talking, but Lucas barely even paused. The floodgates had opened. Something had shifted and all the words he'd held back came pouring out in the faded intimacy of my living room.

They'd been camping one summer on a remote lake somewhere near Canada when Lucas got sick.

"I was fine the first night. We caught fish and toasted s'mores, but I woke up the next morning with my skin on fire and everything hurt. I couldn't even get out of the sleeping bag. Dad thought it was a cold and told me I'd feel better within a day or so. Then I started seeing bugs everywhere. Bugs crawling over the tent, bugs marching on my arms. I don't remember a lot of what happened, but somehow Dad brought me back out of the woods. The next thing I knew I was in a bedroom. A woman was giving me something to swallow, a woman with long, brown hair and flat eyes, like she'd been inside too long."

He shifted his gaze from the ceiling to me.

"I thought it was you. When I got to Congdon—I don't know—there was something different about you, familiar. I thought you were the woman who'd taken care of me when I was sick and somehow"—he shook his head, as if trying to clear it—"that's how the doctors were trying to get me to talk."

"That's why you said you knew me, why you were afraid of me?"

He nodded, lifting the picture of Heather Price again. "It was her. When I woke up in the hospital today and saw her face, I recognized it immediately. I remember her shouting at my dad and his fists, balled tight into his sides. I don't know what they were arguing about. I don't know what happened between them. It felt like I was in that strange bed twisted up with fever forever, until one night—when all the lights were out—I finally felt good enough to get up on my own."

His breathing picked up speed and his eyes darted around the living room, seeing nothing.

"Someone was moving on the stairs, bumping into the wall, walking slowly. I crept to the door of the room and peeked out, waiting for the noise to appear. Then it did. I saw my father's profile moving across the house and I almost went to him, but he was carrying something big, something draped over his shoulder."

"A body," I murmured.

"I watched him haul it out the front door and then a few minutes later the lights of his car turned on and he drove away. I went back to bed and waited. I remember feeling weak and sweaty and scared, but not of my father—I've never been afraid of my dad in my entire life. I was scared of the body, the way the hair swayed each time he took a step and the arm that hung along his back skimming the walls, the furniture. I was afraid the arm would reach out and find me, even though I knew my father was making it go away. He was taking care of it. The sun was up by the time he got back and he made us breakfast and told me we were going to camp for a while as soon as I felt better. I didn't hesitate; I wanted out of that place. I told him I was ready and later that day we canoed into the Boundary Waters and never came out.

"I know what you're thinking," Lucas said, "but he didn't do it. I can't explain it, I just know. Have you ever known something about your parents, like the knowledge is in your blood?"

I had a mother who'd abandoned me and a father who chased ghost ships, trying to salvage the impossible. I looked away, as if Lucas could read the legacy in my eyes.

"My dad spent the last ten years protecting me, providing for me. He hiked out a few times a year and came back with fresh supplies, boots when I outgrew my old ones, books and science experiments for us to try. He taught me everything he knew, including what the world was like and what they'd do to us if we ever left the Boundary Waters. He didn't tell me why. He didn't need to, because I was protecting him, too."

"But you left anyway. Why did you raid the outfitter's store?"

He covered his face with a hand. "In the last few months dad became sick, weak. He could hardly stand up, let alone hike out of our camp. When he started mumbling and sweating through his blanket I made him take the emergency medicine and went to get more, but I didn't even know what I was looking for. I waited until it was night and tried to be quick, to not get caught.

"That was three weeks ago."

Without warning Lucas sat upright and grabbed my arm, almost bruising it with the sudden force. The movement brought Jasper to his feet, but Lucas paid no attention. "If he's dead, it's my fault for leaving him. There's no one else to blame. And if he's alive I've still abandoned him. I have to get back there, Maya. Now. We need to leave today."

Jasper advanced with his ears standing straight up, a nervous growl working up his throat, the rumble of it filling the room. I could feel Lucas's heart racing through the ice pack caught between us. He was too close; I couldn't breathe.

I broke away and tugged Jasper's collar, processing everything as I pulled a hundred pounds of anxious muscle across the room on one good leg. "You want me to help you—" I broke off as Jasper whined in frustration.

"Find my father. We have to go alone."

Was he joking? We barely had one working body between us. "Lucas, you're not the only person who wants to find your father. The entire world is asking what happened to him. Do you have any idea how much attention your story has gotten? And there's Dr. Mehta, Officer Miller, and everyone working the missing persons case. U.S. Forest Service rangers are searching for him right now."

"They won't find him."

"He's not wanted for any crime. No matter what really happened with Heather Price, her case is closed. They won't take you away from each other."

He shook his head. "It doesn't matter. He won't come out. The Boundary Waters . . . it's part of him . . . he couldn't survive in this world anymore. Whatever's killing him is nothing compared to making him leave, and that's what all those other people would do, right? No, we have to go alone."

"Why me? Why did you come here when you could have been halfway to Canada by now?"

I let Jasper pull me back a step and looked Lucas directly in the eye, trapping his gaze in a way I'd never done with another patient. I always gave them a way out, room to be comfortable, the space they needed to grapple with their own voice. This, though, was way past the point of comfort. I wasn't asking him for a fluent, compound sentence; we weren't working through aphasia or a stutter. An escaped psychiatric patient was asking me to reunite him with his potential-murderer father somewhere in the wilderness, with a Minnesota winter bearing down fast.

Lucas stood up and walked over, ignoring Jasper's warning growl. He stopped a few feet away and reached out to take my free hand. "I heard you talking to Dr. Mehta yesterday."

"Jesus, don't you sleep at all?"

He laughed once. "Not really. There's too much noise here." Then, growing serious again. "You didn't tell her about the body. She asked if anything made me run and you lied to her."

"Yeah." I didn't try to explain, even though he seemed to be waiting for me to do just that.

Eventually he took a step closer. "You told me I could trust you before, but I didn't believe it. Not until now. So I'm trusting you, Maya. I'm trusting you with my father's life."

The directness in him—the openness, after so many sessions of careful avoidance—was stunning. I forgot about danger. I forgot about psychology and my job and the relationship we were supposed to have and what was possible and impossible. I had a flash of stumbling through the Congdon grounds on a sprained ankle, thinking of nothing except the trail of blood spreading underneath Lucas's body and getting to the hospital as fast as possible. The desperation had consumed me beyond all reason and only now was I beginning to understand it. I was the girl who didn't need anyone and made sure things stayed that way—no matter how many therapy students had tried to befriend me or occasional, brave-hearted guys asked me out. I turned them all down and I was relieved when Dad went out on the lake and left me with only the dog for company. My life was lonely, but there was something vital in the loneliness, an imperative that I keep the space around me empty and weightless. The only time I let myself get close to people was at

Congdon and even though I loved helping my patients beat down their barriers, it was always so they could stand on their own someday, not near me. My work didn't build relationships; it created more Mayas.

Somehow Lucas had changed everything. If it was possible, he was even more fiercely independent than me, yet he'd broken out of a guarded hospital room and traveled halfway across the city to find me, because he needed me. Not a random therapist doing their job. Not anyone else they'd tried to send to him. Me. And for the first time since my mother left, I wanted to be needed.

I realized I hadn't said anything for a good minute, standing in the middle of the living room with Lucas staring at me, yet he didn't seem bothered by the silence. He wasn't fidgeting or pressing me for a reply like most people would and it occurred to me that his life up until now must have been one decade-long conversation with his father, where a pause could fill a breath, an hour, or several sky-bleeding sunsets.

"Lucas, I—"

Jasper's sudden bark cut off the words in my throat. Hair raised, he broke out of my grip and ran toward the front door. Limping after him, I peered through the peephole and saw a police cruiser pulled up at the curb with its lights flashing. Lucas shadowed me, his eyes darting from window to window.

"What is it?"

"The police." I didn't stop to assess the situation, to rationalize. All I knew was that I wanted more time. I grabbed him by the arm and lunged toward the back door. "Let's go."

11

WE DARTED THROUGH the house as Jasper's barks echoed behind us. At the back door, I took a deep breath and motioned for Lucas to be quiet, then unlocked it and stepped into the night. The wind had picked up, battering us as we crept across the lawn. Each crunch of grass echoed in my ankle as I negotiated the roots and twigs, praying I didn't trip over any of them and give us away. Why were the police at my house? Either Dr. Mehta was worried that I hadn't answered my phone or someone had seen Lucas in the neighborhood. I felt the weight of a thousand neighbors' stares on our backs. Charges raced through my head: *aiding and abetting, accessory, repeat offender*. The last one found its mark and sent a shot of adrenaline through my system, bracing me, numbing me better than any drug as I acknowledged the full implications of what I was doing.

Behind us a flashlight beam arced across the neighbor's lawn. They'd be turning the corner any second.

We ducked into the shadows of the garage and raced to the side door. There were no windows in here. We could wait out the cops and decide what to do next. With shaking fingers, I eased the creaky knob open and pushed against the wood. Lucas was a millisecond behind me as we rushed inside, then both of us staggered to a halt.

Dad stood next to his truck holding a tire iron.

His arm relaxed when he saw me, but he stared at Lucas, obviously trying to figure out what was going on.

"Dad." I checked behind us to see the lawn was still empty. "This is . . ."

A few different lies zipped through my head, none of them really plausible with Lucas standing there in hospital scrubs and one arm bound in a sling. Before I could pick one, he cleared his throat and finished the sentence for me.

"Lucas Blackthorn."

Lucas glanced at me, apparently as unsure as I was about how to proceed.

"Your picture's been all over the news tonight." The surprise on Dad's face melted into suspicion and even though he kept his eyes on Lucas, I knew the next question was for me.

"What the hell's going on here?"

"Dad—"

"Sir—"

We spoke at the same time, both of us stepping forward right as a policeman walked through the main garage door. He surveyed the scene and homed in on Lucas, easily identifying him in the light from the workbench. Without acknowledging any of us, he pulled his gun and radioed his coordinates in, asking for backup. It was over.

With a sinking feeling, I turned my back on everyone else and touched Lucas's coat.

"Don't put up a fight. If you have to go to jail, I'll try to get them to release you as soon as possible. Just ignore everyone like you always do."

His arm was rigid, almost bursting with tension. "But"—he dropped his voice, gaze frozen on the officer—"my father."

"It's okay." I patted the sling, trying to reassure him, to sound like I had the power to make any of this okay. "Be mute. I'll handle the rest."

Dad stood off to the side, obviously listening to our exchange. I lifted my chin, determined not to be ashamed of the choices I'd made tonight. Our gazes met for a split second and then, just as the officer finished his radio call, Dad turned around and set the tire iron on a shelf.

"Glad you stopped by," he said conversationally. "My name's Brian Stark. Look who I found wandering around on the docks."

"Sir, this young man is considered a dangerous individual. I'd advise you to back away. You too, miss."

"Shit, him? More like a lost puppy. Come here, boy. Lucas, isn't it?"

Although digesting the turn of events, Lucas seemed rooted to his spot. I leaned into him, nudging him forward. Shoulders still tight, his free hand fisted, he took a calculated step toward my dad.

He swallowed before speaking. "Yes, sir?"

"You feel like hurting any of us?"

"Of course not." His face, though, said the exact opposite.

"See?" Dad gave Lucas what appeared to be a pat on the shoulder, but I knew that move from the days when I'd run loose on the streets, unwilling to listen to a thing he said. Dad was anchoring him in place. "I brought him here to see what Maya wanted to do with him."

"Sir, you should have brought him immediately to the station." The officer still had his gun trained on his suspect.

I spoke up. "I work with Lucas at Congdon."

The officer's expression made it clear he didn't think I looked capable of much more than graffiti, let alone having a career. "My orders said the suspect's doctor lived here."

"She's a speech therapist working for Dr. Riya Mehta," Dad said. "Great woman. Anyway, we finished detailing the boat and I was headed back to my truck when I spotted this one dangling off the Northland Pier. I'd seen the news of course, so I went over and told him I was Maya's dad and he came along with me. We were just fixing to take him back. Right, Lucas?"

I saw my dad's grip tighten on Lucas's shoulder and there was a beat before Lucas nodded and let his hand uncurl at his side. "I'm sorry if I caused anyone any trouble. I wanted to see Superior. I kept hearing about it and . . . wanted to see the water for myself."

"Jesus Christ." The officer grumbled, relaxing his stance. He waved the gun at the truck. "Go stand over there and put your hands on the hood. I have to pat you down anyway."

Lucas glanced at me and I nodded, so he stiffly walked to the truck and submitted to the inspection. Two more squad cars showed up within a few minutes, their lights flashing all over the alley. The neighbors I'd imagined watching us before were now glued to their windows and I saw at least one phone pointed at us from behind some curtains. I hobbled back to the house where Jasper was losing his mind and sent Dr. Mehta a text to let her know the situation.

After an extensive argument and two calls to superiors, I convinced the officers we should take Lucas directly back to Congdon according to our "original plan." The hospital obviously didn't employ enough security to contain him, the courts had already placed him in our care, and no additional crime had been committed. Eventually they agreed and even allowed Dad and me to drive him, with a police escort. Lucas and I climbed into the back of Dad's truck and we followed the police motorcade out of the alley.

Dad punched the radio off and gripped the steering wheel in silence. Lucas stared out the window at the dark houses and wind buffeted trees, the empty storefronts lined with Lincoln Park's night dwellers—dealers and drunks peppered in with the blue-collar crowd out draining their paychecks—as we drove toward downtown.

"Thanks, Dad."

"What happened to your foot?" He took a turn too sharp, making Lucas lean into me and me brace against the door.

"Why aren't you still on the water?" I countered.

"There's a storm coming in."

"But the *Bannockburn*—"

"The *Bannockburn*'s been out there for a hundred years. It can wait a little longer. Your foot, Maya."

I sighed. When he'd texted about the video and news coverage this morning, I'd omitted the part about spraining an ankle, assuming he wouldn't be back until long after it healed. I should have known better. Briefly, I recounted the Taser incident and the hospital's treatment.

"The X-ray showed no breaks. It's fine. I can barely feel it."

"You don't limp when you're fine," he snapped, and we both fell silent, hitting a stalemate.

As we began climbing the hill, Lucas turned away from the window, glancing between me and the back of Dad's head. Duluth wasn't a big city and the amount of time we had left in this ride was already dwindling. Police lights blinked over his skin, forcing my mind up the hill to what lay ahead.

"You'll go to medical first," I spoke low, ignoring the angry slice of Dad's face in the rearview mirror. "Hopefully you'll be back in ward two in a few days, tops."

He could hear what I wasn't saying. Swallowing, he looked at the tail of the squad car in front of us and the city rushing past. He didn't respond.

"You can't just skip up to the Boundary Waters tonight. You're still weak, it's below freezing, and you don't have any gear."

"Winter's coming." He rounded on me. "What would you do if it was your father out there?"

A bark of a laugh snapped both our heads to the front of the cab. "She prefers me gone. Then there's no one to complain when she half kills herself getting electrocuted or strangled by violent patients."

"Dad—" I tried to jump in but he only got louder, a captain used to bellowing over the wind. Lucas looked shell-shocked when he heard the last part and I reached out to him quickly, shaking my head. Dad hadn't known Lucas was the patient who'd choked me, and it was in everyone's best interest to keep it that way.

"What the hell was going on back there, Maya?"

"She didn't do anything," Lucas said. "I came to find her—"

"I didn't ask you, Blackthorn." The streetlights broke in waves over Dad's face, splintering his irritation as he took another turn. "And I thought you were supposed to be a kid."

Lucas turned to me. "I'm supposed to be a kid?"

"You're nineteen," I told him, "even though you don't look or act like a typical teenager."

Lucas thought about that for a second. "What are nineteen-year-olds supposed to act like?"

I shrugged. "Younger. Stupider."

He smiled. "I'll work on that. So how old are you?"

"Twenty-three."

"And you're acting like a thirteen-year-old," Dad cut in, not ready to let the conversation get away from him. "What happened back at the house?"

"Lucas is my patient. He came to tell me some things we've been working on in therapy. I think we made a breakthrough tonight."

Dad laughed again and it was a hard sound. "You got the lines down, Maya, but don't try to sell bullshit to me, even if you've made it smell like roses. Why were you running away from the police with him?"

I didn't answer. I couldn't even explain it to myself.

"Christ, I knew it was a bad idea when you took the job there. You don't go work at the same mental hospital where you spent time as a patient seven years ago."

Lucas looked at me sharply. His shock was palpable as I stared down at my lap and said in a voice that didn't sound like my own. "Eight years ago."

"Whatever. The point is that you should be in the regular world with a normal job."

"Define normal."

"Out here!" He flapped a hand at the dark, vacant streets. "You could be a therapist in a clinic making twice the money and not getting attacked every day. Do you even know how much you're worth?"

"It didn't go so well when I was out there in the regular world. Besides I do good work at Congdon. I help people." My voice came rushing back and with it, my own anger.

"You're susceptible to this head case stuff. That's all I'm saying."

"It's not contagious, Dad." Lucas laughed once, but I could still sense his surprise. "And I'm probably the least susceptible twenty-three-year-old I've ever met. It comes from being half you."

"But you're half her, too."

Before I could reply, Dad turned onto Congdon's street and I gasped. A reporter stood in front of the gate, filming a segment, next to at least a dozen people crowded onto the cracked sidewalk. They held signs and leaned into the shot, their faces washed blood-less by the camera light. There'd only been a handful of them here when I punched out a few hours ago, but news of the escape must have made them multiply. A girl about Lucas's age with bright red hair stared at the truck as we approached, holding a piece of tag-board that read IF HE'S CRAZY, I'M CRAZY. She pointed and yelled something, causing the rest of them to turn as one while the cam-eraman scrambled to get footage of our procession.

"Get down."

I pushed Lucas by the good shoulder, doubling him over in the rear seat as the guards began herding people back, trying to make way for the police motorcade. The crowd didn't want to disperse.

"Who—?" Lucas began, but anything else he might have said was lost in the yells and clamor of a mass of bodies breaking free from the guards and racing toward us. Signs waved frantically, hands reached out with grasping fingers as I held Lucas's head be-neath the window. One of the police cruisers spun a U-turn inside the gate and flipped their siren on, driving between us and the crowd. As soon as the path forward was clear, Dad gunned the engine and sped through the parking lot to the main entrance where a team of orderlies, nurses, and more security guards waited for us.

I gave Dad's shoulder a squeeze before grabbing Lucas's hand and sliding across the seat to the door. "Thanks, Dad. Don't wait for me."

We hurried toward the main doors, flanked by the remaining police officers. Once inside we were rushed to the medical ward where they performed a series of checks on an uncharacteristically docile Lucas. He submitted to every probe, answered every question, and it wasn't until I saw Dr. Mehta standing at the doorway to the triage area, eyes narrowed in speculation, that I realized I'd barely let go of Lucas's hand since the moment we got out of the truck.

12

THE NEXT MORNING the world was coated in white. A thick frost had frozen every rooftop, lawn, and tree branch in Duluth and as I peered out the staff break room window, rubbing the couch debris out of my sleep-bruised eyes, a powdery snow whipped into the panes and skittered along the ground, as if the wind refused to let it land. Sometime in the night I'd left Lucas in the care of the nurses and headed down the hall for a few restless hours of sleep. The break room furniture was scratchy and reeked of antiseptic, but it beat going home and trying to explain what happened last night while Dad looked at me in that way of his—like I was a vase glued carefully back together and he had to constantly check me for missing pieces, fissures, any sign that I might crumble again. Today was my day off, though, and I couldn't leave Jasper alone much longer. I stared into the blowing white world and listened to the tick, tick, ticks of the snow against the window, each flake hurling winter that much closer.

After checking on Lucas—who may or may not have been sleeping—I took the bus home and made sure the garage was empty before going in to shower and walk the dog. We drove up to Bayfront and paced the lake walk, where Jasper chased snow devils and I limped along the empty boards and scanned Superior's horizon. The powder wouldn't last. The sun would chase it away as soon as the clouds broke, but we were getting closer to November and not even Superior's gales could fight off the inevitable. Normally I liked winter—the four-foot drifts, the nostril-freezing arctic blasts that drove all the tourists away, leaving the town to the hardy, the survivors who bundled up and shoveled oceans of snow before retreating to our mugs and fleece blankets to wait out the endless December nights. Winter in Duluth was antisocial paradise and for someone whose mother suffered from chronic depression, there was a disconcerting comfort in the isolation. A home I recognized, even if I hadn't asked for it. Today, though, I wasn't comforted by the cold blast of wind numbing my ankle. I didn't find relief in the absence of people on the lake walk. Today I was scared for a man I'd never met.

After dropping Jasper off at home, I drove to the library and spent the rest of the morning poring over books and topographical maps. I studied pictures, read travelogues, and stared at the mottled landscape of greens and blues that would be covered in white, frozen over and closed off to even the most adventurous hikers in a few short weeks. Maybe to a young boy it would look like a mountain of salt, vast and impenetrable, but Josiah Blackthorn was out there somewhere, sick, alone. I circled the location of the outfitter's store and drew ranges out from that center point. Five miles. Ten. How far would you go up the mountain to save the person you loved most in the world?

How far would I go to help them?

————

Two days after Lucas's hospital escape I drove through the swelling crowd at Congdon's gate—at least fifteen people were bundled up and waving signs at passing cars—and punched in to find most of the staff either staring or whispering to each other on the opposite side of whatever room I was in. My dramatic recovery of the boy who came back from the dead, which had aired on every major news channel in Duluth, apparently sealed my reputation as something entirely apart from them. I spent the morning catching up on email, planning session activities for my other patients, and trying to ignore everyone whose Minnesotan niceness made them smile before walking hastily away. The one person I could count on for direct address, unfortunately, was the one person I was trying to avoid. Dr. Mehta held me back after our afternoon staff meeting.

"I approved Lucas's transfer back to ward two today."

"That's great, thanks. The group environment is his biggest challenge. The sooner we get him comfortable there, the quicker his recovery." I inched my way toward the door, thankful that my ankle felt almost back to normal.

"Yes, he still needs to acclimate and of course integrate his childhood experiences with the larger world, but Mr. Blackthorn strikes me as someone who needs a path forward. He should be thinking about short- and medium-term goals."

"We'll start working on that right away." Obediently, I made a note of it, turning to leave.

"I haven't decided who his speech therapist will be yet."

"What?" Halting in mid-escape, I swung on Dr. Mehta. "I'm his therapist."

"Shut the door and sit down, please, Maya."

I complied, watching her warily as she sat opposite me and carefully picked cat fur off her pants.

"You haven't told me what happened the night of Lucas's escape."

In a clear, even voice, I told her the same story Dad had given to the police. Unlike the officers, though, Dr. Mehta didn't appear the tiniest bit convinced.

"You weren't answering my calls earlier that evening."

"I'm sorry. I was tired and off duty."

Dr. Mehta nodded and let her gaze slide somewhere closer to my heart. "A perfectly reasonable explanation and if it was any of my other staff, quite in character."

My tongue pressed against my palate and held. After a moment, she sighed and clasped her hands. "And then we have Mr. Blackthorn. He left the hospital almost two hours before your father discovered him, claiming he was standing in plain sight in the middle of one of the busiest docks in Duluth."

"That's where Dad found him." I met her gaze head-on, mixing mine with the right amounts of irritation and confusion.

"It still seems like a long gap of time to me."

"Did you ask him where he went?" I countered.

"We did. He said he was wandering."

Dr. Mehta stared at me with her all-knowing look. Every muscle in my body tensed, and I barely made myself nod and murmur an acknowledgment.

"Lucas Blackthorn doesn't strike me as the wandering type."

I took a deep breath. "So I'll try to figure out what his goal was during our next sessions. I haven't worked this hard to earn his trust for nothing."

"Yes, I have no doubt that you've gained it. He's been asking for you—extremely politely, I'm told—with every new nurse at every shift change. He even struck up a conversation with one of the janitors about you. Your interests. Your background. Hector wasn't extremely helpful in the situation, apparently only knowing you as 'that little punk girl with the shit in her car.'"

"See?" I ignored the sudden upbeat in my pulse. "So why would you make him start all over again with someone new?"

"Because I'm worried about your attachment to each other."

Jesus. She didn't pull any punches. I felt myself flushing, which might as well have been a big fat confirmation of our "attachment." Dropping my gaze, I tried to find words that were both true and harmless.

"I like him."

"Obviously. You spent hours at his bedside in the hospital, off the clock, and when you brought him back here you barely moved from his side all night. The medical team noticed what they called an 'unspoken communication' between you."

"Well, for one, that sounds like gossipy bullshit."

Dr. Mehta chuckled.

"And two," I sighed and tossed my hands in the air. "You're right. I have become attached to him. He reminds me of me, I guess. But is that so bad? I mean, don't you ever become fond of any of your patients? What about Big George? That man is a human-sized teddy bear. How can you not love him?"

"Don't shift the topic. There's a difference between professional compassion and personal attachment."

I made myself laugh. "I'm not going to ask him to go steady, okay?"

"It's against policy, it's dangerous, and to be completely honest I'm more worried about the consequences for you than for Mr. Blackthorn."

"This is insane." I launched myself out of the chair and paced behind it. "In the eight years I've known you, all you've ever told me is that I need to let myself connect with people, to open up to love and loss again and all that crap. Then you force me to work with Lucas against my will and outside my professional scope. And now you're upset because I'm too close to him?"

She steepled her fingers under her chin, undisturbed by my outburst. On the scale of emotional incidents around here, we might as well be having a sedate tea. After a moment's consideration, she nodded.

"I'll authorize you to continue your sessions for the time being, but I'll be monitoring your work closely. And please know, Maya"— she stopped me as I headed for the door—"I believe in you."

———

Belief is a powerful thing. It grabs you, unmakes you, changes the tilt and angle of everything around you into an entirely different geometry. You see the world in a new shape and no matter how horrible the belief, no matter what awful things it makes you do, a part of you is still grateful for the structure.

I'd believed a lot of things in my life, most of them about my mother.

I'd believed in Santa Claus until I found the frosted animal crackers I only got once a year in my stocking, tucked away in

Mom's sock drawer. They were brittle cookies, animal shapes coated with a careless icing like snow drifted into patches along back alleys, and the ones I found were leftovers, crumbled into tiny rocks at the bottom of the bag. She cried when I brought them out, perplexed by my discovery, and after she broke down I immediately wanted to hide the bag, to bury it at the bottom of a snowbank that would never melt. I'd believed our rock garden would make her happy, and that if I could memorize just one more mineral her eyes would blink into focus again and she would hug me with pride. Later, when she left us, I believed every word of her goodbye letter. Everything shifted into place: the jobs she could never keep, the long silences when Dad was gone, how her sadness swamped her at the strangest times—in the grocery store or walking me to school. I'd look up and her face would be wet, eyes averted and unwiped. If I tried to hug her, it seemed to make her worse. If I ignored it, the gap between us only widened. She hadn't wanted me, hadn't wanted this life, and disappeared like the *Bannockburn* before I could demand a reason why. To ask what I'd done that was so intolerable.

Sometimes I even wondered if I'd studied speech so I could dissect my memories of her. I played old videos of us over and over but could never find any hint of her intentions. I hated the counselors who pulled me into their offices, the words that came so easily to them and had been impossible for her. The thing no one understands, when your parent abandons you, is that it doesn't happen just once. They leave every day, every moment that you remember them is a door slamming shut in your face. And with every slam, you believe—a little more each time—that you probably deserved it.

My belief about Lucas Blackthorn was nothing like that creeping kind of blame. It didn't gradually take root in my consciousness over years; I woke up this morning with a certainty flowing through me that not even Dr. Mehta could derail. I hated myself for lying to her—sane Dr. Mehta, sober Dr. Mehta, a woman who had faith in the faithless and confidence in the worst people you could imagine. After all, she'd hired me. She'd challenged me, elevated me, believed in me, but now I wondered how much she really understood me. If she did, she never would have given me this assignment. Before I met Lucas, I don't think I'd even understood myself.

This is what I knew now:

A father had disappeared. A son was desperate to find him.

And I would tell a thousand lies if it brought him one step closer.

The path before me seemed so clear and it gave meaning to everything I'd survived to get to this point. I had to help Lucas find his father. No matter what Josiah had done, no matter what had driven them into the Boundary Waters, they needed to find each other and I was possibly the only person in the world who understood how much. But the clock was ticking. Every day the winds blew harder and colder, the gales raged in a losing battle against the coming winter. Soon the ice would win, soon Josiah might be dead, and we'd be out of time.

I gathered up my session supplies and jogged up the stairs to ward two. I could feel the organs in my body pumping, expanding, the excitement set loose in every nerve ending, flashing with a life I hadn't known was even inside me. Without any premonition of what lay ahead, I badged in to ward two and caught a flash of Lucas's face before the world jerked sideways.

13

A CRUSHING WEIGHT knocked me to the ground, sending the air whooshing out of my lungs. Several people yelled my name, the loudest one right in my ear.

"Tag, Maya! Tag, Maya!" the voice shouted gleefully.

I twisted around and pulled his skull into a headlock as Lucas appeared above us, grabbing a massive arm and ripping it backward. Big George shrieked in pain.

"Back off, Lucas! Now." I managed to order as two nurses came to pry our tag player off me. After we got untangled and de-escalated the situation, the other staff and I led Big George to his favorite squishy chair and sat him down. He held his arm and rocked, refusing to make eye contact with anyone. I nodded to the nurses and they gave us a little distance, returning to the bustle of the adult men's common room. Most of the other patients watched us to see how the show would turn out, but when nothing more exciting happened than Big George sniffling into the crook of his arm they gradually resumed their card games, books, and TV programs. Faces turned away from the window of the classroom, where one of the life skills coaches held up a rainbow-colored chart. Lucas paced behind the row of sofas in front of the TV, and even though he didn't look over once I knew I had his undivided attention.

Big George was holding his throat now and he'd gotten himself into a loop, repeating "Ow" over and over.

"What hurts, George? Tell me."

Instead of verbalizing, he pointed to his arm and neck and then, as he always did when something ached, he doubled over and pressed his palms against his head.

Big George had lived at Congdon for twenty years, ever since he and two friends robbed a grocery store at gunpoint in Cloquet, loaded up trash bags with cash and food, and met a squad car on their way out. The other two began shooting at the police and were killed on sight but George was "lucky"; he'd been hunched over a box of Triscuits when they opened fire and the angle of the bullet through his brain missed every major artery. He had the aptitude of a four-year-old now, ate every meal as if his life depended on it, and was aggressively cheery unless he felt the slightest twinge of pain—reminding him a phantom bullet lived in his head—or if he saw anything resembling a tan, plaid square, which would send him spiraling into a meltdown. Triscuits were strictly banned in the men's ward.

I gave him a second to work through his feelings and then doubled over my own legs, mirroring his pose. When I got his attention, I pointed to the ankle Bryce's Taser had sprained.

"I've got a place that hurts, too." As George reached out to tap my shin, I asked him. "Where am I hurt?"

"Leg."

"This is my leg." I sounded as excited as anyone could about discovering a piece of their body and he caught on to my enthusiasm, pointing to his head.

"This is my ow."

Keeping my grin in place with a Herculean effort, I corrected him. "No, silly. That's your head."

He cackled and we kept going, the body part naming game an old favorite and a comfortable way for him to articulate complete sentences. I'd tucked a bunch of fabric samples in the surprise bag with another exercise in mind, but swatches could wait. We played while tears dried on the dark mounds of his cheeks, until I'd pushed him beyond all the body parts he knew and into the more phonetically uncomfortable territory of forearm and spine, where cognitive fatigue soon settled in. Sessions with George were always brief.

To end, I pulled him to his feet and we sang a version of "Dem Bones," hopping around the common room. "Toe bone connected to the foot bone, foot bone connected to the heel bone . . ."

George loved singing and was oblivious to the snickers and stares. We spun and danced while recapping all the body parts he might need to verbalize to his doctors in the event of illness or injury. After we finished, the easy grin melted into a more complicated emotion and his next words came out in a quiet, but perfectly clear cadence. "Sorry, sorry, sorry."

"What are you sorry for, George?"

"Tag, Maya. I'm sorry."

"Thank you for finding those words." I touched his arm and grinned into his contrite face. "Next time you play tag, you've got to remember you're a big, old bear. You can't go around tagging little gnats like me."

"Bird." He petted my hair and cracked a smile. "Maya's a bird."

"Bears have to be careful of birds, okay?"

"Okay, Maya."

I left Big George in the care of one of the nurses and wandered through the ward with his words repeating in my head. *This is my ow.*

When I was first promoted to speech therapist I'd focused on one thing—helping my patients speak. I spent all my sessions working on palate exercises, pronunciation, articulation, and sound. The goal was form. Whatever coherent subject matter they produced had ended up on their doctor's plate, not mine, but now Lucas was changing everything. I couldn't ignore the meaning behind their words, couldn't keep describing the water in the boat without wanting to plug the holes. *This is my ow.* My heart ached for Big George, for the broke, hungry kid who would probably grow old inside these walls. He had no support network outside of Congdon, nowhere to go if he was ever released, and no hope of becoming self-sufficient. All I could do was point to my forearm, teach him words he would forget by our next session, and try to make him smile.

I poked my head into every room along the corridor, trying to locate the one person in this building who'd actually asked for my help, and who had suddenly—if characteristically—vanished. Finally, I found him at the far end of the dining room and what he was doing stopped me in my tracks.

He ran full speed at the wall and then, without slowing down, ran up the side of it, turned sideways and landed lightly back on his feet, jogging to where he began. The sling he still wore on one arm didn't slow him down at all, or maybe it did. Maybe if he hadn't been wearing it he could've scaled further, gone higher. I had a vision of the fence outside, of Lucas clearing the entire thing in one giant leap. I might have been George's bird, but Lucas was the one who was trying to fly.

I watched him repeat the trick two more times with my mouth hanging open before realizing I wasn't his only audience. The Grinch sat at a nearby table, puffing on an e-cig with a slight head twitch as Lucas went almost horizontal against the cement blocks.

"I think I'm having an episode." He puffed, eyes straight ahead and unblinking.

"Me too."

He grunted in acknowledgment. The Grinch was another lifer, but for far different reasons than Big George. His schizophrenia was well managed with medication and he'd conquered most of his paranoia, even completing some vocational training he would never have the opportunity to use. He'd been found not guilty by reason of insanity for hacking up the young couple and their two-year-old twins who lived next door to him, but guilt didn't matter with some crimes. There would never be any protesters at the gates for the Grinch, demanding his release. People might understand, rationally, that his illness had caused the crime, but they would keep the man locked up long after the illness had been treated. After a decade of perfect behavior, the only concession the system had granted him was a transfer from the state security hospital, where most of Minnesota's criminally insane residents lived, to the relatively progressive environment of Congdon. He would die in the high security ward here, a Scrabble champion who would never feel the breeze of an oe on his upturned face.

My story was the exception, and I always assumed the basis of Dr. Mehta's affection for me. Most of her beds were taken by forensic patients and the longer ones like Big George and the Grinch stayed, the fewer voluntary patients she could accommodate. Rather than treat patients when they actually sought help, she had to wait until their mental illness caused them to commit a crime and then hope the courts would send them to Congdon instead of prison. I was lucky—I'd been in and out in under six months, barely a blink of Big George's eye—and now I had to help Lucas get even luckier.

Finishing his show and not even out of breath, Lucas walked over to the tables. He leaned down to murmur something in the Grinch's ear, then clapped him on the shoulder and walked past me without a word or glance. I was still so stunned that it wasn't until he left the dining room I realized he was blowing me off.

Pivoting out into the hallway, I raised my voice.

"We have a session, Mr. Blackthorn."

He turned around at the other end of the corridor. "You told me to back off."

"That was then. This is now. Keep up with the schedule, will you?"

"So you're done being tackled by huge men?" Even across this distance, his irritation was palpable. I tried not to laugh.

"In the grand scheme of things, let's hope not. But today . . ." I shrugged and went back to the dining room, pulling out papers from the surprise bag and laying them in rough geographic order on the nearest table. The Grinch paced the wall where Lucas had been running, muttering to himself in a monotone and taking drags of his e-cigarette. I kept working even after I sensed Lucas standing behind me.

Once everything was arranged I started marking places with a pen, narrating in a voice that could have easily been just to keep myself company.

"Here's where you were found." I pointed to the blue *X* and talked through the paths that grew like tree branches through the paddle and portage routes beginning in Ely, stopping when I hit the fifteen-mile range and the jagged edge of the international border. I lingered on the line, drawn like a stuttering heart monitor, and finally turned my head to acknowledge Lucas's presence.

"I need to know where you left him, everything you can remember, if we're going to be able to locate him in time."

Lucas took a step forward, swallowing as his eyes filled with tightly-banked emotion. "You're going to help me?"

Swiveling back to the table, I shifted one of the copies a millimeter to the right. "Nothing gets by you, huh?"

When I started to tape the fragments of the maps together, he moved up beside me and held the edges together with his one good arm, helping me create a patchwork whole.

"Thank you."

"Don't thank me until you've heard the plan." I lifted my face to his and smiled. "Let's get to work."

Thirty minutes later, after discussing, debating, and flat-out arguing in whispers too low for anyone else to overhear, I gathered up all the papers and stuffed them away. Lucas wanted to leave for the Boundary Waters *yesterday* and refused to even try to understand how the system worked. He thought my way was irritating and pointless, which made me think it was the most adult plan I'd ever had.

I slung the surprise bag over my shoulder, ready to beat hell across the building for my next session, an OCD patient who would take it badly if I wasn't punctual.

Lucas stood up with me. "Can I ask you another question?"

I glanced at the clock again. I had three minutes. "Only if it can be answered in five words or less."

His mouth quirked up, the first sign of humor I'd seen from him all day. "That's up to you."

He walked me to the cafeteria door and pushed it open with his good arm, easily keeping up with my determined pace.

"What did you mean earlier? By the grand scheme of things?"

It took me a second to remember what he was talking about and then it flashed back—the quip about being tackled by large men. I felt my cheeks getting warm as we headed toward the rear exit of the ward.

"Hmmm. Sometimes . . ." I paused before counting the words on my fingers. "Tackling can be fun."

We reached the end of the hall and I reached for my ID.

"You're talking about sex?"

Badge in hand, I ran out of reasons to avoid his gaze. We stared at each other for a second. Then I smiled and activated the door.

"That's two questions."

14

MY MOTHER GAVE me a necklace once. She called me into her room one day and held it up to the sunlight filtering through the bedroom window. A simple string with a slice of Superior agate for a pendant, the striations of white and burnt orange looked like a depth map, sharp at the edges and polished in the middle. The light caught its brilliance and made it flash into the corners of the room—lake and lighthouse together.

I asked her where she'd gotten it, but she didn't seem to hear the question. She traced the layers with a finger, describing the billion-year-old volcanic eruptions that had tried to tear North America apart.

"But they didn't. The eruptions ended and tiny bubbles in the lava filled with mineral sediments. The white is quartz and the red, oxidized iron, which is the same thing as rust. Have you ever imagined rust looking like this, Maya?"

I shook my head. At ten years old, I hadn't given rust much thought.

"This is what the Earth makes," she said, laying the necklace carefully back in her jewelry box, "out of violence and decay. Do you see?"

I didn't know what she wanted me to see. I saw a semiprecious stone, no different than the minerals in our rock garden, or the four-pound agate she'd found in college and kept uncut on her bedside table—her prize specimen. Our house was littered with rocks as paperweights, doorstops, and decorations. I saw their form and function, nothing more.

"So, it's sedimentary," I offered, but it was the wrong thing to say. She shut the drawer and turned inward, telling me to go play until dinner, which we both knew she wasn't going to make.

I didn't see the necklace again until a few months later when she took the copper study job on the iron range, packed her things, and left before I got home from school. The four-pound agate was gone from her bedside table and the pendant necklace was lying on my pillow. I didn't think about it in those first few days of her bewildering absence, when every sound in an empty room brought me running, stupidly expecting to see the rich tumble of her hair, her thin frame turning to me and restoring what she'd fractured. It wasn't until after Dad read me her letter and we started to accept she wasn't coming back, that I remembered the afternoon she'd shown it to me.

Had I failed some obscure geology test? Was there a hidden meaning in the agate, something that might have made her stay if I'd said the right thing, been the right daughter? I had no one to ask and the questions only grew louder with every milestone she missed, every day without her in it. The questions became my brothers and sisters. They were with me always, in my blood, until five years later when I found an answer that sent me to the depths of Congdon Psychiatric Facility.

———

I must have dreamed about the agate necklace because it shimmered in the shadows of my mind as I lay in bed, unwilling to get up after another late night studying Boundary Waters topographical maps and the restless non-sleep that followed. The necklace itself was gone and I didn't want to think about where, so instead I rolled over and saw Jasper lying patiently in my bedroom doorway, waiting for me.

"You want to take a drive today, Jazz?"

He answered by walking over to the bed, laying his head on the sheets, and licking my elbow.

I sighed. "No kisses. Time to put your game face on."

Today was a huge day. Today Lucas took his first sanctioned step toward the Boundary Waters. My plan was simple: If Lucas could prove himself capable of behaving in public—i.e., not running off or assaulting anyone—then Dr. Mehta had agreed he might be able to join a search party to locate his father. I'd set up different field trips every day, with progressive liberties attached to each outing. First we started by taking a walk around Congdon's neighborhood and worked up to our last test at the end of the week, a drive up the shore to Split Rock Lighthouse with Dr. Mehta in tow.

I showered, gulped down a quick breakfast, and drove Jasper up the hill to Congdon, where at least fifteen "Free Lucas Blackthorn" protesters waved signs and took footage with their phones. Lucas's escape attempts from Congdon and St. Mary's had given fuel to both sides of the fire raging on the social media sites. To those who believed he was a dangerous criminal, it proved his unbalanced state of mind. For the protesters—whose presence outside the gates seemed to grow every day—his actions were a desperate plea for help and the Congdon staff had become the instruments of his oppression. This morning the red-haired girl, who'd led the charge on the police motorcade the night we brought Lucas back, took several halting steps toward my car as I pulled up to the guard-house, talking and gesturing at me. I kept the window rolled up and flashed my badge at the guard, who quickly opened the gate and waved me through. Pulling up to the drop-off zone at the main entrance, I saw Bryce already waiting with Lucas out front to meet us. They'd dressed him in street clothes for our outing, or at least a mental health facility's version of street clothes—he wore a bright turquoise hoodie, sweatpants, and a baby blue stocking cap with cat ears courtesy of Dr. Mehta's wife, who bought cat caps for all the patients and never knew most of them ended up ripped to pieces or shoved into snowbanks within a few days of their annual arrival. At least the hat sort of matched his arm sling.

Jasper rumbled a hello as we climbed out of the car and I let him sniff Bryce's shoes while Bryce looked less than comfortable.

"Is that the same dog that chewed on this guy's foot?"

"I don't know." I nodded to the holster on his belt. "Is that the same Taser you tried to kill us with?"

Lucas's eyes widened and he stepped back, pulling against the grip Bryce had on his good arm. Bryce bristled, but before he could retaliate Jasper's muzzle started wandering up his leg.

"I was doing my job," he said. "Now call off your fucking dog."

"Fucking," Lucas muttered. "Why do people always say that?"

146

I escorted everyone back toward the car. "It's an expression. An all-purpose word for people who don't know very many."

"Fuck you, Maya." Bryce jerked open the car door.

"See? Adjective. Verb. It can be a noun, too. Like, *Isn't Bryce such a dumb fuck?*"

Bryce cursed some more and threatened to call Dr. Mehta while I engaged the child locks and waved the two of them into the backseat. Jasper climbed in front next to me and immediately turned around to inspect Lucas, who was glancing between his sling and the hand Bryce was using to grip his Taser handle.

"Don't get bent out of shape, Bryce. It was just an example." I handed back a blanket covered in dog hair. "Here, put this on him."

Bryce made Lucas double over and covered him with the blanket as we pulled out of the parking lot. The protesters parted as the gate opened, hovering only a few feet away from the car. They were near enough to see the blanket and I held my breath as we pulled through them, not too fast, not too slow, only exhaling when we got halfway down the block.

Bryce uncovered our patient, and we drove for a few minutes in silence.

"Free Lucas Blackthorn."

"What?" I glanced in the rearview mirror.

"That's what those signs said the other night. That's who those people are." Lucas looked behind us, but Congdon was already out of sight. "They want you to let me go."

Sighing, I tried to explain the situation, the controversial celebrity he'd become, but the more I said, the more agitated both passengers became. Jasper whined and tried to pace, hitting me in the face with his tail, rubbing his head nervously against the seats. I steered the car over the cracked and potholed pavement, climbing higher up the hill until we reached the Enger Trailhead.

"Look, it's complicated." I checked the parking lot to make sure it was empty before pulling into a spot. "These people don't understand the legal system or the mental health system."

"Neither do I," Lucas muttered.

Jasper and I got out and then let Bryce and Lucas out of the backseat. Bryce immediately lit up a cigarette.

"All you need to know is that they love you," Bryce puffed. "They hate me, they hate Maya, and they love you, all right?"

"Bryce."

He rolled his eyes and turned away, scanning the perimeter. "I can't even log in to Twitter anymore, I'm getting tagged on so many posts. I had to cancel my Facebook account. One of my cousins is out there protesting and texting me every day. Every freaking day. She thinks I'm the reason he got sent to St. Mary's."

"Bryce, we can talk about this later." We could talk about how I sided with his cousin on that one, but right now Lucas was absorbing every word, his gaze shifting between the two of us.

"Yeah, right." Bryce took another drag. "So what are we doing here?"

I pointed out the Superior Hiking Trail that led into the woods at the south side of the Twin Ponds. It wound up through the park and toward Enger Tower, the five-story bluestone observation building. "And if you try to run or incapacitate Bryce or me in any way during this walk, Jasper is going to have you for lunch. Understand?"

I said it mostly for Bryce's benefit, but Lucas still shifted uneasily.

"I understand."

"Okay, then. Let's hike."

The four of us set off. Enger Park was situated on the peak of the bluff overlooking Superior. Below us to the east, Victorian houses and brick buildings stood in varying degrees of disrepair from the constant punishment of the winds. To the west the land flattened out into college campuses, strip malls, and suburban housing before giving way to forests and the Iron Range beyond. The temperature on top of the hill was always at least five degrees warmer than downtown at the water's edge. Sometimes ten. Today that meant we were flirting with fifty degrees and only traces of the blowing snow from a few days ago remained, swept into the crevices underneath rock ledges and gathered at the base of evergreens. I led our strange little troop on to the trail and up toward the summit.

Jasper led the pack with Lucas and me following and Bryce bringing up the rear. The path was littered with dead and decaying leaves and I sensed Lucas looking around, trying to gauge the extent of the forest. He stared at the tower on the hill and seemed surprised when we descended into a parking lot in the middle of the trees. I kept walking, moving away from the cars and the few people milling near the tower, directing us up a set of stone steps to a giant gazebo with pergolas on either side. A slope of exposed rock—anorthosite gabbro dotted with scrub bushes—provided a perfect outcrop in front of the gazebo to get a panorama of the largest freshwater harbor in the world.

Lucas stared at the horizon of blue. "Where's the other side?"

Bryce huffed out a laugh and shook his head.

"It's out there," I shrugged. "I've never seen it."

"Your dad has."

I nodded, scanning the blur where clouds met water. "He's out there somewhere, too."

After examining the drop-off around the outcrop and eyeing

Jasper's position—within biting distance of the meaty part of Lucas's leg—Bryce wandered back up to the gazebo and lit another cigarette. I watched him pull out his phone and start texting people, apparently too wrapped up in his unwanted Internet attention to worry about our patient escaping. Leading Lucas and Jasper over to a bench, I wrapped my coat around my middle and curled up on the iron slats. After a beat, Lucas sat down next to me.

"What is it?" I asked.

He shook his head, refusing to respond even as he glanced back at the trees again.

"Don't even think about it. Jasper is much faster than you."

He heaved out a sigh and crossed his arms, staring sightlessly at the vista. "Why should I tell you what the matter is?"

The retort, an angry teenager's reply, sent my brain stumbling back. I thought we were beyond this. Keeping my tone casual, I reached down to scratch Jasper behind the ears. "Well, I'm glad you asked. This is what we call therapy. The modern form of psycho-analysis was developed ages ago by a guy named Freud, who inci-dentally could have used some of his own medicine, but informally the idea of communicating to resolve conflict dates back to—"

"I didn't ask for therapy, I asked for your help," he interrupted. "All those people outside Congdon want me to be free. You said you were going to help me, but here we are. In Duluth. Not. Going. Anywhere. Do you know how frustrating it is when someone you love is suffering and you can't get to them?"

I swallowed and stared at the fractures in the rock where the weeds kept growing even with the nightly frost freezing their leaves. They would be back next year and the next, never flourishing, never giving up.

"Yes." I nodded at the rock. "I do know what that's like."

"That's the problem," he said. "I don't know anything about you, do I? I tell you everything and you tell me nothing."

Turning to face him, I looked him straight in the eye, giving him my complete attention. "What do you want me to tell you?"

"Why were you a patient at Congdon?"

My mouth fell open in sheer surprise. Lucas watched me, waiting, until I exhaled, long and heavy.

"What does that have to do with anything?"

"It tells me what kind of person I'm trusting with my father's life." Then his head dropped and his jaw tightened, struggling with the qualification. "If he's alive."

I tried to put myself in his place, tried to remember how it felt before I'd really gotten to know Dr. Mehta—the one-sided revelation called counseling. It had been uncomfortable, exposing, like I was stripping naked and prancing around in front of fully clothed, expressionless people. As Lucas's speech therapist, I wasn't supposed to tell him my life story. But as a friend . . .

"There's not much to tell. My mom . . ."

"Didn't stick around," he supplied, startling me with his uncanny recall.

"Yeah." I plowed ahead, trying to do it quick, like a Band-Aid. "I didn't handle it well. Neither did my dad. He disappeared out there"—I waved to the lake—"as much as he could and left me with a woman who didn't care what I did so long as my dad's checks cashed. She lived over there."

I pointed to an area even further south of our house, where violence, drugs, and drunkenness saturated the neighborhood with a reek even the lake winds couldn't blow away.

"I started hanging out with random kids on the street. Getting into trouble."

"What kind of trouble?"

"The usual. Stealing, destruction of property, breaking and entering. I discovered I had a knack for picking locks, which endeared me to a certain group of people."

"And that's why you got sent to Congdon?"

"No." Bryce stubbed out his second cigarette and headed across the outcrop toward us. I turned back to Lucas, my face carefully blank, and told him what I'd never shared with anyone outside of Congdon's walls.

"I got committed because I killed a man and painted my face with his blood."

Lucas gaped as Bryce reached us. I stood up and stretched.

"Are you done yet?" Bryce asked.

I patted Jasper on the head. "Yeah, let's go."

15

SOMETHING HAPPENS to you after you kill a person.

I'm not talking about the guilt or the doubt or the nightmares that make you do it over and over, each time a little different, each time like you have a chance to change it but you never can. What happens, in the daylight hours, is a bubble forms between you and everyone else, invisible and impenetrable. Everyone on the outside is all the same. They work and they hustle and they complain about what they don't have and then they go home and crawl into their beds and drift away. And you can never be part of them, because something is awake in you that doesn't know how to sleep.

I still remember the crunch of his skull, how it didn't feel broken as I smashed the rock into it—there was no sudden give, no tremor of anything reverberating through my fingers—but I heard the pop of fracturing bone. It was a dull sound, the kind of noise that would have been forgotten in the next breath if it meant anything else and it wasn't even the sound itself that haunted me; it was the feeling that washed through me the instant I heard that crack and saw his body go limp. Not horror. Not regret. Not even relief. It was happiness, a raw, savage joy that flooded my veins as I stood over him.

I was fifteen, I had just ended someone's life, and I was happy.

The week started out on a crap note to begin with. Some cheerleader named Hope—why not call her Glass Half Full, you unsubtle helicopter parents?—picked a fight with me before class and of course I was the one who got suspended, not pom-pom girl. Dad was somewhere on Lake Ontario and wouldn't be back until Saturday, so I spent the week roaming Lincoln Park with all the badassery of an unsupervised spring ninth grader. I walked the train tracks, stole Twinkies from the gas station, and finally decided to break into an abandoned warehouse, where I ran into two guys smoking weed.

Their names were Derek and Rex and they called themselves D-Rex, or rather Rex did and Derek put up with it. I'd seen them around before. They'd just gotten into town and had hung around the fringes of our group for the last month or so. One was short, the other fat. I didn't think I had anything to worry about from some short, fat rookies, even if they were a lot older than me, so we spent the afternoon wandering the neighborhood together. Rex, the fat one, kept wanting to find things to eat. Derek, the short one, played music on his iPhone and scrolled through the crappy pictures on my old flip phone. One of them was a picture of a picture—a shot of me and my mother standing in front of the cabin. When he asked, I shrugged off a few details, touching the agate necklace I wore beneath my shirt. Yes, that was me. My mom used to take me up north every summer, before she left us.

"I swear to God I saw her the other day. Rex and I came from up north."

"From Ely?" I spun around.

"Yeah, Ely." I didn't even register the glance between them at the time. "You still have the cabin, right?"

I didn't think; I reacted. Rex knew how to hot-wire cars, so we found a rusted Ford parked in an industrial lot with no surveillance cameras. Before I knew it, we were driving out of town and it felt . . . right. Even though I'd always thought of the cabin as our place—hers and mine—it made perfect sense that she would have retreated there. The place had been in her family for generations, it belonged to her, and my dad had refused to take me there since she'd walked out. I'd just assumed he couldn't stand the memories, but maybe they'd made an agreement without telling me. Maybe she'd been living there all along.

The sun was setting by the time we arrived and my heart practically beat its way out of my throat. I had tears in my eyes as I crept up the front walk and felt ten years old again. I'd taken the agate necklace off and clutched it in my hand for most of the drive. I didn't know what I was going to do, if I'd clasp the pendant around her neck, throw it at her, or break it into a thousand pieces on the doorstep. The Earth took violence and decay and made agates, she'd said, so maybe I'd take agates and make violence and decay. There weren't any lights on inside and I didn't know the security system code, so I went to ring the doorbell, thinking the guys would hang back and let us get our angry reunion on. They dogged me right up to the door, though, and kept asking about the code.

"Maybe you'll remember," Rex prodded. "I'm sure one of your parents told you."

I looked from one to the other and slowly the veil of stupidity lifted. They couldn't quite hide it in their faces and I knew then that no one was on the other side of the door. They'd never seen my mother in their lives.

"Wait," I said, feeling a different kind of tremor taking hold. "I think they hid a copy of the code in the boathouse with the spare key."

The walk took forever. I scanned the horizon with every step while they flanked me the whole way down to the water. Our lot was large and wooded. The nearest neighbor, a recluse name Harry, spent most of his time fishing and probably wasn't even home. There were no boats on the lake when we approached, only a single loon bobbing like a black speck on the sunset orange waves. Our boathouse was a creaky shack on the beach and I threw open the unlocked door, knowing right where to look. A loose piece of plywood covered not a key, but the gun my mother had always hid out here because this was bear and wolf country.

I dug underneath the plywood, scraping against studs and cobwebs, finding nothing. Where was the gun? One of the guys stepped into the doorway behind me, blocking the little light that trickled inside, and I spun around and kicked him right in the stomach, sending him flying. I ran out of the boathouse but didn't get four steps across the beach before the other one—Rex—tackled me. He flipped me over and said not to scream, that if I told them how to get in the house, they wouldn't hurt me.

Derek walked over, bracing his gut and smiling. He wanted me to scream.

As they grabbed me I didn't think about why they were

doing this or why it was happening to me. Those were questions Dr. Mehta gave me later, the kind of questions people had when they believed their lives were worth something. It didn't even occur to me to question them. They were animals being animals. The only refrain playing in my head was what an easy mark I'd been.

Stupid, I kept thinking. *So stupid.*

Rex, the fat one, held me down as Derek tried to take my clothes off. I fought and yelled at him, which was what he'd been waiting for. He started hitting me, close-fisted, over and over until even his friend told him to stop.

"Leave, then," Derek said. "I'll teach her a lesson by myself."

Rex stayed for a little longer, nervously checking the horizon before he slunk into the trees. As he left, I heard him tell Derek, "Shut her up, for chrissake." In response, Derek flipped me onto my stomach and clamped his hand over my face, cutting off my voice, and that's when I saw it. It was tucked among the other rocks forming a circle around the lakeside firepit, the place where we had built bonfires and roasted s'mores and watched the sunset over the water—heavy, jagged, the exact size of my hand. It didn't belong in that firepit and I knew instantly what it was and who had put it there.

When I went quiet, Derek released his grip on my face so he could yank my jeans the rest of the way off. Then I grabbed my mother's prized, four-pound agate and smashed it into his temple.

His hands flew up and I kneed him in the groin. When he dropped I rolled up and drove the rock into his head again and again until I heard his skull break. There was a gurgling sound, his muscles seized, and then nothing. I stood over the body, cradling the bloody rock in my hands, and cried tears of absolute gratitude.

I knew the answer. I understood what my mother had been

telling me all those years ago. Agates can only form when something in you is destroyed, when the hollows of grief or depression can never find the light, and the sediment that accumulates inside them is dense. Their power changes you. She had changed into something that wasn't able to be my mother, but she'd left me a way to survive. As clearly as I knew I was standing on a shore next to a dead man, I also knew she'd wanted me to find this rock.

The pool of blood spreading underneath Derek's face seeped over the sand until the water got at it, pulling it away in streaks of deep red shot with amber. I dipped my fingers into the blood and painted it over my forehead and cheeks in a fortification pattern. Then I walked back to the cabin.

Rex was waiting by the car. As soon as he saw me with the rock in hand, blood mask congealing over my face, and murder in my eyes, he jumped in the truck and gunned it out of the driveway. I never saw him again. I kept walking until I got to Harry's cabin and sat in front of his door, waiting for it to open while new minerals formed deep inside me, filling the hollows with a type of strength she'd never had.

―――――――

I could feel Lucas's shock as I told the story. The wind had picked up as we walked back through the park, whipping the dead leaves into a white noise that made conversation almost impossible. Almost. I spoke in a low, monotone voice as the air slapped me in the face, stinging tears into my eyes and drying them before they could fall. I barely registered the trail ahead of us as I related how Harry had found me and the investigation that followed.

"The coroner counted over twenty contusions on Derek's skull. They said I wasn't hurt enough to justify murder, especially when there was no evidence of rape. I told them the truth, the truth I'd felt so shining and clear in that place and then had to lie about later so I could leave Congdon behind.

"I told them my mother spoke to me through rocks and that she'd given me the agate to kill him."

Our group came out of the woods at the trailhead and crossed the Buckingham Creek bridge toward the parking lot. I could hear Jasper's pants again and the click of his claws on the pavement. Bryce, still bringing up the rear, gave no sign he'd heard any of my story; he ignored me as I glanced back, one thumb in constant motion on his phone. Lucas, though, had caught every word. It was surging in his eyes, lighting them with an overwhelmed understanding. Instead of heading for the car, I steered us toward a floating dock on one side of the Twin Ponds and Jasper, eager for the detour, pulled on the leash until we reached the end of the narrow planks.

"What are you doing, Maya?" Bryce called from the parking lot. "I'm going to be late for my next patient."

"Two minutes."

Facing the water, I let out a breath. "I've never told that to anyone except Dr. Mehta."

Lucas squatted down and leaned against the railing, staring at the pond. "Thank you." And then, after picking at the metal for a second, "Why did you think your mother gave you the rock?"

It was impossible to explain it, the instant certainty when I saw it nestled in the fire ring. I'd felt the riddle of her life unfolding, the briefest flash of her attention and love before I was abandoned again, left with the mark of the agate and a corpse leaking out its

blood. I'd never questioned the sanity of that day, not in the deten-
tion facility, or in court, or the months at Congdon that followed,
but it wasn't a reality I knew how to translate, not even eight years
later.

I shrugged. "It wasn't something I thought. It's what I knew."

He nodded, but he didn't understand. I didn't expect him to. I
was about to suggest going back to the car when he surprised me
by asking, "Was there much of his skull left after you were done?"

I cocked my head, curious. "No."

Lucas looked at me for a long moment before standing unsteadily on the swaying dock.

"Good."

We stood there with the wind pulling at our clothes while
Jasper ran up and down the floating walkway, making us struggle
for balance. I'd spent my life separated from the rest of the world,
first by my mother's illness, then her ghost breathing in every rock
around me, and by the dead man whose eyes wouldn't stay shut
when I fell asleep. I couldn't get rid of them and suddenly I was
furious that they might keep me from knowing the one person even
further disconnected from the world than I was. I didn't want to be
unreachable, not anymore. Not to Lucas.

I stepped forward, about to speak, when Bryce's warning cut
through the air.

In the parking lot I saw a streak of bright red hair. The girl from
the protesters ran toward us, leading a group of cell phone—and
sign-wielding fans. I stepped in front of Lucas, calculating the distance to the car, when Bryce grabbed his Taser.

16

No!"
     Cinching Jasper's leash and holding Lucas behind me by his good elbow, I navigated the narrow dock as it dipped and swayed. Bryce had his arms spread wide, holding the Taser and blocking the group from getting to us. The red-haired girl recognized him and, pointing at the weapon, started in on the Eighth Amendment and cruel and unusual punishment. Shouting above her, Bryce swept his arms forward, trying to make a space for us to get off the dock where we were trapped. Phones pointed at us and I squeezed Lucas's arm. "Get ready."

I could hear him saying, "They want me free."

The hair on the back of Jasper's neck stood entirely on end. He growled and shifted his weight, unsure of what to do. I choked up further on the leash, steadying him, until Bryce had pushed the fans back far enough for us to duck through.

"Excuse us. Please allow us to pass." I tried to make myself heard as we edged forward. The closer we got to the crowd, the more Lucas stiffened against my grip. His head jerked as someone called his name, a girl young enough that she should have probably been in school, who ran forward and yelled, "I love you!" Bryce caught her just as she launched herself at us, holding her by the arms and glaring at me.

"Go!"

"Come on." Jasper barked as I dragged him away, shielding Lucas's face with my free hand. The red-haired ringleader began shouting at Bryce to release the girl while two more of them chased us across the parking lot, holding their phones in front of them like talismans. I unlocked the car and Lucas got in immediately, bending at the waist and covering his ears. Jasper climbed in front and, ignoring the shouted questions and yells, I asked everyone to please move back so I could pull out of the spot and return our patient to Congdon. They swarmed the car instead, holding their phones to the backseat windows and making it impossible to see where Bryce was. Revving the engine, I inched back, finally spotting Bryce in the center of the crowd. Angrily, he holstered the Taser and gestured to the road. *Go.*

I went. We took the fastest route back to the hospital with Jasper pacing, falling whenever I turned, and anxiously checking the windows. Lucas stayed hunched over for the entire ride, only sitting back up after we cleared Congdon's gates and were driving through the parking lot.

Pulling up to the main entrance, I put the car in park and turned around.

"What was that?" He still looked shell-shocked.

"One of the reasons it's not entirely safe for you out there."

"I don't want this." Without warning, he ripped the sling off his arm and threw it on the floor of the car. "I don't want any of this. Maya—"

"I know." I reached a hand over the seat. "I'm going to get you there. I promise."

He took several deep inhales, using the meditation breathing, and then wrapped my hand in both of his, squeezing down to the bones.

———

The next few days passed in a blur of emails and phone calls crammed between near-constant sessions with Lucas and updates to Dr. Mehta. I checked the ice in websites, making sure none of the Boundary Waters lakes were freezing over yet, and also monitored news sites and social media. Other than a bear sighting near Twin Harbors and photos of the last of the fall colors, it was quiet up north. I wished I could say the same for Duluth. Footage of Lucas at Twin Ponds had swept through the media, causing backlash at the protesters and throwing Congdon's practices even further into the spotlight. Dr. Mehta had given a news conference explaining patient reintegration privileges and appealing to the public for their support.

With Lucas in attendance I held the first meeting for the search party, who were surprisingly easy to recruit. Everyone wanted to be part of the rescue effort, winter be damned. Two orderlies volunteered within ten minutes of when I sent the email and Dr. Mehta offered up one of the associate psychiatrists as the medical resource on the expedition. A U.S. Forest Service ranger named Micah was going to be our official guide and within two minutes of meeting him—and without asking—I learned that he'd grown up in Michigan's Upper Peninsula, he'd needed to find some direction after his discharge from the military, and he had no, absolutely no, problem with crazy people. Officer Miller, who was sitting in on the meeting, stifled a laugh as I shook the ranger's hand.

I started by displaying the same picture showcased on all the news outlets and taped up on my fridge, the Blackthorns sitting on a dock together before they'd disappeared. After repeating the story everyone in the room knew, I told them the part they didn't know—that the Blackthorns had lived happily off the grid for ten years until a few months ago, when Josiah got sick.

"It's been twenty-five days since Lucas last saw his father and time is running out. Our mission is to rescue him before the ice sets in."

I went over the details of the trip. Due to Lucas's "inability" to pinpoint Josiah's location on a map, we'd backtrack his journey starting from the outfitter's store. Lucas would lead us to his father, our doctor could administer any emergency medical treatment, and Micah the forest ranger would be able to radio in for an airlift to transport Josiah to the hospital.

"What if he's already dead?" one of the orderlies asked.

That question sparked a debate about whether a helicopter would be called, under increasingly extreme conditions, merely to transport a body and who was going to pay for all these extraordinary measures. The doctor suggested towing an empty canoe for the remains, but—after accidentally catching Lucas's murderous look—quickly amended that it could be used to haul out any extra stuff from their campsite, too.

"After all," he appealed to everyone else, careful to avoid Lucas's corner of the table, "that's the motto in the Boundary Waters, right?"

Lucas grunted, drawing the table's attention. "We don't need lessons on how to disappear."

I directed the conversation quickly back to the list of supplies, cautions about entering the Boundary Waters in November (cue smug grins from the ranger), and general preparations for monitoring Lucas, who needed to be supervised at all times by Congdon staff. He would sleep in a tent with the orderlies, paddle with me, and wear an ankle bracelet in the event he got separated from the group. As long as Dr. Mehta gave the approval, our target departure date was November 1, three days away.

———

Sometimes when things moved forward, they moved backward, too. It was a strange sensation, a déjà vu carnival ride. I'd spent years trying to forget Ely, Minnesota, and now it had clawed its way back into every corner of my life. Past and future, a man killed, a man who might be saved; everything converged in Ely. There was no hiding from it anymore, so on my last day off before the search party was scheduled to leave, I left Dad a note and drove north.

If Duluth was considered small by most urban standards, Ely was hardly more than a dot on the map. It had been an iron town until the mines gave out, drawing all the miners to the taconite under the towns to the south. Now it was a collection of small businesses, a hub for the forest service, and of course, a gateway to the Boundary Waters. Soon after my discharge from Congdon I'd read that Ely was named The Coolest Small Town in America, referring to possibly more than the temperature.

Driving through the small grid of streets I saw a mix of old and new—Babe's Bait and Tackle, Steger Mukluks, and the Northland

Market sitting adjacent to places with vague names like Insula and very specific ones like Gator's Grilled Cheese Emporium. I drove past Pillow Rock, the one place we always stopped when Mom and I came to town, our tradition, like some people went to the Old-Fashioned Candy store. Bigger than a car, the ancient greenstone could be found nowhere else in the world, but what I remembered most was that she never let me climb on it, never let me lay my head on those inviting, almost fluffy looking puffs of minerals.

In the center of town, I found a large camping store in a clapboard building whose foundation was lined with flowers. Wilting plants, crosses, and wreaths with ribbons that whipped in the wind crowded next to black-and-white pictures of a lined, laughing woman's face. A hand-painted sign in the center of the memorial had Monica Anderson's name with her dates of birth and death. Across the street, a tax office's window was crowded with signs. One of them said, FRIENDS OF THE BOUNDARY WATERS. Another, in large red letters, read, REMEMBER MONICA. KEEP BLACKTHORN IN JAIL. I parked outside the camping store and took a deep breath.

Inside there was enough gear to outfit the entire Forest Service. I browsed the all-terrain boots, the tent covers, and varieties of powdered eggs, picking up items here and there and starting a pile on the abandoned counter. I was on my fourth trip back up to the register when a man appeared on the stairs at the back. Moving stiffly, he unfolded a pair of glasses from his shirt pocket and scanned my selections with flat eyes.

"Planning a winter trip?"

"Yeah." I set a box of fire starters on top. "Going to find Josiah Blackthorn."

His head snapped up. I gave him a bland smile.

"I don't know anything."

"I didn't say you did, Robert. I'm just here to buy some gear."

His throat worked and he seemed to be weighing the benefit of a thousand-dollar sale against the urge to throw me out of his store. Eventually he stepped closer and picked up a pair of top-of-the-line boots. "These are men's. This size won't fit you."

"They're not for me."

He braced both hands on the counter then, and stared at the stack of clothing, gear, and provisions. He might have been anywhere from fifty to seventy, with stone gray hair standing up in odd places, and a series of faint red lines zigzagging through one side of his forehead and temple, like the edges of puzzle pieces if the puzzle had been bleeding. A huge silhouette of a moose against the sunset hung behind the counter, framed in driftwood. There were other touches through the store—painted paddles mounted near the ceiling, product explanation cards written in an elegant flourish—the undeniable traces of a woman who'd left her mark, even if she hadn't planned on leaving.

"Take your business elsewhere." He didn't look at me.

I moved to the door but stopped before opening it, glancing through the window from one end of the street to the other. "Why didn't he?"

"Excuse me?" It was the closest most Minnesotans would come to telling you to fuck off.

Ignoring his implication, I looked through the store, filling in the shadows of struggling bodies, the spill of fluids. "Why didn't Lucas go somewhere else? Why did he come here, to an outfitter in the middle of town, when there were three other stores closer to the edge of the woods?"

"I don't know."

"He strangled me. See?" I moved back to the counter, approaching carefully, lifting my chin to reveal the faint bruise line. "He could have killed me, but he didn't." Robert looked at my neck and his jaw started working.

"There are two kinds of violence, Robert. Violence as an end and violence as a means. Lucas's violence is a means, and we both know what the end is, don't we?"

I let the silence drag out. No one came in to interrupt us, the store virtually dead in the off-season. Picking up a premium winter tent, I added it to the pile.

Robert heaved out a long sigh and shook his head, then pointed me to a model that cost half as much. "That'll give you the same protection with less draft and an easier setup."

I smiled and made the switch.

After ringing up the sale, Robert flipped the closed sign and invited me upstairs for coffee. He showed me pictures of him and Monica at the store's grand opening. It had been their second career, their dream. He wasn't sure what to do with it without her and could hardly bear to look at the flowers laid outside the building. Then, swirling the grounds at the bottom of his cup, he began talking about Josiah Blackthorn.

"I told the police I didn't know it was him until they started showing their pictures on the news. Josiah came in a few times a year, and he didn't look any different than most people exiting the Boundary Waters. No one would have noticed him in town. You can't throw a rock around here in the summer and not hit a guy wearing a backpack. He always said he was stocking up for next year and always paid cash. Rations, lures, clothes, and I only remembered him because he cut the tags off everything and packed it up right in the store." He swallowed. "That's what I told the police."

I set my cup down. "I'm not the police."

Robert looked out the window, where the KEEP BLACKTHORN IN JAIL sign was posted across the street. "I met Josiah Blackthorn when he and his boy moved to town. He bought a secondhand canoe off me and started coming in regularly after that. Not a big conversationalist, always had his son in tow, but we talked paddle and portage routes, fishing spots, all the regular stuff. Then one day he came in by himself and something was different. He asked to speak to me privately and I brought him up here. He was sitting right where you are now and I noticed . . . I noticed dirt on his clothes and under his fingernails. It was early in the season—the ground hadn't even thawed yet—and I remember wondering how he could've gotten all that dirt on him.

"He said he and his son were moving, leaving town, but he wanted to keep buying his camping supplies from me. He gave me a list of items and two dates. April first and October first."

"And you agreed."

He nodded. "I knew right away when I looked at the list. Preppers and survivalists are good customers for outfitters. I figured the Blackthorns were going off the grid somewhere and true to his word, he came in like clockwork twice a year after that, right up until this fall. He didn't show up this October first and I was worried, wondering if I should do something. I'd given him . . ." Robert covered his mouth, as if trying to keep the coffee from coming back up. "I always gave him my card when he came in, and I told him if he or his son ever needed anything, they knew where to find me."

The words trailed off and a storm of emotion worked over his face, pumping the scars on his temple with fresh blood.

Robert sold me Josiah's unclaimed supplies, which I packed into the car along with the rest of the gear. I was fitting the last of the boxes in the trunk when a vintage Chevy drove by, the rasping putt-putt noise unmistakable, and I lifted my head in time to see the driver stop in the middle of a left turn. His hunched frame swiveled in the window and we stared at each other, neither making a move. Before I could decide on a reaction, an oncoming car honked its horn and the driver stepped on the gas, pulling onto the side street.

Slamming the trunk, I walked straight to the police station a few blocks away. I had the business card Officer Miller had given me along with Josiah's arrest records, but I didn't need to look at it when the desk sergeant asked who I wanted to see.

"Sergeant Coombe, please."

It took fifteen minutes for the guy to waddle out into the waiting area and when he spotted me, his eyebrows shot up to underline the furrows in his forehead. Waving me back, we went to a messy office littered with empty vending machine wrappers and enough stacks of paper to suggest he thought the computer age was a giant hoax.

I unfolded a piece of paper from my backpack and set it on top of one of the stacks. Heather Price's creased face smiled up at both of us.

When he saw it, he gave a shocked laugh and leaned so far back in his chair the hinges shrieked. Then he crossed his arms and looked me up and down, as if checking for weapons. The last time he'd done that, he'd had to take a bloody agate out of my hand, so he probably assumed anything was possible when it came to me.

"Heard you ended up at a mental hospital. How'd that work out?"

I shrugged. "I'm still kind of there."

"Better there than here. Especially when you seem to have a

thing for dead bodies." He grunted and nodded at the picture. "Officer Miller, huh? I was wondering about that request when it came through."

I got down to it, giving Sergeant Coombe a slightly different pitch than what had worked with Robert Anderson. Instead of victim solidarity, I went for the unsolved case angle, but I'd barely outlined the situation before he was in stitches.

"*You're* his shrink?" He couldn't stop laughing and, in all honesty, the man had a point.

"I'm trying to figure out what drove them into the Boundary Waters in the first place."

After wiping his eyes with a napkin, he wadded it up and overhanded it into the waste basket. "Never thought they stuck around. Frankly, I was shocked as shit when your boy turned up here. Back when those two went missing, I assumed they hightailed it to Canada."

"Why Canada, then? What were they running from?"

He nodded to the paper. "You already filled in your own blank."

"The medical examiner's report said she died of a heroin overdose."

He rifled through a drawer and pulled out a few packets of Cheetos, offering one to me. I happily dug in as he took me through the finer points of the autopsy with a mouthful of orange mush. Heather's body had shown evidence of chronic heroin use including scar tissue on her veins, abscesses on her lungs, and even tissue death in her heart.

"Her heart was dying?" I scooped up the last of the Cheetos crumbs. "That doesn't sound like Josiah's fault."

"No," he licked his fingers, "but listen to this."

The heroin hadn't actually killed Heather, not by itself. The medical examiner also found a contusion on her brain. Somehow, she'd received a blow to the head before she died and the pain-inhibitors in the drug prevented her from getting help before a blood clot formed.

"So she fell and hit her head?" I asked.

"Maybe. Or something—or someone—hit her."

Someone with a history of violence. I carefully folded the empty Cheetos bag and laid it on the desk. "Why did you close the case? Why was it ruled an overdose?"

He tossed his own bag and wiped his fingers on another napkin. "Believe you me, I searched that scene for any evidence of wrongful death. We couldn't come up with anything and according to the M.E., the drugs and the contusion were kind of a chicken and egg thing. We found her dealer and he confirmed she bought and shot alone, so my chief closed the case."

I picked up Heather's picture. "What do you think happened?"

"Why, you know something about it?" His voice changed; it became threaded with that universal flint edge handed out to every cop along with their gun and badge. My pulse reacted, but I smiled as I deliberately folded the paper and slipped it back in my backpack.

"Back then I was still learning how to pick locks in Lincoln Park."

He shook his head. "Well it's probably good you ended up where you did . . . and lucky for Josiah Blackthorn he ended up wherever he did."

"Why do you say that?"

His lips thinned out. "Cops are pretty fair psychologists, too. I don't know exactly what happened to Heather Price, but I do know Josiah Blackthorn was hiding something."

The Cheetos had sucked all the moisture out of my mouth. Clearing my throat, I thanked Sergeant Coombe for his time and got up to go, but he stopped me, making me wait while he left his office—to do what? Get a tape recorder? Another officer? I wasn't at liberty to reveal anything Lucas had told me, but maybe he could see it in my eyes. A body—Heather Price's body—draped over Josiah's shoulder. I checked my phone and thought about leaving before he could come back, but as I moved toward the door he appeared again, handing me a box that looked like it held files. I set it on the desk, lifting the lid.

"That came up for disposal a while ago. I'm not sure why I had them keep it."

Reaching in, I pulled out a plastic bag holding the agate, my mother's agate, still crusted with remnants of dried blood. It felt lighter than I remembered, the colors less vivid, but still warm to the touch.

"I've never given anyone back a murder weapon before."

"Don't worry." I dried my eyes and put the bag in my backpack next to the picture of Heather Price. "I won't tell anyone."

17.

Modern science says: "The sun is the past, the earth is the present, the moon is the future." From an incandescent mass we have originated, and into a frozen mass we shall turn. Merciless is the law of nature, and rapidly and irresistibly we are drawn to our doom.

—*Nikola Tesla*

JOSIAH

Damaged people recognized their own. Josiah could smell it on Heather Price as she led him and Lucas through the vacant apartment.

"The ad said it was furnished." He opened a few cupboards and glanced in the fridge, where a brown ring stained one of the empty shelves. A folding table and two chairs sat under the bare bulb in the dining room, coated in a fine layer of dust.

"There's a bed." Lucas, already far ahead of the adults, reported from one of the bedrooms.

"Partially furnished." Heather held her elbows and walked to the couch in the living room. "You're not going to find that in Ely at this price. Trust me."

She pivoted and gave him another once-over without any attempt to disguise what she was doing, her gaze settling somewhere near his wallet. Her hair was limp and tangled, falling almost to her waist, and any luster it might have possessed had leached out a long time ago. Her skin looked brittle, her movements jerky, and it seemed like all the life in her had been sucked into those too-bright reptilian eyes. For someone who'd moved as many times as he had, Josiah had seen plenty of landlords and no matter what the exterior looked like they all spoke the same language.

"Two hundred and fifty a month? I can give you the first and last month today."

She backed into the shadows, unblinking. "I told you the first month is free."

"Dad, the toilet sounds like a frog. Come listen!" Lucas called from another room.

He glanced at the trampled carpet, the yellowing walls, and the hook in the corner of the ceiling where someone had maybe tried to hang a plant once, as if a tiny gasp of green could make any improvement to the place.

"Nothing's free. You can put it toward a damage deposit if you want."

That made her blink and after a fraction of a pause she reached a hand out of the shadows. He didn't want to, but he shook it.

———

Over the next few weeks, he and Lucas settled into the duplex and bought their usual necessities—sheets, toilet paper, bleach—lots of bleach—and also found a secondhand canoe that they stored in the living room. Lucas did his homework every night in the belly of the boat, balancing his worksheets and library books on the thwarts and afterward he wrote and illustrated stories about their adventures, which always ended with treasure and ice cream. Josiah taped all his stories to the walls, next to maps of places they'd been, places they were planning to go, and some places they could only imagine.

They did everything together—cooking, grocery shopping, spending afternoons at the library to surf the Internet and read back issues of *National Geographic*. He refused to leave him with strangers. The entire concept of exchanging money for childcare hinted too much of his own childhood and then there was the other problem; when Lucas was out of sight, a quiet panic began building in Josiah's chest. When Josiah had to work evenings, his boss let Lucas hang out in the office. He got up at least once a night to watch the hypnotic rise and fall of his son's chest and sometimes when he woke up, Lucas's frame was illuminated in his own doorway, checking on him, too. When he was younger he asked questions from those shadowy doorways. "What was Mom's favorite holiday?" "Did she like cats or dogs better?" By the time they moved to Ely, though, Lucas just blinked sleep-swollen eyes and turned around, heading back to burrow into his bed. Josiah worried about his son's lack of friends. He knew what it was like to grow up alone, but every time he mentioned it Lucas scoffed. "I'm not alone. I've got you, Dad." And for the rest of the day he would stand a little closer, talk a little more, showing Josiah with every word and action that there was nothing missing. Together they formed their own discrete ecosystem.

Within their first month in Ely, it became obvious Heather Price was part of no such community. No visitors came in or out of her side of the duplex. She never spent time outside and when Josiah found a citation for yard maintenance in their mailbox, he had to knock on her door for a solid minute before she answered and then she tumbled into an incoherent speech about mayors and her work schedule and neighbors who were trying to repossess her house. Josiah left her mid-rant and found a broken lawn mower in the garage, showed Lucas how to take it apart and fix it, and then mowed the tiny lawn every week until the snow came. Heather watched him from her window, her seemingly lidless eyes following his every move. Lucas studied her in his turn and, like a budding naturalist, called out his observations from their living room window. "It's Work Heather today" or other days "Ugh, Home Heather" and the two were easy to differentiate. Work Heather had wet hair pulled back into a ponytail and white lab coats frayed at the edges; she stumbled down the street toward some job that required breath mints and hastily applied lipstick. Home Heather, the one they'd seen during the duplex tour, rarely went anywhere and when they did run into her outside it felt somehow calculated. She fawned over Lucas, who at nine years old was long past the age when boys wanted to be fawned over, petting his hair and telling him bizarre facts about his classmates as Lucas jerked out of her spindle-armed reach.

Then, as winter set in, the price of her free rent started coming due. She began asking for money early each month, knocking on their door at two in the morning when they both worked the next day, always with a reason ready—the utility company was screwing her over or she'd gotten scammed by a credit card collector. When that didn't work she started offering up her body, not like a barter so much as something she wanted to be rid of. Josiah stopped answering the door. He listened to the knocking while lying in bed, staring at the water stains spreading over the bedroom ceiling like an insidious cancer.

In a perfect world Josiah would have helped her, invited her into his life and tried to show her she was worth something, but in reality he just wanted her to stay as far away as possible from him and his son. At the very least they should've moved, they should've packed up and found some other place in Ely or even Babbitt, which was only twenty minutes down the road, but two hundred and fifty a month was dirt cheap. He was saving more than ever, stockpiling money for all the things Lucas might someday need—casts for broken bones, his first car, college tuition, or maybe a trip around the world. He might actually be able to see the Amazon or the Nile, all the rivers he pretended to navigate from the carpet-grounded canoe in their living room. So they stayed. He shot down Heather's advances, installed a chain lock on their door, and put the cash in her mailbox on the first of every month. It didn't take someone with his police record to smell the trouble reeking from the holes in her arms. He itched to move on, counting down the days until Lucas finished third grade, and in the meantime they found sanctuary in the Boundary Waters.

Camping most weekends and on school holidays, they explored the giant wilderness where civilization was strictly prohibited. No motorized boats. No cans. No bottles. Any stain of human habitation had to be scrubbed when you left. It was the guiding principle, the bedrock rule for entering the Boundary Waters Canoe Area Wilderness, a place that changed even the language people used to describe it. When passing other paddlers, everyone asked the same questions. "When did you come in?" "When do you go out?" The paradigm shift was subtle, but complete. This world where bear and moose still roamed, where loons cried like melancholy ghosts and the Milky Way raged overhead in a storm of shadows and stars, this place was the pulse, the center, the *inside*, and everything else, the stuff people built their lives on, was merely the *out*.

They camped from the end of summer through the fall, and in the winter Josiah bought his first auger and they taught themselves how to ice fish. Robert Anderson, the man who'd sold them their canoe and the auger, helped them map out some of the best spots to tap the labyrinths of underwater boulders and find the elusive winter fish. They experimented with snow packed tents, heaters, and chimney positions, testing the limits of snowshoes and sleds. Sometimes entire days passed during which they'd hardly spoken a word, bundled up in their hoods and scarves, but they worked together with an implicit understanding, shifting positions on the sled with a touch on the shoulder, signaling a firewood expedition with just a nod to a shrinking pile of kindling. Lucas seemed wise beyond his years and Josiah watched, awestruck, as he grew stronger by the day. Subzero temperatures didn't faze him. He paced his strides to Josiah's, reaching his legs longer and farther, and then giggled—transformed into a nine-year-old boy again—when he fell over into a pile of fresh powder. The kids at his school played sports and video games, and when Josiah asked if he wanted to get a Wii, Lucas shook his head and frowned. "Why would I want to sit around and pretend to do things when we really do them?" It wasn't a question either Blackthorn could answer.

On the first day of Lucas's spring break, they packed for a week-long trip and set out on the freshly thawed Fall Lake but had to turn around when Josiah remembered he'd been in such a hurry to leave he'd forgotten their tent. Laughing, they drove back to town and Josiah told Lucas to stay in the truck while he jogged inside the duplex only to find Heather trying to break into the safe where he stored all his cash.

"What the fuck?"

She panicked and bolted for the door. Grabbing her, he dragged her out of the bedroom and threw her into the wall in the hallway. She bounced off it, unfazed by the pain or maybe too far gone to even feel it. Her eyes were bloodshot and the corner of her mouth was cracked and scabbed over. She screamed and swore at him, accusing him of withholding rent, of stealing from her, and threatened to call the police. He pushed her back into the wall, and right as he heard the satisfying crack of her head against the plaster, there was another noise, this time from behind him.

"Dad?"

He whipped around and saw Lucas wavering in the front door. His eyes were wider than Josiah had ever seen them, but his narrow shoulders tensed and shifted, squaring up, ready to come to his father's aid.

"Get back in the car."

Lucas hesitated, his hands creeping into trembling fists at his sides, before Josiah barked the order again and he jerked backward, running to the truck that was still idling in the driveway.

"It's just a few bucks." Heather's voice was broken, panting. "Just a loan. I gave you a free month's rent, remember? You owe me. I'll pay you back on Tuesday, as soon as I get my next check." Then with barely a pause for air, "I took you in with no questions, no applications, or background checks, and everyone knows you're a goddamn felon. Get your hands off me. I'm calling the police."

He gave her one last bone-crunching push into the wall and walked back to the safe, emptying the whole thing in front of her, stuffing thousands of dollars in a bag with the tent just so she could smell the ink before tossing two hundred-dollar bills at her face.

"There's our first month's rent, minus lawn mowing fees. Go put that in your fucking arm." He didn't know how much heroin cost, but two hundred dollars had to be enough to keep her high and out of his house for the rest of the week. Dragging her across the living room to the patio door, where Lucas wouldn't be able to see them, he shoved her out onto the concrete. "When we get back from this trip, we're moving out."

Then she raged about the lease and taking him to court, hitting him with the wadded-up bills clutched in her fist until he swatted her off and she fell into a heap on the filthy remains of last winter's snow. Neither of them saw the neighbors frozen in their kitchen window, one holding a coffee cup suspended halfway to his mouth and the other bent over the sink as the unexpected altercation spilled into their weekday breakfast routine. Josiah wouldn't find that out until seventy-two hours later when the police interrogated him, telling him he was the last person to see Heather Price alive.

18

"IT CAN'T BE a good sign, can it?" Dr. Mehta muttered as she stepped her kitten-heeled boots carefully up the gangplank to my dad's tugboat. "The top isn't supposed to be wet."

"It's only mist." I swallowed a smile, trying not to be amused by Dr. Mehta's surprise aversion to boats. Who would have thought psychiatrists had phobias, too?

After the confrontation at Twin Ponds, I'd modified my field trip plans. Split Rock Lighthouse was one of the most famous landmarks on Superior and far too public a venue for Lucas to make an appearance. If he was chased down at as quiet a place as Twin Ponds, he'd be mobbed at Split Rock, so I'd modified the agenda with a little help from Dad. Yesterday Stan and I had taken Lucas to the docks by the longest route possible, driving up through the University neighborhood and weaving our way down the hill to Garfield Avenue, where we doubled back through the industrial stretch twice to make sure no one was following us or hanging around. Dad's dock was in the middle of the harbor and Lucas spent the morning learning how to detail the boat while Stan and I watched with Jasper on the sidelines, pointing and yelling our advice. Butch taught Lucas several key swear words to use on us, but Lucas just kept working, absorbing the nautical nuances and the industry surrounding us on all sides. He didn't flinch at sudden noises and was even laughing by the end of the outing, scratching Jasper's scruff as the dog barked at some circling gulls.

Today was our last field trip—a sunrise cruise on Dad's tugboat—and after that, with Dr. Mehta's approval, the Boundary Waters. At the moment, though, she was having trouble focusing on anything besides the giant orange and white hull in front of us.

"When was the last time this vessel has even been serviced? Did you check?"

I started to reply when a baritone voice cut in over my shoulder. "She was dry docked last winter and we do weekly inspections during the shipping season."

Turning, I caught Butch's indulgent wink and introduced Dr. Mehta to my dad's first mate. He offered a tattooed arm to assist her the rest of the way up and started pointing out the early morning activities around the harbor, doing his best to put her at ease. I didn't see Dad anywhere and assumed he was on the bridge.

Below us, Lucas leaned over the rail and peered into the water as if trying to see to the bottom. Bryce squinted up the gangplank with bloodshot eyes and steered Lucas onto the boat, with the other hand resting on his Taser.

"Do you really need that?" I muttered as they boarded.

Bryce glared at both of us before releasing his grip on Lucas.

"I don't have any other patients who try to jump fences or sick their crazy fans after me."

"Lucas didn't sick anyone on you. Anyway, that's why we're here before dawn. Crazy sleeps in."

He grunted and stalked away. When I filed the incident report for Twin Ponds I'd specifically asked for Stan on the rest of our field trips, but today was Stan's day off and none of the other orderlies had as much experience with Lucas, so we were stuck with Bryce.

Once everyone was on board Butch brought us into the cabin and gave a quick safety talk as we chugged out into the harbor and waited for the lift bridge to raise. The boat boasted a 3,000-horsepower diesel engine that could steer thousand-foot freighters with ease. Its two decks were full of lights, winches, and rope that an F-16 fighter jet couldn't break. The lower deck cabin had only a single wooden bench for us to sit on, otherwise we could climb up to the open-air deck behind the glass encased captain's bridge for better views. Butch pointed out the bathroom, which wasn't a huge step up from the latrines dug at the Boundary Waters campsites and nothing like the facilities on the yacht-style passenger cruisers that catered to the tourists on Lake Superior. The tugboat, though, was infinitely safer, a controlled environment away from the general public. When I'd texted Dad at the beginning of the week, he agreed to take us out and even turned down a job to arrive back in port early. After the safety talk, Dad came down to the lower deck and showed us the map tacked up on one of the walls, pointing out their attempts to locate the *Bannockburn*, before moving on to describe the shipwreck of the *Onoko*—our destination for today's cruise.

At the top of the hour, the lift bridge closed to car traffic along the peninsula and cranked up its metal scaffolding to the accompanying scream of fire alarm bells. The bridge was an icon, the symbol of Duluth and as far as alarm clocks went, a piercing start to the day. We filed out of the warmth of the cabin to watch the bridge rise. Bryce smoked a cigarette in the bow, legs wide and taking the slap of the wind head-on. Lucas watched in silence, absorbing the spectacle while Dad stood behind him and Butch's head moved around on the bridge. The only person missing was Dr. Mehta.

I let the wind blow me back to the cabin and found her braced on the bench, watching the cement canal pass outside the windows. She looked paler than normal, smaller. It took a few minutes, but I convinced her to come out for the sunrise. We cleared the canal and cruised along the shoreline while Butch pointed out landmarks on the loudspeaker that no one looked at. Instead everyone faced east, into the endless sightline that showed the curve of the Earth itself and watched in silence as the thick gray morning became infused with an illumination that seemed to have no source. A haze of clouds shrouded the water, but somewhere behind them the sun was rising. A shimmer of pink glanced off the waves and made the buildings on Duluth's hillside glow. It was a sunrise with no sun, a morning without light, and before anyone could do more than huddle into their jackets and gaze around, it vanished and the day began.

I turned to Dr. Mehta, eager to share the moment, but she was quaking against the rail.

"I always get seasick. It's not the boat or the water I'm afraid of," she admitted. "It's vomiting in public."

Biting my lip, I gave her a hesitant pat on the back. "Dad says seasickness comes when your body insists on being vertical. If you let go of that need, stop focusing on the horizon and what you think should be up or down, then the sickness will pass."

She squinted across Superior, where the gray below met the gray above. "There is no horizon."

I tried not to smile. "One less problem. Just try to remember: up isn't up. Down isn't down."

Dad came over and, after hearing the situation, offered to take her back to the cabin. She accepted his arm, too queasy to even grumble about being led around like an old lady, while he told her about the *Onoko*'s hull failure and spectacular flipping explosion and sinking, presumably to cheer her up. When Bryce took Lucas inside for a supervised bathroom trip, I climbed the stairs to the second deck and curled up beneath the sightline of the captain's bridge, using it as a buffer against the unrelenting wind. The gales had begun.

Shivering, I watched the churn of the water until Lucas appeared on the stairs. Bryce's head popped up behind him and I waved him off, agreeing to supervise. Negotiating the deck unsteadily, Lucas leveraged the winches and coils of rope to make his way to the bench and sit down. Silently he gripped the rails of the seat and I wondered if he was going to be sick, too.

The boat progressed up the shore where the sprawl of Duluth gave way to secluded mansions, towering homes sitting regally on the cliffs, and then we turned and headed into the open water toward the site of the wreck. Dad climbed up to the captain's bridge and passed us without comment or hurry, seemingly immune to the blast of wind, the Arctic's first attempt to take Superior.

As the shoreline receded, I felt Lucas relax and start to absorb the morning. This. *This* is what I wanted to show him, the moment I'd secretly hoped for when I planned these field trips with Superior lurking behind every outing—first a view from the hill, then a trip to the docks, now cruising over the water itself. Duluth lived at the mouth of this inland sea, at the whim of the water. We took the wind, the squalls, the snow, and the flooding. We took everything the lake gave to or inflicted on us, knowing there would always be more. This was a resource we could not exhaust. It wasn't protected like the Boundary Waters, it didn't sink quietly into your soul; it dominated everything it touched and we were the ones who needed protection from it. The water would always win, no matter if it was beating at the basalt cliffs that tried to contain it or reforging our empty bottles into lake glass as beautiful as gemstones. This gray wind-tossed water, raging at the gales, the water that sucked ships into oblivion, that roared so loud you forgot the storm in your head, this was what I loved most about Duluth—the absolute reign of Superior.

I didn't realize I was shivering until Lucas slid over, closing the gap between us and slipping his arm around my shoulders. I stilled. Even the tremors died as I felt the length of him press into my side, offering his own body heat.

"Your ears are red," he murmured, so close I could hear him above the wind and the roar of the engines. Too close.

I pulled away, putting distance between us. Someone was walking in the bridge behind our heads and Bryce and Dr. Mehta were right under our feet. I should have joined them downstairs and ended the insanity of this stolen, frigid moment before someone discovered us, but not even that threat was enough to make me sever it completely. I threaded our gloved fingers together on the bench, trying to pretend I was watching the few gulls screaming overhead, fighting the immense pull of the air currents.

Lucas gripped my hand. I could feel him searching my profile but after a while—when I refused to do anything more than stare at the birds—he turned to the water. "The search party."

"What about it?"

"I won't lead them to him. I told you we had to find my father alone."

I'd already explained to him several times that working with the police and the U.S. Forest Service was the only chance of getting Congdon's approval for the trip. It was the only door we could walk through. The problem was he knew part of the plan, but not the whole thing. I couldn't share everything, not with staff and patients constantly prowling around our sessions. Here, though, where the wind whipped our words away, where there was no one to overhear, I took a deep breath and told him the rest.

"You'll go alone. I have to organize the search party so Congdon will let me get you up there, and then I expect you to disappear, okay? We'll get the medicine, the supplies, and then it's up to you to slip into the shadows. Understand?"

The surprise on his face was almost funny, but he quickly recovered and another emotion flooded his eyes. "I shouldn't have doubted you." Then he thought of another obstacle. "The ankle bracelet. How am I supposed to disappear if they're tracking me?"

I squeezed his hand. "Don't worry. I have a plan."

"Do you always have a plan?"

He turned his head, studying me, waiting patiently for my answer, and it struck me how absorbed he was in every single thing I said. I'd revealed my big secret; I'd told him I killed a man and all he wanted to know was whether I'd bashed his head in hard enough. If anyone else had asked me a direct question about myself I'd shrug it off with an easy lie, something to redirect the conversation. With Lucas, though, I wanted to excavate the truth. Right now, sitting here together, there wasn't anything I couldn't tell him.

"I guess the worse things are, the better prepared I am. I started working at Congdon because it felt like home. Sad, I know, but I can't help it. People are honest about who they are in a psychiatric facility. They don't pretend things are fine. My job reviews always say I'm good in a crisis, that I'm the first person to jump into a dicey situation."

"Like wrestling down a patient who tried to strangle you and escape?" Lucas grinned.

"Yeah." I smiled at the stern. "They think I'm brave. The truth is I'm not comfortable unless something's on fire or someone's having a meltdown. I don't know what to do with things that aren't broken. The quiet times . . . it's like I'm just waiting for things to go bad."

"And they always do?"

"I've never had to wait too long."

Moving carefully, a fraction of an inch at a time, Lucas tugged my zipper down to trace my neck with one finger, the faint but still visible line where he'd choked me the first time we met, and his expression filled with regret.

"Lucas."

He tilted his head, leaving his hand on my neck, his touch falling somewhere between penance and petting. "Are you waiting for me to break, too?"

"You know this is completely inappropriate." I glanced around us to make sure the deck was still empty, wondering how much longer this privacy could last. "Dr. Mehta will remove me from your case."

His answer was entirely nonverbal; he leaned in, pushing my hood back to nuzzle my temple and smell my hair, as though he needed to learn as much about me as quickly as possible.

"It's unprofessional. Unethical." I turned into the bulk of his jacket, trying to make myself get up, to end this now.

"You just said you're helping me escape so I can get back to my father."

"So you're saying I've already crossed the line? Why stop now?"

"Yes." I opened my eyes to see his breathless, wind-slapped smile, but as he said my name and started to lean in, a movement caught the corner of my eye.

Bryce stood on the deck, watching us.

19

"GETTING OFF WITH Tarzan? Now it makes sense why we're doing all this crap for him. It's not therapy, it's a freaking date."

That's all Bryce got out before Lucas exploded off the bench, aiming his full weight at the center of Bryce's body. I was half a second behind him but had to duck out of the way as Bryce doubled over, swinging wildly in all directions. He made a grab for Lucas, who twisted to protect his bad shoulder and the two of them flipped around like clashing bulls, ramming into the equipment and railings on the platform.

Ordering them to stop, I wedged myself between their bodies, trying to push them apart.

"What the hell?" came a shout from somewhere above us. A door banged open and feet reverberated against metal. Just as I pulled Lucas's good arm back, an elbow flew into my face and sent me reeling backward into one of the giant steel pulleys. The world went black and someone shouted, then a long guttural scream seemed to be ripped apart by the wind before it cut off.

A scuffle nearby, flesh on flesh, heaving breathing. I shook my head, desperate to get my sight back. When the stars finally cleared Butch stood in front of me holding Lucas's arms behind his back. Both of their heads bowed toward something beyond the rail.

I ran to the railing and saw Bryce sprawled on the main deck, not moving. Shit, oh shit. I climbed down the ladder and reached the deck right as Dr. Mehta came out of the cabin, clinging to the door. Above, I could hear Dad's voice joining the mix in the sudden silence of the idling engines.

Before anyone could reach him, Bryce kicked out, looking for a foothold, and rolled over to boost himself up on all fours.

"Bryce—"

"Don't move." Dr. Mehta ordered, but he didn't listen. I crouched down next to him and he shoved me back, catching me in the hip and sending me stumbling toward the railing. Holding Dr. Mehta off with a warning hand, he dragged himself to his feet.

"What happened?" Dr. Mehta asked.

Dad's voice came from above and I had to crane my head to see him, standing with his hands on his hips and hair whipping in the wind. "Lucas started fighting that orderly. He attacked him and shoved him off the deck."

"Bryce was antagonizing him," I jumped in.

Bryce leaned back against the railing and clutched his side, lip curled with equal parts pain and loathing. When he spoke, every word landed like angry spit marks on the deck.

"Maya was making out with the patient."

A horrible silence followed, where everyone on the entire boat looked at me. I stepped instinctively away from the weight of their collective gaze, gripped the freezing railing, and tried to think of any justification for what I'd done, any reason for Dr. Mehta not to fire me on the spot.

I turned to her. "It's not—"

She held a hand up, a look of total disappointment swallowing her face, until it turned into something else, a sickness. Then she ran to the edge of the deck and vomited.

―――――

The trip home was short, but the amount of panic I crammed into it could have filled several terrifying weeks. I sat in the captain's bridge, wedged between two control panels, while the rest of the Congdon staff supervised Lucas on the main deck. Butch threw sympathetic glances my way every now and then, and once even broke the silence to say, "I don't blame you, Maya. That kid's hot."

"Butch," Dad barked.

"What? I'm comfortable with my masculinity. I can say it."

I stared at the North Shore, the pine, spruce, and birch trees that began here and stretched hundreds of miles to the north and west, into the Superior National Forest, the Boundary Waters, and beyond. Josiah was out there somewhere, maybe suffering, maybe a murderer like me, maybe just a father, freezing and alone. An hour ago I'd had a plan that would have given him back his son. Now all three of our futures were in jeopardy.

As soon as we docked, I followed the van with Lucas, Dr. Mehta, and Bryce back up the hill and stood outside Dr. Mehta's office for a good part of the morning. Wherever she was, she was either too busy or still too nauseous to look at me. When one of my sessions came up on my calendar I went and conducted it, counting each minute as closely as I counted speech errors in the oral reading passage, waiting for someone to seize my badge and toss me out of the building. Nothing happened. Afterward I raced back downstairs, feeling as unstable as Dr. Mehta had on the deck of the boat. Up wasn't up. Down wasn't down. Before I reached the administrative area, I ran into her in the main corridor and she started talking as soon as she saw me coming.

"I spoke to the Forest Service this morning. They'll continue their search without Congdon's involvement." She didn't slow down or even glance in my direction.

"How? You said yourself they've turned up nothing. Without Lucas, we have no path to Josiah."

She stared at the floor tiles ahead of us. "I know that, Maya, but he had a serious violent incident on the boat today. I can't approve Lucas to leave the facility. Josiah Blackthorn has spent ten winters in the wilderness. All we can do now is believe that, if the Forest Service can't locate him, he can make it eleven."

I didn't believe it. The odds of two healthy men surviving a brutal Minnesota winter were incredible enough. One sick man, by himself, had no chance. Cursing Bryce, cursing myself, I cast around desperately for some way to salvage all the work I'd done. There had to be a way to find Josiah.

"Maybe," I shook my head, the words hopeless even before I'd spoken them, "I could get Lucas to point them in the right direction. Narrow down the range. I can ask him."

"You won't be speaking to Lucas Blackthorn again."

Even though I'd expected it, my frame jerked like I'd crashed into a wall. We'd reached the administrative offices and Dr. Mehta held the door open to hers, waving me inside. I glanced at two clerks by the copy machine—both staring at the papers in their hands and trying to pretend they weren't eavesdropping—and woodenly walked into the office. She shut the door behind us.

"It's not what you think."

"I blame myself more than anyone else." She sat heavily in her chair and propped her elbows on the desk, rubbing her temples. "To place such responsibility on your shoulders, against your will, and with little prior clinical experience . . ." She trailed off.

"I did everything you said." I could feel my face flushing, my fists clenching. "I reached him. I've been acclimating him, preparing him to enter the world. He doesn't hide from group environments anymore. He can handle noise, stress; he independently initiates relaxation techniques."

"You'll no longer have access to ward two. All your patients in that ward are being redistributed."

I should have been relieved that I still had a job, but all I could think about was Big George. The Grinch. I was losing them all because of one stupid mistake. Because for once in my adult life I'd wanted to be close to someone, and this was the result.

"I screwed up, okay? I admit it. I care more for him than I should because I know what he's going through." I smacked a hand over my heart, ready to dig it out and show it to her if it would change her mind. "You have no idea. You don't know what it's like to lose a parent."

"Really?" She folded her hands and carefully laid them on the desk in front of her. Suddenly the whine of the copy machine outside became the loudest noise in the room. I shrank back, unsure of the depth of the water I'd just splashed into. Dr. Mehta smoothed her face, a masterful veiling of muscle and skin, and looked directly into my eyes.

"I'm sure you know India is a very traditional culture. In Bolly-wood, it's rare to even see a man and woman kiss onscreen. Can you guess, Maya, how most Indians feel about homosexuality?"

I shook my head, even though the last ten seconds gave me a pretty good idea. Then Dr. Mehta told me, in carefully modulated tones, a past she'd never shared before. Growing up in Mumbai, she'd been exposed to a deep-seated prejudice against gay culture. Same-sex relations were a crime, committed by people with a "genetic flaw" according to her father, and she'd accepted his opinion with a daughter's deference. She had no idea that when her parents sent her to school in the United States for a Western education, she would meet her future wife. Conflicted and ashamed, she'd kept their love hidden for four years, until her parents announced at graduation that they'd arranged a marriage for her back in India. She had to choose between going home and obeying her family's wishes or telling them the truth. When she chose honesty, they cut all ties. They refused to meet her girlfriend and stopped answering her phone calls. In the twenty years since her confession they hadn't spoken to her once, not even when she fulfilled her father's dream of seeing one of his children become a doctor.

The longer she talked, the more callous I felt. How had I never wondered about Dr. Mehta's family before now? She'd been my therapist, my boss, my mentor, and friend. If my mother was the shadow of my life, Dr. Mehta was the light. I ached for her even as I wanted to hide from her unrelenting, quiet gaze.

"There are many ways to lose one's parents, Maya," she said. "In my personal and professional experience, it seems to happen in the manner we least expect. I didn't know my family wasn't able to put their daughter before their culture. You could never have known your mother would abandon you when you were ten years old, and

I doubt Lucas Blackthorn could have predicted the chain of events that began when he broke into that outfitter's store."

I leaned in, letting her see straight into me. No anger this time. All emotion carefully banked.

"I promised I would help him. Please. Let me keep that promise."

There was a split second where I thought she might change her mind, until she sighed and her eyes filled. "I'm so sorry. I'll be acting as Lucas's therapist going forward and you can consider this a disciplinary warning in your employee file. If you'd like to talk about any of this, in a session or simply off the record, I'm here."

I pushed myself up and walked out of her office, feeling all the purpose I'd had over the last few weeks draining out of me, taking every good thing with it. When I got to the door, I paused, and some monster inside me roiled up, teeth gnashing.

"I'm sorry, too. And on the record? You just killed Josiah Blackthorn."

———

Jasper was sniffing through the dead grass in the yard when I came home and he immediately ran to the gate, tail wagging, and looked hopefully toward the end of the street. I ran my hands over his rough coat and told him to wait a second, running inside to grab his leash, but Dad called my name from the kitchen.

"Please don't." I paced to the doorway. "It's none of your business."

"You made it my business when you brought him on my boat." He pointed at the refrigerator, still plastered with all the disappeared families. "You made it my business when you brought him into our house."

Grabbing my wallet, I started dumping bills on the table that I couldn't see as my vision started to blur. "There. Your services are paid in full. The boat, rent, whatever. Go back to hunting for the *Bannockburn* and pretending that it's going to bring her back."

The mug Dad was holding banged on the counter, sending coffee drips flying. I flinched and blinked the tears away, afraid to look up. When he spoke, the words sounded like they were escaping from a clenched fist.

"And what do you think you're doing with that bathroom? You think if you remodel it enough, it won't be the same room where she tried to kill herself?"

"No. I don't know. I can't do this right now." Stuffing the wallet back in my pocket, I headed for the door and almost reached it before Dad's hands clamped down on my shoulders, holding me in place. Breaking away from a man with the strength to fight Superior every day was impossible, and I didn't even attempt it. Sniffing, I wiped my eyes.

"I'm sorry," I said to the door. "I want you to find the *Bannockburn*."

"I know I worry about you more than you like. You think I don't see what a strong, capable woman you've become, but that's not it. I see all of you, every version of Maya you've ever been and all the storms you've survived to get this far. I just don't want you to have to weather any more." His breath hitched and he paused before speaking lower, his voice unsteady. "I didn't know your mom that long before we got married. I didn't understand how ill she was, and she really wasn't bad until . . ." His fingers shrunk away from me and he cleared his throat. "The doctor said postpartum, but it never got better, not really. It was probably there all along and I just didn't want to see it."

He wasn't touching me at all anymore. He spoke to my back, which began to tremble. "I don't want you to make the same mistakes, Maya. He's a mental patient. He's violent and he's—"

It was all I could bear to hear. Grabbing the leash, I nodded and left. I turned my phone off as Jasper and I disappeared into the cold streets, working our way from bad to worse neighborhoods. Street kid territory. It took almost a mile for Dad's words to recede far enough to notice something was different. The drunks seemed drunker, the dealers bolder. "What are you supposed to be, honey?" one of them asked, and I let Jasper have a little more leash, flash some canines. It wasn't until I passed two women wearing blood-soaked scrubs with black eye sockets and cracked faces that I realized it was Halloween.

South of the railroad tracks I passed a group that stopped me in the middle of the street. A man and woman, both dressed in heavy coats and carrying steaming thermoses, followed a pack of kids bubbling over with excitement. Some had plastic pumpkins rattling with candy, others clutched half-full pillowcases. They circled the end of a residential neighborhood, ready to plunder another street with bouncing flashlights, red, dripping noses, and nonstop chatter. The adults were quieter, but enjoying themselves, too. They told the kids to steer clear of Jasper, sipped their drinks, and smiled at me as they passed.

I watched them go with an ache I could barely contain, gut-punched by the careless laughter of those kids. They had no idea what walked behind them, anchoring them, because they had never been unmoored. And they shouldn't have to know.

20

THE NEXT DAY at work, while I led a new group session with four nonverbal women, Lucas tried to escape again.

We were doing deep-breathing exercises and humming out our breath, or at least I was and maybe one patient. The other three sat in their wheelchairs staring at the walls. Hard to blame them. Staring vacantly at the walls was pretty much what I'd done all night after getting home to a dark house and Dad's closed bedroom door. He'd already left by the time I got up this morning, but there was a note on the counter next to a paper bag. The note said, "Going out for one last run at the *Bannockburn*. Maybe we'll get lucky this time." I opened the bag and found copper-plated drawer handles, polished on the edges and shimmering with deep mahogany and streaks of gold. She would love them, if she ever came back.

I stopped humming and looked around at the group.

"It doesn't get better, does it?" I glanced from face to wrinkled face, searching for any hint of reaction. Their expressions sagged, unresponsive. Only one woman, the one who had been breathing with me, met my eyes. Tears leaked out of hers, but she didn't look away. She kept breathing, the exaggerated deep inhale that lifted her shoulders, and then hummed the air out in a noise that turned to a lament, her tiny, soprano ode to sorrow. I crouched in front of her wheelchair and held her hands.

"Maybe coming here was your only way out."

The tears fell silently off her chin. Her fingers rustled underneath mine like little birds in a cage.

"Let's just breathe."

And that's how the attending day nurse found me, kneeling in front of a crying woman as we whistled our breath in and out together.

"Maya! Your boyfriend's trying to escape again."

"Jesus Christ."

I shot up and out of the ward, shouting at the nurse to help the women back to their rooms. I ran down a flight of stairs and sprinted through a vacant corridor of offices. As I neared ward two a thought almost sent me stumbling.

Whose side was I on?

The badge slapping against my thigh was a Congdon badge. I was a Congdon employee, here to rehabilitate and protect patients, especially from themselves.

But everything in me wanted to find Lucas and keep running.

Just as the realization hit, two orderlies rushed out of another stairwell and the three of us barreled through the door into the high security men's ward. A crowd of people had gathered at the far end of the ward near an emergency exit, crushing any impulse I had to do something crazy. As I slowed to a walk, I noticed nurses kneeling in the center of the huddle and a surge of fear shot through my chest.

"What happened?" I elbowed my way to the front. "Who's hurt?"

"I believe that would be me." Blood covered the side of Dr. Mehta's head, dripping from a place in her hair where one of the nurses applied a compress.

I scanned the bodies, searching for any sign of Lucas.

"Get out of here, Maya."

"But . . ." My attention snapped back to Dr. Mehta.

"You don't have clearance for this ward. Go."

The rest of them shifted uncomfortably, glancing at me then away. The two orderlies who'd arrived with me worked their way through the crowd to the emergency exit. Had Lucas gotten that far? Was he gone? I took a step toward the exit, but Dr. Mehta's look stopped me. Even with blood streaks smeared over her face, sprawled in the middle of the linoleum floor, she still managed to impart that shrinking, piercing stare. Like she knew exactly what I'd been thinking.

I swallowed and nodded, withdrawing from the group, and walked slowly back down the hall.

After my shift ended, I pretended my sprained ankle was hurting again and went to the medical ward where the gossipy nurses reigned. One of them set me up on a bed and examined the bone while the others filled us in, peppering the story with knowing glances in my direction. By now, everyone had heard about the incident on the boat and my demotion.

"According to Stan, all he would say during his session was, *I have to go find my father.*"

"Nothing else?"

"Nope. Totally silent after that, wouldn't answer any questions about where his father is so other people could, like, actually go look for him. Only glared at Dr. Mehta and stared out the window. He won't even talk to Carol when she brings him meals now, and you know he used to ask her about . . . other people . . . a lot."

Nurse Valerie, the information queen, pointedly ignored me as she parted with this tidbit. I kept my expression neutral, focusing on the narrow bone boxed in one of the other nurse's hands.

"So when Dr. Mehta tries to give him a book, the kid bashes Stan over the head with it and takes Dr. Mehta hostage."

The other nurse wasn't even pretending to examine me anymore. She gasped, putting a hand over her mouth.

"He got a lot farther without this little firecracker"—Nurse Valerie nodded toward me—"around to stop him. He handcuffed Stan to a table, took his badge, and forced Dr. Mehta through the ward to that emergency exit that leads out to the parking lot, but the nurse's station saw him right away and the guards met him at the door. He threw—literally threw—Dr. Mehta at them and took off. Fell down a flight of stairs and kept going, until three of them tackled him at the main door."

I closed my eyes. The guilt doubled and redoubled as I sat on the hospital bed, oblivious to the continued chatter of the nurses around me.

"Where is he now?" I asked, opening my eyes to look around. "Doesn't he need medical treatment?"

"Dr. Mehta wouldn't let him be treated here." The nurse who was wrapping my perfectly healthy ankle replied, glancing up with a smug look, like she thought it was obvious I'd come to the ward to see him.

Nurse Valerie piped back up. "I've been given clearance to visit him three times a day in his isolation room—where he is in full restraints, mind you—to administer pain medication and check for infection and swelling. That is, until I leave for my Cancun trip."

Her voice turned gloating and one of the other nurses groaned. "Do you have to rub it in?"

Nurse Valerie glanced at me and seemed to soften a fraction, answering the unspoken question.

"No serious injuries this time. His right side is going to look like a burger patty, but luckily the shoulder didn't get any more damage. I put it in another sling just as a precaution. Don't worry," she patted my bandaged ankle. "Sounds like that kid's got stamina. But you'd know better than us, right?"

The other nurses snorted, ducking their heads. I felt my face flush as I swung my legs around and put my weight gingerly on the "bad" ankle, shrugging into my coat.

"He's only on pain meds?"

She nodded as she turned away. "Tylenol 3, three times a day."

I thanked them for the wrap and pretended to favor the leg as I left the ward.

Everyone knew the definition of insanity. Lucas had tried to escape from Congdon three times now. Three episodes of the same behavior, expecting different results. How many more attempts would it take, how many crawling days and nights in isolation, how many times could he beat his head against the wall before his mind started to crack? Before he became what everyone thought he already was?

A string of storms raced across Superior and slammed into Duluth over the next few days, bringing blinding lake-effect snow squalls that buried the city, while only a few miles west the ground remained brown and bare. Dr. Mehta hadn't gotten any updates from the Forest Service rangers and I could tell she was getting tired of me asking. I hibernated in the house after work, spending half my nights on the Internet. The backlash against the protesters who'd chased us down at Twin Ponds had helped some new voices rise on social media, people calling for Lucas's privacy, to let the system help him and focus public efforts on finding Josiah instead. I looked up Boundary Waters maps, sometimes scrolling the satellite images to the tiny break in the green that showed the roof of my mother's cabin. Other nights I googled everything I could find on Heather Price: her life, the scant details of her death. A drug addict's death, apparently, was even less noteworthy than a mental health patient's. Society turned away, pretended the body had never been a person. No one demanded to know how she'd gotten the blow to her head. I found a small, archived post on the website of the dentist office where she'd worked, offering the usual thoughts and prayers to a family who didn't seem to exist, and the only person who might know more had disappeared from the known world.

After half a week, the snow stopped and the gales began tossing it around the city, whipping drifts of white over the streets, tearing at anyone who braved the cold. I left work one day and the wind picked up the tails of my jacket, invaded my hood, and froze my earrings the second I muscled open the security door. I jogged toward the parking lot, intent only on getting to my car and starting the heater, before stopping dead in the middle of the sidewalk.

Lucas, two orderlies, and Nurse Valerie were walking in the side yard near the therapy garden. Lucas was restrained in a full strait-jacket with an orderly holding each arm. His head listed to one side and he stared dully at the flakes whipping along the ground. Even from twenty yards away it was obvious he was drugged. His movements were sluggish and awkward, reeking of a massive dose of some life-sucking, behavior-correcting prescription cocktail. It looked like Nurse Valerie was trying to hurry them back inside, but Lucas could barely put one foot in front of the other.

Until he saw me.

His eyes wandered over the sidewalk and roamed up my body like I was just another static feature in the landscape. A moment passed when it didn't even seem like he recognized me until he blinked and jerked upright.

Maya. I saw his mouth form my name even though no sound came out. He lurched forward, throwing his handlers off balance, and tried to close the distance between us. Confused by his sudden mood change, Valerie put a hand out to steady him before she turned and saw who he was trying to reach. She snapped back around and said something to the orderlies, who abruptly stopped walking and grabbed Lucas, preventing him from moving. Lucas struggled, but he was no match for the combination of the strait-jacket, two burly orderlies, and whatever chemicals they'd pumped into him. Thrashing in place, he mouthed my name until he finally managed to work the ragged sound out of his throat, and he reached me the only way he could.

"Maya. Help, Maya. Maya, I'm sorry. I'm sorry." Tears started to run down his face. "Don't leave me here. Please, Maya. Please."

Nurse Valerie stepped in front of Lucas, blocking him from my sight, and gestured to the parking lot.

"Go on. Dr. Mehta's orders state that he can't have any contact with you."

I couldn't move, even as the wind slapped my cheeks and stung needles into my fingers. I forgot where I'd been going. Lucas dragged one of the orderlies a step forward, bumping into Valerie.

"Go!" She pointed to the cars, trying to keep her hood from flying off with her other hand. "We're going to freeze out here if we don't blow away first."

It took strength I didn't even know I possessed to walk toward the parking lot. Lucas's voice grew weaker and weaker before dying away in the wind, and I didn't know if he stopped calling my name because the group had gone inside or because he'd lost all hope. I didn't turn around to check.

By the time I climbed inside my car, I was shaking. Snowflakes clung to the ends of my hair and my hands were red and raw. I stared at Congdon's brick walls and barred windows rising like a fortress out of the angry, white blur of the gales, and everything became suddenly clear. As clear as a sun-soaked sky over the lake. As clear as a bag of carefully chosen hardware. As clear as the layers of an agate, sliced and gleaming in my mother's hand.

I knew what I had to do. I had to rescue Lucas Blackthorn.

21

STEALING A PATIENT from a psychiatric facility is a little harder than your basic B&E. Congdon had multiple layers of security, beginning with the outside gates where a guard was posted twenty-four hours a day and the ten-foot tall iron fence enclosing the rest of the property. Then there was the building itself. Every exterior door locked from both sides and could only be opened with a security badge, except the main entrance, where visitors passed through metal detectors and checked in with another Taser-armed guard before being escorted to the appropriate room. Each floor and ward had their own entrances with their own electronic security. Not every badge opened every door. And if you happened to be trying to kidnap someone from an isolation room, no badge would work. The entrances to each seclusion unit opened with individual keys which were only held by the attendants on duty or the night security staff. Cameras in every hallway fed video back to the guard desk at the main entrance. If an emergency was spotted—like, say, someone trying to make off with a high-security patient—they could hit a button that would deadlock all doors, trapping everyone inside until the lockdown was lifted.

That was getting in. Smuggling the patient out and figuring out how to get as far away as possible without drawing attention was the other obstacle. People tended to notice stumbling mental health patients in straitjackets, even when they weren't celebrities.

For three days I planned the rescue, making lists and detailed plans before burning the pages immediately afterward. It had to be a night job, when staff levels were the lowest. I began staying late after my shifts to catch up on paperwork and then stopped to chat with the front desk guard on my way out, pretending to be outraged at the rumors flying around about me while watching the security monitors and the pattern of the night rounds. Jason, the guard, had apparently been accused of sexual harassment once and was sympathetic in a way that made me immediately want to shower. On the third day, he told me he got off at eleven and had a growler with my name on it. We could watch Netflix and chill. I told him no thank you, marking the end of my first attempt at friendship. All in all, I called it a success.

The supplies I'd bought for the original search party were still piled in a vacant office in the administrative area, including extreme weather tents, subzero sleeping bags, and—most important of all—the locked, waterproof box filled with a random buffet of medicine: antibiotics, anti-inflammatories, cortisol steroids, every broad-spectrum pill or shot that might have provided Josiah the emergency care he needed. When we'd been preparing for the search, I'd brought the box so the associate psychiatrist could fill it and dutifully secure it with a Master No. 3 padlock, universally acknowledged as the easiest lock on the planet to pick. And, as an added bonus, the building's security cameras were only used in patient wards. Over my three days of planning Lucas's rescue, I exchanged ward bedding for sleeping bags, Advil for steroids, swapping items so the gear appeared intact and smuggling the supplies out one by one in the backpack I always brought to work.

On my next day off, Jasper and I took a longer than usual walk. We headed north out of Lincoln Park and started climbing the hill into nicer neighborhoods until we reached a two-story Victorian with window boxes full of spruce branches and an honest-to-God porch swing with snowflake-printed decorative pillows arranged on it. Rounding the block, we doubled back through the alley. I stopped near the house's garage, pretending to pick up some dog poop while checking for motion in the house and then we slipped inside the gate and around to the side door. Houses in Duluth were built so close together that only the next-door neighbors could have seen me working on the lock, and luckily their blinds were closed.

I hadn't used my lock picking skills in eight years and it wasn't exactly like riding a bike, but luckily I'd saved my bump keys and the door was old. Closing my eyes, I put myself inside the lock, feeling the weights and springs, and tapping the bump with a screwdriver until the key turned. Jasper pushed ahead into a sun-soaked laundry room. I reined him in before he could get too far.

"Anyone here?" I whispered.

Jasper nosed the air and we both listened, waiting for any signs of life while my heart raced. When I broke into places as a kid, I'd never cared about getting caught; I had nothing to lose then. Now Lucas's mind and freedom hung in the balance, and I couldn't stop hearing his drugged, desperate voice. *Don't leave me here. Please, Maya. Please.*

After a few minutes of total silence, I forced myself to relax and crept further into the house. It was like another world— a Martha Stewart world. Curtains with gauzy stuff at the top set off the rich colors of the walls and sleek couches. Vases, books, and art filled the built-in shelves lining every room. I thought I'd done a good job with our bathroom, but every inch of this house felt manicured. The containers in the pantry had tiny chalkboards attached to their fronts that were scrawled in hand-written cursive. Red lentils. Protein powder. Each drawer had an organizer and each bin had a label. A church bulletin lay on top of an ornate-looking Bible near the fireplace. The air even smelled different here, like vinegar-dipped roses. Framed pictures of the ocean were scattered everywhere and I paused at one sitting on top of a piano.

In the picture Nurse Valerie sat at a table with a balding man as they held up some fruity drinks. They were both sunburned and smiling in that overly wide, forced way when you hold one pose for too long.

"Hey, Val." I grinned at the picture and kept moving. "Hope you and the hubs are having fun in Cancun. Nice digs, by the way. My dad might need your advice on our kitchen."

I checked all the coats in the front closet, the purses in her bed-room, the kitchen drawers, even the pockets in her dirty laundry. Nothing. This was a house where everything had a place, so why couldn't I find what I was looking for?

After twenty minutes of frustrated searching, I spun toward Jasper. "Are you thinking what I'm thinking?"

The door to Valerie's detached garage was more exposed.

I watched the nearby houses until I was sure no one was looking out their window and then Jasper and I ducked into the yard with the ring of keys that was thoughtfully hung right next to the back door. In the glove box of the Chevy Malibu I finally found the prize—her Congdon security badge, newly upgraded with isolation ward clearance.

"Aww, Valerie." I dangled the strap from one finger and watched her perky photo spin as the rope untangled. "You shouldn't have."

Putting the keys back in the house, I relocked the door on my way out. I was practically skipping when I opened the gate and led Jasper back into the alley, until a man came out of the yard on the opposite side at the exact same time and did a double take when he saw me. Shit. Shit. Shit.

"Oh, hey!" I smiled and jogged over, pulling Jasper into a sharp heel at my side. "Do you know Valerie? I was supposed to meet with her today, at least I think it was today, and she's not answering her phone."

I scratched my temple like I was confused and made sure the stocking cap fully covered my head. As long as the maroon hair and earrings were covered, I could pass for a completely nondescript college kid, one of thousands in this town.

The neighbor looked me over, not replying, and I could sense him cataloging, judging. Jasper tugged on the leash and let out a growl, making the guy back up a step. Apologizing loudly and repeatedly, I ordered Jasper to sit and took the opportunity to duck my head, shirking away from his gaze. I glanced back at the house, as if unsure I had the right one.

"That's Valerie's place, right?"

He finally spoke. "She and Rick are out of town."

"Oh crap, she's in Cancun *this* week? I must have written the dates down wrong." I pulled my phone out of my jacket pocket and pretended to check it, playing it out, waiting for him to make any wrong move. If he went for his phone or backed into his yard, I was going to have to choose between knocking him out or running. This was the first real test. Surveillance, breaking and entering, stealing—that was kid's play, literally the toys of my childhood. It hurt no one. But now this forty-something, UMD Bulldog sweatshirt–wearing guy waffling in the back alleys of the hillside was barging into my plan. Why hadn't I stolen some jewelry or pulled out a few drawers? I could've at least made it seem like a random robbery if I was spotted, which would have sent the police in a different direction than Congdon. Breathing carefully, I slipped the phone back into my pocket and closed my fingers around a jagged rock. If all else had failed, I'd been prepared to break a window to get inside. Now I prepared myself for the first innocent bystander.

He seemed to ease up a bit, though, when I dropped the Cancun reference. I flashed him a self-deprecating smile. "She's my mentor for this life skills program at our church. Or she's trying to be, anyway."

I laughed and he loosened up more, chuckling with me, a man who wasn't going to take a rock to the head. We talked for a minute as he put his trash out, until I remarked on the cold and how I didn't want Jasper's paws to freeze.

"Thanks for your help. I guess I'll catch up with her next week."

I pulled Jasper down the rest of the alley, acting like I was checking email or something, while adrenaline flooded my chest and Valerie's security badge bounced comfortingly in the pocket against my hip.

———

The next day I went to Congdon prepared to kidnap Lucas.

It was a strange thing walking into your job—a place where you'd worked so hard, followed all the rules, and turned yourself inside out to be accepted as a professional—suddenly hoping everything went to plan so you could commit a felony. The delinquent kid inside of me was on high alert, noting every detail down to the number of clouds in the sky as I drove to Congdon. I parked and came in through the front door with a large duffel bag that immediately set off the metal detectors.

"Hey." I unzipped the bag on the search table and nodded to the guard who resentfully got out of his chair at the monitoring station.

"We're having a jam session today. Want to come up to the third floor around three? It's gonna be epic."

The guard poked through the mess of tambourines, hand drums, sleigh bells, and whatever else I could find at the second-hand music store yesterday. "Um, I think I'll pass."

"Your loss, man." I zipped the bag back up and flung it over my shoulder, heading for the employee locker rooms.

It was early enough that the night shift was still on, yawning into their sleeves and ready for the late winter sun to end their day. I nodded to a few of them and some even acknowledged me without smirking. Walking past the lockers, I took the bag through another exit into a stairwell and jogged down to the basement. There was no badge access down here and no video cameras as far as I could tell, so I set the duffel down and went to work on the lock. Twenty minutes later, just as I was starting to lose hope, the catch sprung and I swung the door open, peeking inside. A dim, open room housed a pile of miscellaneous furniture and on either side of the mess two hallways disappeared into blackness. I took the one leading right, mentally tracking the map of the building above me, until I got to the stairwell exit I wanted. Opening the duffel bag, I reached through to the bottom where I'd cut the lining, pulled out the tools I needed, and tucked them behind a dusty fire extinguisher.

"See you in a few."

Then I left the basement and started my shift.

22

JASON HOUSLEY—MY fleeting front desk friend—had worked as a second shift Congdon security guard since he graduated high school fifteen years ago. In the last few days I learned he liked to sit in the break room telling anyone who would listen that he made more money than half the guys he knew who had gone to college.

"And no friggin' loans to pay off, either," he'd add, slopping up whatever microwave meal he'd overcooked that day and filling the room with mystery meat or fake butter smells.

The picture on Jason's security badge showed a not-bad looking kid trying to seem tough, probably taken a few days after he was hired. The real Jason had the shape and appeal of a rancid turkey. He was a mountainous, slack-jawed guy who'd harassed the only unmarried nurse until she'd threatened to go to H/R and bragged to everyone about his pristine, collector-registered Pontiac Trans

Am. He mattered to no one, which made him desperate to seem as important as possible. He always carried his flashlight out when he made rounds, scraping it along every door as he puffed and sweated through each ward. After I rejected his offer of a growler and a groping, he waited for me at night as I left the building, throwing out some bizarre comment he'd no doubt been refining all day.

"You're too late." He sneered from the monitor station today. "The high school let out already, so you missed all the underage boys."

I didn't slow down. "I prefer undergrads. All that sexy book learnin'."

He grunted as I left, acting offended, like it wasn't the highlight of his day someone actually talked to him, and today I was going to make sure of that.

On Monday nights, Congdon had late visiting hours, so there were still plenty of cars in the parking lot after five o'clock. I wove through the rows until I came to my beat-up Civic, parked right next to a shiny, black Pontiac Trans Am. The guard station faced the street, the protesters had all dispersed a few days ago, no one else was coming in or out of the building, and Jason had considerately parked his collector wheels right next to a giant spruce tree that blocked the view from most of Congdon's windows. The car was backed into its spot and ready to floor it off the property. It was now or never.

I pulled a tire iron out of my trunk. The nicest thing about old cars was how easily everything came apart.

Six hours later I parked in an alley a block away from Congdon's eastern fence. The building rose up over the top of the line of houses, a black silhouette towering at the crest of Duluth. I took a few deep breaths and stared at the outline of the institution that had given me a fresh start, not once in my life, but twice.

For the last several days I'd obsessed over the logistics of this kidnapping—the exact sequence of events and every tool I'd need—ignoring the hovering cloud of my betrayal. I wasn't naive. I understood exactly what I was doing, the line I was crossing. No matter if I succeeded or failed in the next hour, the life I'd been trying to live was over. I was going to prove everyone right who'd whispered Dr. Mehta was wrong to hire me, that once a mental health patient, always a mental health patient. The costume was gone, the show over. Just like my mother. I wondered if she'd been as sure as I was now, if she felt this thing in her core that told her she'd found a greater purpose. Maybe her abandonment of me was as inevitable as my abandonment of Dr. Mehta and Congdon now. Maybe it wasn't my fault she left. I would probably never know. And I'd never know if she took a moment like I was taking now, sitting in this car at the point of no return to face the roil of sorrow in my gut. Acknowledging the emotion, like I'd been taught to do.

"I'm sorry, Riya." Dr. Mehta's first name felt wrong on my tongue and I embraced the alienness, the separation of what she'd been to me from what I had to become to her now.

I took one last giant breath before double-checking everything in my backpack and slipping out of the car. It was time. Lucas was waiting.

Cutting across the block to the sidewalk that bordered Congdon's grounds, I glanced in the windows of nearby homes. Briskly, I paced to the far end of the block and checked the front gate, making sure no protesters had decided to make a reappearance, but the sidewalk in front of the guardhouse remained empty. I crept along the fence, to the spot where my shoes crunched over a pile of broken glass from the streetlights I'd knocked out last night. Hip hop thumped out an open window of a nearby house, but I didn't see any movement other than a lone squirrel ducking through the fence's iron bars. Pulling out a knotted length of rope from the backpack, I swung the looped side over the top of the fence and threaded the other end through, drawing it tight. I scaled easily up to the top and teetered there, carefully gripping the bars between the spikes to ease one foot over, then the other. Once I'd swung my weight over I grabbed the rope again and scaled down the other side, noting how much time it had taken while I tucked the trailing section along the fence. If someone searched the perimeter of the grounds they'd spot it, but to the casual observer it blended into the shadows.

I put on a full ski mask and cinched the hood up on my jacket. The gloves, baggy black sweatpants, and shoes had all been purchased at Goodwill, with cash. I crept through the grounds, sticking to the trees, until I had a view of both the isolation ward and the edge of the parking lot. There were no lights in the windows of the isolation rooms and I still didn't know the night shift's exact schedule to do their checks, but I did know when the shift changed.

At exactly 11:15, after the transfer of keys and notes, Jason Housley lumbered out to his Trans Am. I crouched under the bows of a pine, clutching Nurse Valerie's badge, and held my breath. He started the car and floored the engine, then let it idle for what felt like an hour. Jesus, what was he doing in there? I couldn't see him through the glare of the parking lot lights and started to get nervous. Could he tell something was wrong? He hadn't hesitated before getting in the car. I edged to the far side of the tree, ready to run.

When he shot out of his parking spot and gunned out of sight, I waited, listening. Sooner or later he was going to have to turn to exit the parking lot. And sooner or later his tires—missing all their lug nuts—were going to come barreling off his baby.

The crash came seconds later, followed by an ear-splitting car alarm that jerked me into movement like the starting gun of a race. I sprinted to the emergency exit door and badged my way into an empty stairwell, ran down to the basement and opened the door I'd sealed with duct tape before my shift this morning to insure it wouldn't latch. My tools—a hacksaw and can of spray paint—were exactly where I'd left them behind the fire extinguisher. I grabbed them and shoved the saw into my backpack, taking the stairs two at a time until I reached the emergency exit of the men's isolation ward. I paused for a second, peering in the lead glass window, as the car alarm still shrieked in the night. No one was at the desk on the far side of the ward by the main entrance. I badged in just as the car alarm stopped. The quiet was deafening.

I breathed once, then pushed the door further open and slipped inside. It was impossible to tell from this angle if any patients were up and looking through their doors. Shaking the spray paint can and cringing at the noise, I aimed it at the corner of the ceiling directly above me, where a security camera was mounted to capture the entire corridor down to the main entrance. Hopefully the front desk security staff were still in the parking lot dealing with Jason's accident and—with any luck—they'd think a black screen was a shorted-out wire before coming to investigate the camera. Once I had the lens covered, I duct taped the door latch, then crossed to the main desk to see which room Lucas was in. My fingers shook as I ran them over the check sheet, finally finding his name by room six. I had the lock pick ready as I sprinted to his door, attacking the knob and tripping myself up with the adrenaline rocketing through my body. Bump keys wouldn't work on these doors. I had to pick through each individual weight and spring.

There was rustling and scraping in one of the rooms behind me, then a broken, singsongy voice started chanting words I couldn't understand. It sounded like he had respiratory issues. A clavicular breathing pattern? I shook my head, forcing the voice out, and concentrated all my energy on the piece of metal separating me from Lucas. How much time did I have? Every second wasted was one second closer to failure.

I couldn't hear anything inside Lucas's room, or maybe I just couldn't hear him over the combination of the singer and the pounding of my heart. More seconds ticked by. Sweat dripped down my temples under the mask and I started praying to the god of lock picking, to anyone who could help me break through this door. I was running out of time.

Finally, after what seemed like an hour, I popped the latch and turned the handle, pushing inside.

It took a second for my eyes to adjust to the dark. When they did, I saw a body strapped to the bed in full restraints, unconscious.

"Lucas," I whispered, going to work on the handcuffs, which were a walk in the park compared to that freaking door. I had both his feet free before he even blinked his eyes open.

"Lucas, can you hear me?"

It took him a moment to focus on me and when he did, the ripple of fear over his face broke my heart. I paused at his left wrist and tugged the ski mask up, squeezing his hand.

"Had enough of this place yet?"

As soon as my face came into view, his entire body lifted and his breath caught. A strangled noise came out of his throat.

"Maya," he breathed, looking at me like he was drowning and I was the only buoy in all of Lake Superior. I swallowed a wave of emotion and smiled before pulling the ski mask back down.

"Let's get the hell out of here."

I opened the last of his handcuffs, which was more difficult now that he'd woken up because he started tugging against them. When I'd finally gotten them all, I unfastened the straps on the straitjacket and pulled it off him as he staggered to his feet and then fell back on the bed heavily. I boxed his head in my hands, tilting his face to the light streaming in from the corridor. His pupils were contracted and he couldn't stop blinking.

"Swallow this. Quickly." I handed him two NoDoz pills from my pocket and he ate them without question.

"Can you walk?"

He made himself stand up again, slower this time, and inhaled slowly. "I'll crawl if I need to."

"Okay, let's go."

I peeked out of the room. The patient with respiratory issues had stopped singing and there was no sign of any staff yet. Ducking into the corridor, we moved awkwardly to the emergency exit. Lucas braced one arm along the wall while I pulled him by the other. We made it through the door and down the stairwell with Lucas falling twice and me helping him back to his feet. At the bottom of the stairs I pulled Nurse Valerie's badge out and swiped it against the electronic pad.

Nothing.

I tried it again and the light turned red.

"Fuck." I threw my weight against the door once, but it was solid metal.

"Plan B."

"What's a planbee?" Lucas asked as I dragged him back up the stairs. The respiratory patient was giggling when we got back to the isolation ward. Laughter echoed down the hall and met the distant sound of walking feet. I pulled the can of spray paint out and shoved it into Lucas's hands.

"Spray everything."

"What?"

"We need another decoy." I ran to the giggling patient's room and went to work on the lock. Now that I knew the model it was easier to spring the catch. As soon as I opened the door a bone-skinny white guy ran out and started making circles in the middle of the corridor, singing at the top of his lungs, his shoulders heaving up and down with the effort.

"Hey!" I grabbed the can out of Lucas's shaking hands and tossed it to the guy. "We did this hall, but you have to get the rest. Can you paint the basement?"

I opened the emergency exit and he ran through it on pale, quivering legs, tottering down the stairs and spraying a trail of paint all over the walls and himself. There was no time for the stab of regret that lanced through me. Voices came from the other direction, getting closer.

"Get into bed." I pulled Lucas into his room, shutting the door behind us.

"No!" He struggled against the straitjacket as I tried to cover him with it.

"Shut up! Do it now." I forced him back to a lying position and was tucking the handcuffs up so they didn't dangle off the sides, just as we heard the dull thud of the main ward door opening.

"Oh, Jesus H Christ." A man's voice came from the end of the corridor. Someone else replied, but I couldn't hear what they said. I crouched against the wall next to the door, fighting the panic that swelled in my throat.

Lucas's breathing had sped up, which meant the NoDoz was starting to kick in and counteract the sleeping pills, but other than the quick rise and fall of his chest, he lay motionless on the bed with his eyes closed.

The guards ran past us to the end of the corridor.

"Spray paint? Are you fucking kidding me?"

"Radio the desk. Check the rooms. Now."

One of them called the central monitoring station while the other's footsteps came closer and closer, pausing at each room. Stride. Pause. Stride.

I held my breath as the feet stopped outside Lucas's room. A flashlight's beam shone through the window and bounced off the bed; I could see the glare of the handcuffs clearly open, the strait-jacket straps hanging loosely. As noiselessly as possible, I pulled a utility knife out of my jacket pocket, waiting for the shout, for the door to spring open.

"Here!" The yell made me jerk and the flashlight beam disappeared as quickly as it had come, but the door didn't open. Footsteps ran across the corridor, in the opposite direction of Lucas's room.

"How the hell could he have gotten out?"

"Crazy people, man. They do crazy shit."

"He must have gone this way. Come on."

They hurried back to the emergency exit and into the stairwell. As soon as the door slammed shut, I sprang up and ran to the window, opening the casement and cranking it up as high as it would go. There was enough room to fit through and barely reach the bars.

"The bed."

Lucas and I dragged it under the window and I jumped on top, retrieving the hacksaw from the bag and starting to saw the middle bar, putting every ounce of muscle into my dad's diamond tipped blade. Before I'd finished four strokes, Lucas's arms appeared on either side of me and he gripped the handle, adding his strength to mine. I felt him brace his feet wide as he leaned against me for support.

"Is this . . . going . . . to work?" he asked in my ear as we frantically sawed through the bar.

"Diamond . . . beats . . . rebar." I puffed as we broke through the other side. I repositioned the saw at the top of the bar—a harder angle because of the window—but we barely got halfway through before more footsteps thundered through the stairwell.

"Shhh." I stilled our arms and we waited, catching our breath while more guards burst into the ward and examined the spray paint damage not thirty feet away from us. All they had to do was shine a flashlight into this room and it would be over. Hear a noise. Take ten steps this way and send up an alarm that would condemn Lucas to this cell and send me to jail. I felt Lucas's heart race against my back as we stood, frozen.

Just as one of them started to come closer, they got a call over the radio. It was too muffled to hear, but they immediately headed back into the stairwell and the ward was quiet again. Lucas and I whipped back to the window and sawed as hard and as fast as we could. We hadn't taken more than a few strokes when a light hit the side of my mask.

"Hey!" A guard—who must have stayed behind when the rest of them left—pointed a flashlight through the door. He tried the knob, but I'd shut it fully, engaging the lock again.

"Central station, I've got an escape attempt in ward four. I repeat, ward four, room six. Need immediate backup both inside and out." His shouted instructions grew disjointed as he ran down the corridor toward the main desk, probably to unlock some emergency keys.

There wasn't time to saw through the whole thing. I tossed the blade and pushed the partially detached bar as hard as I could to one side. The metal screeched as it slowly opened a hole large enough to squeeze through. The guard returned, still yelling for backup as he stuffed key after key in the lock.

I shrugged off the backpack and shoved it through the opening, hearing it drop on the ground below. Then I turned to Lucas.

"You first."

His glance shot to the door. "Maya—"

"Go! Now! There's a rope on the fence straight ahead through the trees." I braced my stance and lifted his leg.

He started to climb up, pulling himself to the ledge. "But, Maya—"

"Watch your landing."

I pushed him forward until he fell, vanishing from the window so suddenly and completely that for a second I couldn't move. He was out. I had gotten him out.

The doorknob turned and footsteps rushed into the room. I pivoted on top of the bed and kicked instinctually, catching the guard straight in the throat. He stumbled and I grabbed one of the window bars, hiking myself up and through as a flood of victory, of total confidence, coursed through my body. I had almost cleared the sawed-off bar—could see Lucas's shadow hunched below, waiting for me—when two hands grabbed my boot and pulled me sharply back and down.

I screamed as the jagged stump of rebar tore through my jacket and gouged deep.

"Where do you think you're going, you—"

He didn't get any farther before my other foot smashed into his face, sending him toppling off the bed, into the desk, and landing hard on the floor. Ignoring the pain, I pulled myself through the opening and dangled from the ledge before dropping to the ground. At least this time I didn't sprain my ankle. I didn't see any flashlights in the grounds yet, but voices shouted near the front of the building. Lucas's hand reached through the darkness, finding mine. He pulled me up and we moved as fast as we could toward the rows of evergreens. His gait was unsure and I began slowing as pain wrapped my middle in a wicked vise grip, hobbling me. Suddenly a light illuminated us from behind and I looked back to see it was coming from Lucas's window. The same guard I'd just kicked in the face yelled, "Over here! Into the woods!"

More lights bounced around the side of the building, followed by three guards sprinting toward us as the flashlight beam stayed trained on our backs. We disappeared into the trees fifty yards ahead of them and darted through the rows, running on pure adrenaline, breath pumping and feet driving hard into the shadows.

"There," I whispered, stumbling out of the far side of the woods at the exact spot where the rope was tied to the fence. "You first. Don't argue."

He hoisted himself easily. He was becoming more lucid by the second, temporarily winning the drug war I'd waged in his veins. He dropped lightly to the ground on the other side, wearing the backpack. I grabbed the highest knot I could reach and tried to lift myself up, which made pain shriek through my body and tore a groan from my throat.

"What is it? What's wrong?"

He reached through the fence, searching for the wound.

"Don't touch it. Give me a boost."

I'd barely said the words before his hands swept down and I stepped into them automatically, feeling the wind rush by my mask as he pushed me up into the night. I grabbed the rope and pulled, gritting my teeth. Lucas guided me from below and I climbed to the top, wobbling precariously over the spikes as the guards broke through the trees.

"Jump!" Lucas shouted and I did, without any thought for the fall or the consequences of the ground rushing up to meet me.

Lucas caught me, taking my weight easily, and carried me as he jogged across the street. The guards' shouts faded as they retreated back toward the main entrance to pursue either by foot or car, not even bothering to attempt climbing the fence. They were calling the cops if they hadn't already.

"Turn here. Half a block. Down the alley."

He followed my panting instructions as I reached behind him and pulled the car keys out of the backpack.

"Here. Stop."

He dropped me by the Chevy and opened the door.

"You're hurt. I'll drive."

"Nice try."

I pushed him through the driver's seat and fell onto it, slammed the door closed behind us, and turned the car on, throwing it into gear and shooting out of the alley with the lights off. I took us two blocks down and swerved into another alley, working our way north in that zigzag pattern as police sirens blared in the distance. Pulling the ski mask off, I sucked in a deep breath of air and flicked the headlights on, slowing to a sedate twenty miles an hour as we pulled out in a completely different neighborhood and headed toward the University campus. We crested the hill past Amity Creek and Hawk Ridge, and we kept going until we were driving due north on a single country highway where the houses spread further and further apart.

The clock on the dash inched toward midnight and the more the woods took over the skyline, the more I accelerated, speeding away from the city. In Duluth the street kids would be roaming the shipping yards looking for the next unlocked door, Jasper would be pacing the perimeter of the house, growling as the wind beat against the windows, and the downtown bars would be in full swing, ejecting the belligerent too-drunks into the chaos of downtown. I could hear the bustle and traffic, smell the water as it lapped against the shore, see the glow of red and yellow on the neon peninsula that jutted into the lake, the world I was leaving and might not see again. After another ten minutes the homes began receding further into the forest, distant lights shrouded in branches, and Lucas finally turned to face the front of the car. He'd spent the entire drive crouched against his seat watching our tail for anyone in pursuit, but now he reached out and touched the dash.

"This isn't your car."

"No." I answered shakily, fighting against the black edges of the pain. "Butch, my dad's first mate, lent it to me. He won't find that out until they get back."

"No one"—the road started to fade in the headlights—"will report it"—my view of the road slipped lower and lower as I slumped against the driver's side door—"missing."

The last thing I remembered before the darkness swallowed me was the jolt of the car hitting the ditch and my body slamming into the steering wheel.

23

DRIFTED IN a world where clouds descended over tree covered cliffs, spreading their mist in pockets that roiled with dank threat. Clutching the agate, blood ran up my hands and into my eyes, coloring the forest red. Something stalked me from within the mist, something that was both Derek and not-Derek, dead and not-dead. It closed in behind me, readying for the kill. Running over moss covered boulders and rotting logs, I stumbled and fell at the water's edge, losing the agate in the waves. I jerked around, sightless and terrified, trying to find the teeth that had clamped into my side, slicing my flesh apart.

"Get off! Get off me!" I woke up screaming in the backseat of the car, clawing at the pain and finding only soft, wet cloth and a smooth line of tape fastening it to my stomach.

"Maya!" Lucas's voice came from the front seat. Slowly I began to register things. The staccato of broken pavement bumping underneath the car's tires. The scratch of upholstery against my cheek. The chill of freezing air leaking in from the doors.

I looked down and saw a white square of bandage under my rib cage, peeking out from a twisted belt of red-splattered fabric that I recognized as my shirt. The contents of the first aid kit I'd brought were spilled over the floor like a gale had caught it in a fury. I tried to sit up, failed, then took a deep breath and forced myself vertical, bracing my feet and shoulders between the front seat and backseat of the car.

"Don't get up. You're still bleeding."

Lucas's hand reached backward and the car swerved as he tried to force me down to the seats. I leaned out of the way.

"Where are we?" I huffed. The road was a dark, two-lane stretch of asphalt lined with trees clawing in at the edges of the headlights.

"Lie down."

"All the supplies you need are in the trunk. Clothes. Tent. Food." I spoke slowly, needing to get the words out clearly and before I lost consciousness again. "See the compass on the dash? Keep heading north."

"Lie down, Maya! We need help. Medicine."

"All roads lead to Ely."

"Fuck Ely!"

Even through the pain I had to smile, proud to hear his first contextually appropriate curse. I was his speech therapist, after all. Had to celebrate the victories.

"We just passed a town called Aurora. Is there a hospital near here? A doctor?"

Aurora? I started shaking uncontrollably, my skin and brain

both suddenly freezing. How did we cover so much distance already? I remembered passing the reservoir when . . .

"The crash. Are you okay?"

He laughed once, not turning around. "You're asking me if *I'm* okay?"

"We hit the ditch. I don't remember after that."

Lucas explained pulling me out of the car and how he thought I was dead when he saw the blood soaking my clothes. Then, finding the laceration on my torso, he bandaged me and cinched the shirt over the wound to staunch the bleeding like his father had taught him. Knowing we had to keep moving or at least get out of sight, he laid me in the backseat and pushed the car out of the ditch. He'd never driven before, but with a mechanic for a father he was familiar with the basic principles and he'd watched me enough during our field trips to memorize the motions. The car started without a problem and after a few experiments with the gear shift and pedals, he figured out how to get us back on the road.

Now he held the wheel awkwardly, constantly correcting the car as the headlights roamed between the edges of the lane. "I know we can't go back to the city, but we're getting help somewhere. Tell me where to go before you pass out again."

The shivers wracked my body and I started to slide down, losing the strength to keep myself wedged between the seats.

"We're coming into the Iron Range. Ely's right beyond—"

"Maya!" he bellowed, rivaling my dad for volume and irritation.

Shaking, I pulled the burner I'd bought out of my jacket pocket and punched in an address, then heaved the phone forward with the last of my energy. The chills knocked me down to a fetal position on the seat and it was all I could do not to vomit on the floor. My voice sounded like a child as I gave him the name. "Harry. Harry McKinley."

———

The next time I woke up I was being carried into a cabin with a sagging roof that loomed like a ghost from my past. Fat snowflakes poured from the sky, mingling with the scent of wood smoke and pipe tobacco. Somewhere in the distance a truck engine roared then faded into the night. Lucas had found, whether he knew it or not, the border between our worlds.

Lucas laid me down on a couch and a squat man with a graying beard ambled over until his head eclipsed the lamp shining weakly in the corner of the room, the same man who'd spotted me from his vintage Chevy in Ely. One side of his mouth tilted up a few degrees.

"I thought that was you in town the other day. Took me by surprise."

Nodding, I blinked him into focus. Until I'd encountered the Blackthorns, Harry McKinley had been the closest thing I'd known to a hermit. I hadn't expected to see him in town, either. The only places I'd ever seen him were puttering around outside this cabin or tucked into a fishing hole somewhere on the water.

"You like to bleed on this couch, girl."

I let my chest rise and fall a few times, gathering the strength to reply.

"It wasn't my blood last time."

"Damn snickity, it wasn't." I felt rough fingers lift my arm away from Lucas's makeshift tourniquet. "You leave any bodies behind this time?"

I didn't have any more words in me, so I just shook my head weakly.

"Are you a doctor?" Lucas's voice came from somewhere above my head.

"Nope. Rebuilt a few trolling motors over the years, but I doubt she works like a Minn Kota." He laughed at his own joke and then I heard feet shuffling away. "You wait here, eh?"

After a minute I could hear a door open then slam shut. I tried to concentrate on something—the faded cross-stitch sampler hanging on the wall, the cracks running through the ceiling—anything that would help me stay conscious and aware. Then Lucas was there, smoothing the hair away from my face, and I didn't need any help finding a focal point.

He had deep, black hollows under his eyes and he was sickly pale, but the worry in his expression was lucid and his pupils were dilating correctly. The chemical cocktail Nurse Valerie had been feeding him was already leaving his system. We stared at each other for a while, not speaking, and gradually his worry shifted into something else, a kind of desperate happiness.

"You came for me." He breathed it more than said it, stroking down the side of my face and reaching for my hand. I gripped it hard as another stab of pain shot through me.

"I told you I would." I managed a shaky but genuine smile.

"You saved me. I couldn't escape, couldn't get free. I didn't even know where I was trying to go, except I had to go somewhere and they weren't letting me. It was a nightmare and I couldn't wake up. Every time I almost surfaced, they would feed me another dose, push me back down. I was lost until I saw you. I think I saw you." Confusion flickered over his face as he tried to remember. "You were walking away from me and I was screaming for you to come back, but you wouldn't turn around and I couldn't reach you. I kept calling for you. I was afraid if I stopped saying your name I would forget again. I would forget you . . . and if I forgot you, then I would forget me."

He leaned his forehead into my temple. I could hear him swallow.

"When you lifted that mask tonight, your face was the most beautiful thing I'd ever seen."

I closed my eyes and pushed the words out slowly, patiently. "When someone kidnaps you, the proper response is thank you."

He laughed, more a rumble of chest against my shoulder than actual noise.

"Thank you, Maya Stark, for saving my life."

"You're welcome, Lucas Blackthorn. Any time."

The sound of boots thumped up a set of stairs and then a door opened and slammed again.

Harry came back into the room carrying an old, metal case and a folding chair. Lucas moved to crouch near my head while Harry examined me and I noticed for the first time I was shirtless and my sports bra was stained with sweat and blood. Unwrapping the bandage, Harry leaned over and smelled the wound, then mopped up the area under my right rib cage with alcohol swabs that felt like acid. Once clean, it looked strangely like an Easter egg had been carved out of my stomach.

"What did this?"

"Rebar. And a douche bag."

"Good. No splinters or shrapnel from rebar or douche bags." He consulted a small, worn manual. "Might have nicked your liver, but it doesn't look too deep. We can disinfect and sew you up. I don't have much for pain, though."

Lucas went to the car and brought back the first aid kit, where

I'd stored all the stolen medicine from Congdon. I argued—those pills were for Josiah, not me—but Lucas wouldn't even acknowledge that I was speaking. He handed the whole thing to Harry and wrapped his hands around mine, maybe for comfort, maybe to keep me from knocking the kit away. Harry found some lidocaine spray and doused the area, then stared at the blood still pooling in the center of the wound while waiting for the anesthetic to take effect.

"That'll help some, but might still hurt when I stitch it. Do you drink?" Harry asked.

"No."

"That's good. But it's not a bad day to start."

I could feel the needle when he began piercing the skin, but the lidocaine dulled the worst of it. After Harry stitched the wound he told us we needed to eat. I didn't think I could, but Harry cooked us venison steaks and fries like it was the most natural thing to do at three in the morning, then pulled up chairs in front of the couch so he and Lucas could dig in. He didn't ask us what we were doing here, why Lucas wore a state-issued smock and pants, or why I looked like the loser of a vicious street brawl. He joked about the patchy electricity as his lamp flickered and turned off at random. Raccoons in the lines, or maybe mice.

"It's been a while, girl," Harry said as Lucas practically licked the juice from his empty plate.

"Eight years. Give or take."

"She don't call. She don't write. She just shows up, bloody, every decade or so."

Lucas sat up straight. "Is this where . . . ?" He let the question hang.

"I used to see this girl every summer when she and her mom came up to their cabin over there." He waved through the wall, as if Lucas could see it. I tried not to think about what lay beyond the wood paneling and the darkness outside. "Only neighbors I could stand. Quiet. Kept to themselves. Probably ran into them more paddling the Waters than I ever did on our property line."

Lucas dropped his fork on the carpet and barely noticed. "Wait. We're in the Boundary Waters?"

Harry nodded. "Starts at this shoreline here and stretches right out to heaven."

Lucas half turned and his eyes lit up with the knowledge. The impulse to get up, to escape into the forest, shimmered through him as clear as sunlight and I felt torn in half—wanting him to disappear, to leave before the authorities found us, and yet aching for him to stay, to keep looking at me the way he had ever since I lifted that ski mask and showed him who I was.

"The last time I saw this one"—Harry gestured to me with his steak knife—"I'd been out fishing on Basswood all day and what do I find when I pull up in front the house? A gangly girl, sitting cross-legged on my front step with dried blood covering her face. She stared at me like she'd been waiting all day and I was late.

"*Are you all right?* I asked.

"*I killed someone over there.* She pointed toward their cabin. *With this rock,* she added and held it up, like she'd be happy to use it again if I took a wrong step. It gave her a power, I saw. She was safe with that rock.

"I went to the cooler in the back of my pickup and held up the pike I'd caught. *I fished these today,* I said. *Have to go around back and clean them. Do you want to come?*"

Harry rocked a little as he told the story, looking past this room to a place where only the two of us could go. I closed my eyes and let myself remember.

"I didn't know what she was going to do. She might have disappeared if I turned away, so I was careful not to move quick, not to get too close, and she stood up and followed me to the fish house with that rock still in her hand.

"She watched me fillet each fish while I tried to figure out what to do. I'm not what you'd call a social man. I mind my own business. Don't have much use for townsfolk or police, but in the end I didn't see what choice I had. Brought her inside and she sat right where she's lying now while I made the first 911 call of my life and she turned that rock over and over in her hands. When the police came, they asked her who she was. *Maya,* she told them before she handed over the rock. *Red Maya.*"

The room was quiet after Harry finished. Both men looked at their plates in the shadows of the room.

"I never thanked you," I said after the silence had stretched out.

"Hell, it wasn't a count your blessings kind of day."

"But you let me in. You're letting us in now." The simple, rough-edged space wasn't designed for company. There was a single couch, an old cathode ray TV sitting on a block of wood, and a row of books neatly lined on a homemade bookshelf made out of planks and stones. He'd tacked blankets up over the windows to keep out drafts and the scuffed wood floors had seen better days. In all the summers of my childhood, I'd never noticed another person on Harry's property.

He nodded to the cross-stitch on the wall, the one piece of color in the room. " 'Be not simply good, be good for something.' "

I tried to think of a way to voice my gratitude, but an overwhelming drowsiness had begun to blanket my brain. The lidocaine was still working, easing away the pain of the stitches, inviting me into the blackness. I struggled against its pull.

"Sleep, girl. There's still a few hours until sunup." Harry put a small quilt over my shoulders, leaving the stitched up wound open to the air. "I'll set your protector up on the floor next to you."

I gave in and let myself drift off, but not before mumbling into the blanket, making one last thing clear.

"I'm *his* protector."

•

24

WANTED TO leave right away the next morning, but Harry and Lucas took one look at me and both insisted I needed to rest. My heart stuttered every time I heard a car pass, knowing the houses weren't tucked far enough into the trees to be completely invisible, not with November's bare branches. A blanket of snow had covered Butch's car during the night, but even that camouflage wouldn't be enough if the police connected me to the kidnapping and started canvassing the area. My mother's cabin would be the first logical place to look. We were exposed here, vulnerable. How long would it take them to knock on this door? How long would it take my father to come home and for Butch to report his car stolen?

"Hey, it's Maya." I'd left a message on his voice mail before leaving the house last night. "I'm taking off for a little while. Jasper should be fine until you get back."

My voice had almost broken on Jasper's name, just like I'd bitten back tears when I installed the pet door going out to the backyard and topped up the automatic feeder to the three-week line. He wouldn't need nearly that much—Dr. Mehta would contact Dad, too, as soon as it was clear I was missing—but I still felt horrible leaving him. My loyal German shepherd, my guardian and friend, had watched me go with sorrowful eyes.

The provisions, the cash purchases, the untraceable phone—none of it would have been necessary if I'd rescued any other patient in Congdon. The authorities couldn't care less about Greta, or suicidal Eliza, or Big George. None of them had been featured on national news. They hadn't been written about in *Time* magazine, or garnered over a hundred thousand social media fans who picketed outside the gates, or been vilified with signs reading KEEP THEM IN JAIL in the last town they'd known as home. This was Lucas Blackthorn, the boy who came back from the dead, and they weren't going to let him off the grid again, not without a fight. So, I put Jasper out of my mind and concentrated on the present and on the fact that—so far—I was winning. I'd gotten Lucas out.

I only agreed to rest longer because of the pain. Although it was more manageable this morning, a slow walk across the living room was about all I could handle. Harry gave me some of the antibiotics from the first aid kit and didn't listen to any of my arguments about not taking the pain pill—they weren't meant for me, someone else needed them more than I did—and made me swallow one anyway, which turned the flame down to a warm ache and made everything else uncomfortably fuzzy. He went fishing after breakfast, trying to get the last catch before ice-in, he said, but I suspected that, even though he'd insisted we stay, three people in his house were two too many. After he left I sent Lucas to the car to retrieve the clothes I'd bought for him, and it was jarring when he walked out of the bathroom a few minutes later, to see him dressed normally.

When I commented on it Lucas gave me his this-place-is-beyond-messed-up look. "What's normal?"

I waved to the blue all-terrain pullover and cargo pants. "That's normal."

He grinned. "You think that because you were born and raised in Duluth. Normal might be completely different if you came from somewhere else."

I sighed and rolled gingerly onto my back, swimming in the medication and fighting to keep my head clear. "The answer is always a pullover, cargo pants, and hiking boots."

"I used to make myself bracelets out of bark."

"And that's why they assigned me to be your cultural ambassador."

"Right. Thanks for showing me that part about prison breaks. I think I'll fit in pretty well now."

I laughed and immediately clutched my side, wincing.

Lucas crossed the room, laying his hand on top of mine and waiting as my breathing evened out.

"Better?" he asked.

"It's fine." I ignored the pain growling through the drug haze, ready to lie to anyone if it meant we could leave sooner. Most people appreciated bullshit, especially when it helped them dismiss you, but Lucas wasn't having it. He sat next to me on the couch looking awkwardly out of place, a model for *Outdoorsman* magazine trying to play nurse. I attempted a smile and it didn't hurt.

"Swearing. Sarcasm. I think your speech therapy is almost complete."

"I'm a quick learner." He returned the smile and we stared at each other as the wind blew snow dust against the window. Sitting with Lucas, arguing with Lucas, being able to smile at Lucas without wondering how many people at Congdon were watching us—it was almost worth being shish-kebabbed on a stump of rebar. He must have been thinking along the same lines, because he bowed his head and gave my hand a hesitant kiss.

"It's still hard to believe I'm free, that we're here together."

The warmth of his breath against my knuckles cut through the medication in my system, providing a sudden, not unwelcome point of focus. "They're going to be looking for you. You're not safe here."

"I dreamed about this, about being with you." He worked his way up, tracing the outside of my arm like he was drawing a picture in the snow, then his eyes flickered up, narrowing. "Except in my dreams you weren't bleeding."

I propped myself against the cushions and trapped his face between my hands, arresting his attention. "Ice-in is almost here. Soon the lakes will be frozen over. I want to come with you, but—"

He stopped my mouth with a kiss. I didn't have a lot of experience with kissing, and none where the kiss softened you, inhaled you, twisting into your fingers and toes and making you forget, for a mindless second, that you had a seeping hole in your side. Maybe I could've been more clinical, felt it less, if he'd been like every other guy, steeped in all their insecurities and sexual myths about what a kiss did or didn't mean, but Lucas possessed none of that crap. He moved slowly and artlessly, cupping my shoulders like I was a snow sculpture come to life and might break apart if he wasn't careful.

I wove my fingers through his hair and pulled, anchoring him to me as we explored, pulses thrumming, beating faster and harder

against each other in a race neither of us knew how to finish. Then
I made the mistake of stretching, bowing my body to get a fraction
closer, and broke away in a sharp gasp of pain.

"Are you okay?" Eyes dilated, breath unsteady, he watched me
clutch my stomach.

"This is my ow." I breathed through clenched teeth.

He laughed once and hovered anxiously, waiting until my
breathing returned to normal before easing me back against the
cushions. We stared at each other, inches apart, until the drugs
smoothed everything over and I forgot about my stomach again.

"What will they do if they find you?" he asked.

I added up the charges. Grand theft auto, B&E, identity theft,
kidnapping, and assault. "Jail. Probably prison. That'll be a change
of pace."

He shook his head. "No. You're coming with me." Then he
touched my cheek, frowning. "I'm not losing you now. I'm not
going to trade you for him."

"I'll be a liability. I'll slow you down." My eyes drifted closed
and I struggled to blink them back open.

"Get stronger." He murmured and before I could respond, the
sound of tires on gravel cut through the front yard. Lucas jumped
up and checked the window, relaxing as he saw who it was. "Harry."
Then, glancing down at his new cargo pants and clearing his throat,
"I'll be back in a minute."

I grinned as he retreated down the hall.

———

For lunch Harry fried walleye and I was able to walk to the kitchen
without too much trouble and eat at the table. The two of them

talked fishing through the whole meal, swapping stories and techniques, and Lucas asked a hundred questions about licenses, regulations, and enforcement. By the time we were washing the dishes, we'd gotten a full retrospective of the DNR, the evolution of sport fishing in the Boundary Waters, and the fight against a new copper mine some of the locals had convinced Harry to join. Harry was working through a list of invasive species when Lucas glanced at me as he wiped and stacked the plates. In some other world this could be our life. A warm room at the edge of the woods, chipped plates, laughter, the call of the wind in the eaves. It flared in his eyes, too, longing for a homecoming we'd never have. After everything was cleared and cleaned, I retreated back to the couch, feeling heavy and listless, and fell into an instant, dreamless sleep.

When I woke up, I was curled into a sweaty ball. No one else was in the living room and the house was quiet.

"Lucas?"

No answer.

Carefully, I stretched my arms and legs and sat up. A jar of ibuprofen lay next to the couch and I ignored it, examining my abdomen instead. Harry's stitches were neat and even, reminiscent of the cross-stitch that hung on the wall. A stain of blood still coated the skin around the wound, but it was dried and dark—no bright red to speak of—and when I got up to go to the bathroom the raw pain had dulled to a nagging throb. With slow movements and deep breaths, I was good as new.

I splashed some water on my face and found a rag to do a quick hospital-style sponge bath. I had clean clothes in the car if I'd felt motivated enough to attempt the trip. Instead I traded my bloody shirt for Lucas's hospital scrubs and crept through the house, peeking in doors, looking for any sign of life.

"Harry?"

Harry's house wasn't big. It was a single-story rambler with a few small bedrooms clustered on one side and a living room and kitchen on the other. I found a door that led to a pitch-black basement, but I didn't feel like pushing my luck on the stairs.

"You guys down there?"

Then I heard it—a cracking, punching noise from outside the cabin. I crossed to the kitchen window, searching for the source, then hurried back into the living room and pulled on my boots and coat to head into the blinding sunshine. Harry's classic Chevy was parked next to Butch's car in the driveway and everything from the trees to the steps were covered in a thin veil of snow. A sign posted at the end of the driveway said the same thing I'd seen in town: FRIENDS OF THE BOUNDARY WATERS. Everything was bright white and silent until suddenly the punch of noise came again, louder now, echoing off the snow-covered branches. I ran along the siding, each step becoming more painful as the hacked-up muscles in my side took the impact, and rounded the edge of the garage, wincing and panicked.

Harry sat on a tree stump, arms crossed, face into the sun, as Lucas chopped firewood. Neither of them noticed me.

I heaved out a sigh and checked the tree coverage between them and the road, gauging the distance and speed of any potential cars. If someone wasn't looking for an escaped mental health patient, they'd drive right by without a sidelong glance and Lucas, whether by design or accident, was facing away from the street. He looked more comfortable than I'd ever seen him, swinging the axe expertly, easily breaking logs with one or two swings and stacking them into a fast-growing pile of firewood. He'd probably performed the chore a thousand times. As the landscape settled into me and the pain quit snarling, my attention drifted to a log building obscured by pine trees in the distance. The cabin. My mother's cabin.

I could only see the snow-covered roof and part of one wall, the logs dark and worn by countless winters. Sometimes birds had built nests under the eaves, defying gravity, weaving them from forest floor debris, and as a girl I'd crept up and listened day after day, waiting for the morning when I heard those first weak cheeps.

"Here."

Harry startled me out of my fixation. He reached out from his perch, a glint of light cupped in his hand. When I stepped closer, the light turned into a key.

"Your dad asked me to keep an eye on the place, check the pipes and furnace and whatnot. He keeps the heat and electricity going, so nothing freezes. One year I had to put a cat over there to clean out the mice. Haven't been by in a while. You should go."

I didn't want to touch that key, but I forced myself to pick it up and fold it into my hand. Lucas caught sight of me and started to come over, but I waved him off. He smiled and picked up another section of tree trunk, cleaving it in half with one swing. Apparently his shoulder was all healed.

"I've never been inside without her. Even that day . . . I didn't know the security code."

"0-6-1-2."

The tears blurred everything into a painful, sun-washed brilliance. She'd used my birthday.

I shook my head, furiously blinking the water away. "It's been twelve years, Harry. Over half my life ago."

"Couldn't've been that long. Ten years at the most."

"It's not the kind of thing you forget, your mother abandoning you."

"Yeah, I know you guys stopped coming for a while but then she brought you back."

"What?" My vertebrae popped I snapped my head so fast. "What did you say?"

Harry uncrossed and recrossed his arms, rocking back, and frowning. "It wasn't more than ten years since she came back here with you and that new man. I didn't see you myself, but she came over here to borrow my *Merck Manual* because she said you were sick. Down with the flu or something."

Every word hit me like a truck, one body blow after another. Harry kept on in his meandering drawl, completely unaware of the effect his speech was having.

"You only stayed a little while that time and I guess you were sick so maybe you don't remember. Caught a glimpse of her and that guy sitting on the beach together, talking over a fire. They, uh . . . well, I went about my business after that."

"They what?" I demanded.

"They were just hugging, seemed about as cozy as you two." Harry nodded at me and Lucas, then hauled himself up with cracking joints. "I didn't mention anything to your dad. He'd already told me she left, and it's not the kind of thing a man wants to hear about."

Then he squinted into the sun and stretched. "Mighty nice to have help chopping wood. Guess I'll go start some soup for dinner."

I stood paralyzed, reeling in the harsh November sun that bounced light off every snow-covered surface between me and the cabin in the distance. All my life, no matter if I'd spent it with or without her, I'd known my mom was depressed, a woman who couldn't seize the world around her, who shrank away from me and my dad and hardened into her shell like a slab of basalt, porous and brittle. She'd tried to kill herself when I was eight years old, for God's sake, and I'd spent the better part of my teenage years learning a story, the narrative I built for her with Dr. Mehta's help, and it went something like this: Her depression wasn't my fault. There was nothing I or anyone else could've done to help her recover. She loved me, but it wasn't enough to battle back the chemical imbalances in her brain. And without batting an eye or lifting a finger, Harry McKinley had smashed that story into oblivion.

My mother had never come back for me.

I'd never seen her with any man besides my father and not here, not in the one place where we'd been happy together, *our* place, *our* cabin in the woods, *our* paddles dipping in time through the pristine, mirrored surface of the Boundary Waters. She couldn't have. She didn't—because if she did, everything I'd told myself about my mother's disappearance was a lie. It wasn't true that no one could save her. We just hadn't been good enough to save her.

"Where are you going?"

I didn't even realize I was moving until I heard Lucas's voice behind me, farther away than it should have been, and felt the edges of a bush scraping against my side. I gripped the key, gouging it into my flesh as I crossed the uneven ground between the cabins. The driveway was cracked and strewn with snowcapped piles of leaves and needles. Cobwebs rippled against the door frame and my hand shook as I pushed the key into the lock.

"Are you sure you're up for this?" His voice again, this time close to my ear, and a hand I barely registered smoothed over my shoulder. "How's your stomach?"

The shriek of the alarm kept me from having to answer. I punched in the code, my birthday, the day we'd always spent here because I knew she couldn't handle throwing me a party with friends and cake and the chattering of strange mothers at our door. Instead we drove up here as soon as school let out, going "Up North" like all true Minnesotans, and we roasted the first s'mores of the summer over a birthday bonfire at the water's edge. She only made those bonfires for me and sometimes my dad on the few days he could leave work during the busy shipping season. No one else was ever invited into this house.

With the alarm silenced, I looked around, slowly pivoting to take it in. The living area and kitchen took up the main room, with a screened-in porch opening up to the lake below. A small bedroom—my bedroom—and the bath were tucked under a stairway that led up to a loft in the rafters, where her sleeping area overlooked the first floor. Everything was the same. The same rag rug laying in front of the fireplace, the same stack of *Rock & Gem* magazines on the coffee table, the same rips in the vinyl of the 1950s kitchen chairs, tucked underneath the metal soda shop table. I moved through the main floor, touching nothing, a shell-shocked investigator who'd somehow traveled back in time to search for evidence.

When I turned the light on in my old bedroom, a mouse scurried across the floor and disappeared under the twin bed. Nothing was out of place. The bed was made up with the faded daisy quilt I used to hide under with a flashlight to read stolen copies of her geology magazines, scouring them for tidbits that might impress her or something I could ask her, anything to engage her attention. She came alive when she talked about minerals and sometimes we even went on rock hunts, scouting the wilderness for days on our geology adventures. I opened the closet, pulled out drawers, and found nothing except a few rocks here and there, which—when I held them up to the light and ran a finger over the waxy surfaces—I found were all agates. Turning to go upstairs, I glanced at Lucas's face and stopped dead.

"What?" I glanced at the spot where he was staring, a faded picture on the wall of a cliff and a man dangling off the edge by one hand. *Believe,* it said in thick black letters underneath the image. I'd never been sure what I was supposed to believe by looking at that picture. That he was strong enough to hold on? That the cliff wouldn't crumble? Or that his grip would eventually give out, that no matter how capable he was he couldn't hold on forever. I looked back at Lucas, who'd gone as pale as the petals of the daisies on the bedspread. "What is it?"

He didn't answer. Walking to the bed, he sat down on the pillow and stared at the picture again, now directly in front of him, then he craned his head to take in every detail of the room. There wasn't much to see and nothing to justify his sudden agitation.

"No." He ejected himself off the mattress and ran to the door, leaning into the frame as his breathing became ragged.

"Lucas, what?" I pulled his arm and, when that had no effect, shook him as hard as I could, suddenly angry for no reason I wanted to name.

His eyes bounced around the cabin, unable to settle, and he lifted his hands to squeeze his head, heaving air in and out, manifesting all the signs of a panic attack. I tried to pull his arms down and get him to look at me when he began chanting and shaking violently. One unbroken "Nononononononono."

"Lucas!"

"It was here." He broke away, lunging back into the great room and pacing the edges like a caged animal.

"What are you talking about? What was here?"

"I was." He stopped dead, lifting his shocked face to mine.

We stared at each other across the room as I tried to make sense of the words, but what he was saying was impossible. A delusion. When I moved toward him, he jerked back, ducking away.

"I don't understand."

"My father and I—we were here. This is where I was sick. That guy hanging off the cliff in the picture. I remember it." He swung an arm toward my bedroom before his eye caught on a dust-covered picture frame orphaned on a corner table. Grabbing it, he wiped the dirt off and stared at the unsmiling woman and girl. My dad had taken the photo, not fifty feet from where we were standing. "She told me the cliff was made out of salt and I couldn't stop thinking about it. A mountain of salt."

A dawning horror began to clench my body, gripping me, choking me. I couldn't feel my feet. The fish we'd eaten for lunch began moving in my stomach, threatening to swim back up my throat. I stepped closer, until the woman in the picture snapped sickeningly into place.

"Basalt," I whispered. "The cliff was made out of basalt."

Tears spilled down his cheeks as he looked at me.

"It wasn't Heather Price's body."

25

I DIDN'T REMEMBER falling to the floor or clawing at the sudden burst of pain in my abdomen. One minute Lucas was across the room, the next he was prying my fingers off my side, his face too close, the breaking glass of the picture frame still echoing against the walls of the cabin.

He knelt in front of me, pleading, sucking all the oxygen from the air. It was too much. I pushed him off and scrambled as far away as I could, wedging my body into a corner of the kitchen and holding a hand in the air—a warning. Still kneeling, the entire story poured out of him, all the thoughts and feelings I'd been so patiently working to get him to reveal and to which now I could barely force myself to listen.

When Lucas had been brought to Congdon and met me, he said, he began fighting a war with his memories. I'd reminded him of the woman who'd nursed him when he was so sick as a child, the pale lady with long brown hair who questioned him about his symptoms while reading a little book. The same little book, I realized, my mother had borrowed from Harry. The Merck medical manual. She'd laid cool rags on his forehead and told him about the salt cliff, she'd stared at him from the end of the bed and didn't reply when he asked for his father, making him squeeze his eyes shut and wait for her to leave. One night, after he'd begun to feel better, he'd heard noises on the stairs and crouched behind the door as his father carried a body outside. The car engine started, headlights flashed across the living room—this living room—and he never saw the woman again. Ten years later, when he barely remembered what she looked like, I'd walked into his isolation room.

He didn't make the connection immediately, not until I brought the minerals and began explaining them, forcing his mind back to the bedrock of his life in the Boundary Waters, the reason for their disappearance. That's when it clicked, when the horrible connection was forged. *I know you.* Every time he saw me after that was torture. He felt drawn to me, compelled to confess and find out who I was, yet afraid at the same time, trusting nothing and no one in the place that had stolen his every freedom. He began to think Congdon knew about the body and they'd deliberately planted me to get him to hand over his father. Ward two had no shortage of paranoia, and some of it had worked its way into his mind as the strange noises kept him awake every night, never knowing what the next day would bring. It culminated on the day I took him into the grounds, when he thought I was tricking him into betraying the only person he loved.

It wasn't until he woke up in the hospital and saw the picture of Heather Price that he questioned his own memories. He'd been so sick when it happened, hallucinating about bugs in the sky. Mountains of salt. Maybe he'd hallucinated more than he'd thought—and layered on top of the doubt was certainty, a bone-deep certainty that he'd known the woman in that picture on his hospital table, he'd seen his dad fighting with her. And whoever she was, she wasn't me. He was overcome with the need to find me, away from the eyes and ears of Congdon, and when he did the details I gave him about Heather's death made sense—the timing, the overdose—in a way that made him believe.

"That's why I went to your house when I escaped from the hospital." He inched closer and I jerked back, knocking my head into the cupboard. His face contorted and he sat down, keeping his distance as he explained looking through my house that night for anything he might recognize, even trying to find the mountain of salt picture he'd thought he'd seen. It became obvious he'd never been to my house before and he convinced himself that I looked like someone who'd only been a figment of his fevered imagination. That's when he told me what he'd witnessed. That's when he asked for my help finding his father.

The words rolled over my head, landing in some distant part of the cabin. I heard the tremor in his voice, the rush of air as the explanations tumbled out, one on top of the other, as if any of it could change what my brain was still working to grasp. Harry's story had shocked me enough. To think about my mother here, with another man and child, was already as much revelation as I could handle. I'd been reeling from the idea that my mother had replaced me, that she'd found happiness with a new family.

She hadn't adopted a new family and run away to a better life.

A new family had murdered her and escaped into the wilderness.

That's why her rocks stopped coming. It wasn't because I was inadequate or worthless. She hadn't forgotten me or moved on. She was dead. She was dead and so was the insane dream that someday I would see her again, that she would find her way back to us and we could start over. I'd imagined her walking into the bathroom I'd remodeled and seeing how I'd made it into the Boundary Waters, how it would be a place she could thrive and she'd never again have to feel like the soft rock crushed beneath the weight of overpowering forces.

My mother was dead.

"I didn't know you had this cabin. How could I know?" As if he didn't understand the world had stuttered to a halt, that nothing he could possibly say would matter now. He was babbling, creeping toward me again, his face etched in a bald, unbearable need for sympathy. *He* wanted *my* sympathy.

I pushed myself off the kitchen floor and ran toward the front door.

"Wait!" Lucas caught me before I could escape and we fought in a silent struggle of hands and arms, his grasping, mine trying to wrench themselves free.

"You let him take her." I threw blind elbows and heels behind me, thrashing against his grip. "You let him get away with it."

"Maya. Please. Stop." He grunted as I landed a blow to his gut, but the jab doubled me over, too, reverberating back into my muscles and setting fire to the stitches in my side. We fell into the counter like one creature, tangled beyond separation in our rage and grief and pain. I clutched the bandage that had become slippery against my skin and tried to control the sobs that began heaving through my chest, because if I let them out I didn't know if they would ever stop.

"Lucas—" I choked out, but a flash of movement through the kitchen window killed any other words in my throat. A car turned off the highway and pulled through the trees into the driveway. A police cruiser.

I stumbled back and looked wildly around the cabin. My heart, already abused beyond repair, kicked into a sprint. Every room on the main floor had at least one window and there was no basement, which left only one place to hide. Locking the front door, I ran to the stairs and was halfway up before I remembered.

"The picture frame. The light," I hissed and we flew back down. I hit the light switch off in my bedroom and Lucas shoved the broken frame under a couch as the sound of a slamming door echoed in the front yard. We rushed back up the stairs that creaked and groaned with every step, dove to the loft floor, and lay side by side on the scratchy carpet littered with mouse droppings, reining in our breath, listening.

The rap on the door sent a jerk through my entire body. Silence. Then another knock. No voices. The upstairs loft was open on three sides, with only a railing gating the platform from the rafters. If we crawled to any of the edges, we could see what was happening on the first floor. But then anyone on the first floor could see us. After a long pause, one of the living room windows rattled and a beam of light glanced off the rough beams of the ceiling. They were circling the perimeter of the cabin, looking for signs of life. Signs of us.

We listened as they worked their way along the foundation, crunching leaves underfoot, shining flashlights throughout the main level and even illuminating the headboard of the loft bed, so close that we could see the dust motes spinning in the air. At one point, when the silence stretched out and it was impossible to tell where they were or what they were doing, Lucas reached over and covered my hand.

I squeezed my eyes closed and gulped back the silent convulsions in my chest. I could feel his warmth next to me, his absolute stillness save the fingers that pressed into mine, offering what he could never articulate—not even if we had the world to ourselves and all the languages in it—and I had no choice but to twist my hand into his, gripping the very thing that had shattered me.

After another minute, we heard a branch snap in the distance. Lucas rose up and crawled silently to the tiny, second floor window to peek outside.

"There's two of them. They're following our tracks back to Harry's house."

I still couldn't move. Lucas watched from the shadows, eyes trained on the neighboring property.

"It doesn't look like Harry's answering his door. They're walking around his house, too." A pause. Waiting. "Now they're back in the driveway. They're looking at the cars. One of them is wiping snow off the back of ours."

"They're running the license plate." I covered my face, trying to steady my breath. If Butch hadn't come home and reported his car missing yet, there wouldn't be an immediate link. We might have a few hours, a day tops, before they put the pieces together and got a warrant. They'd find me, arrest me, and send me where I'd been heading before Congdon had stepped in all those years ago and postponed the inevitable. At least my mother would never know. She'd never have to witness what her daughter had become.

"They're coming back now. One of them is on the phone."

I wiped my leaking eyes, fighting for control. Lucas, fixated on the threat outside, kept narrating the policemen's progress in a low whisper. One was taking a photo. The other came back to a ground floor window and tried peering inside again. Turning away from the bouncing flashlight beam, I caught a glimpse of something under the bed, an object that—in one swift moment—wiped every tremor from my body and left behind a piercing calm.

The police car's engine fired to life in the driveway on the other side of the house.

"Go check, make sure they're both leaving together."

Lucas obeyed without question, creeping silently across the carpet and down the stairs. As soon as his head disappeared below the floor of the loft, I reached underneath the bed and pulled out the gun.

———

We hurried back to Harry's house, this time pulling pine branches behind us to obliterate our tracks. Lucas kept a cautious distance from me. We'd spoken little since the cops left and then only logistics: when it was safe to come out, how long we'd have until they'd be back, our next steps. The magnitude of what just happened in the cabin haunted his every look, but the police hunt snapped us back to the present danger.

"Maybe you're right. Maybe I should go alone," he said as we made our way through the trees.

"I'm coming."

"But you're still hur—"

"I'm coming." Gaze forward, I felt the weight of the gun bumping my hip with every step, the missing gun from the boathouse, the one I'd desperately been searching for the day I'd come here with Derek and Rex. I finally found it. My mind raced with reasons it had been moved, and every version circled back to the same basic motivation; she'd felt scared and wanted to protect herself. A decade later, the gun lay unused under her bed and her body was rotting wherever Josiah Blackthorn had dumped it.

As we approached the house Harry appeared in the woods coming up from the lake, carrying strings of charred, brown fish. He waved them at us. "How's about some smoked trout chowder?"

"The police were here, Harry." I glanced down the hill, gauging the distance of his fish house to the main cabin. It was possible he hadn't heard them, especially since they'd walked over instead of driving.

He didn't comment on it, didn't even seem interested that the police had been here. Instead he pulled open the cabin door and let it thwack against the siding. "Come on, you can chop some onions."

The pain started getting the better of me as we helped Harry prepare dinner, so I changed the bandage and took half a pill. I didn't want to be foggy or jeopardize the absolute clarity the gun had given me, but I also couldn't be crumpled in pain on the couch while Lucas disappeared into the wilderness, either. He might suspect enough to never emerge again.

I peeked around the blanket hanging over the front window every ninety seconds and stopped cold whenever I heard an engine in the distance.

"We go tonight, after Harry's asleep," I murmured as we set the table, my attention deliberately focused on laying spoons one by one at each chair.

Lucas paused, holding chipped mugs of water. He wanted me to look at him, to let him in, but I couldn't. Finally, after I took the water out of his hands and finished the place settings, he whispered. "I don't know where we are, in relation to him."

That turned out to be no problem. Harry was happy to produce a tattered old Boundary Waters map as we ate chowder, pointing out his favorite fishing spots. Lucas studied our location and let his eyes move over the terrain, jumping from lake to lake, finding our route. He nodded almost imperceptibly after handing it back, while I stirred the congealing contents of my bowl. The food was good, but I had no appetite, no interest in anything besides the comfort of metal against my ankle. The gun, which I'd transferred to my boot in the bathroom, had absorbed so much body heat that now it was warming me.

After dinner, we moved to the couch—Harry relaxing on one side while Lucas and I sat rigidly on the other. Harry flipped the TV on and we watched a reality show that I absorbed absolutely nothing from, instead watching the clock with obsessive focus, and waiting for Harry to get tired. As soon as the show ended, the local news came on.

My entire body jumped as Lucas's face filled the screen.

"Still no word tonight in the missing persons case of Lucas Blackthorn. Blackthorn, who was rescued from the Boundary Waters after being presumed dead for the last ten years, was kidnapped from Congdon Psychiatric Facility where he had been recuperating since his now famous return to society.

"Authorities believe this woman"—my Congdon badge picture flashed on the screen, complete with extra spiky maroon hair and deadpan eyes—"is responsible for removing the patient in the middle of the night, injuring a guard and destroying some hospital property in the process."

The screen flipped to the news anchor, but both our pictures hovered over her shoulder, refusing to fade away. "A substantial reward is being offered for any information that can lead to Lucas Blackthorn's recovery. Please call this number at the bottom of the screen or contact your local authorities."

They moved to the next story, which was the weather. They always opened with the weather. Why hadn't they opened with the freaking weather? I could have reacted then—made Harry change the station before it was too late.

I felt Lucas looking at me, but my eyes were glued to Harry. He'd sat motionless through the whole thing, legs sprawled, fingers linked across his flannel shirt. Another story passed, then another. I kept waiting for him to say something, but he was like a statue—*Hermit in Repose*—and no hint of what he was thinking crossed his face. At the first commercial break, Harry finally broke his position and sat up tall, reaching his arms toward the ceiling in an exaggerated stretch. Was I crazy or was he refusing to make eye contact with us?

"Well, I'm to bed."

"Harry—" I started, not knowing what should come next.

He stood up and nodded vaguely toward us as we sat frozen on the couch, waiting for him to make a move.

"Get some rest, Maya. You need your energy."

I couldn't tell if he was offering to protect us or trying to get out of the room so he could make that call, the call that would send us tumbling into the bowels of the world, Lucas back to the Congdon and me to prison.

"Harry, it's not what it looks like."

He chuckled, flipping the TV off. To hear us better from his room? "Looks like a couple of nervous kids in trouble. I could have told you that when you staggered in here yesterday. Rest up, okay?"

And then he was gone, shuffling to his bedroom at the end of the hall. He shut the door, but his light stayed on.

I turned to Lucas, who looked as unsure as I felt. "We have to go. Now."

26

WE CREPT THROUGH Harry's house as quietly as possible, folding the bedding and stacking it on the couch, getting our cold weather gear from the car and changing into it. Lucas filled up our water bottles while I retrieved all the bloody bandages from the trash and bagged up every other trace of our stay I could find. Right before we left, I laid three hundred dollars on the kitchen table. It was nowhere near the "substantial reward" he would have received, but it was all I had and I wanted him to know I was grateful for his help, no matter what he thought of us now.

When everything was ready I climbed into the car and put it in neutral so Lucas could push us out of the driveway. He threw his weight into it and we started rolling, crunching quietly over the gravel, until Lucas snapped upright and shouted a warning. I whipped around and saw a figure standing directly in our path.

Slamming on the brakes, I stopped the car inches before we collided.

Our brake lights illuminated the person's face. It was Harry.

I shifted into park and gave Lucas a warning look before sliding out and bracing my weight against the door panel. Harry wore a dark robe and slippers and held something in his hands. He wasn't smiling or moving out of our way.

"You might need this."

"What is it?" I didn't move, either.

"Something for a journey."

Lucas stepped up to my side and we both scanned the black horizon, listening. The snow was powdery enough to muffle any footsteps, anyone approaching from the sides or stationed behind the house.

"Stay here," I whispered and walked to the end of the car where Harry stood holding a knife.

The gun was still tucked in my boot, but before I could decide whether to pull it out Lucas cut in front of me, shielding me from Harry.

"Hey!" Harry held his hands up and retreated a step. "If I meant harm, I would've done it when you were sleeping, right?"

"You didn't know our situation until an hour ago," I reminded him.

He laughed now, his deep, thoughtful Harry laugh. "I hate to disappoint you kids, but his mug"—he waved at Lucas, who stepped back and scanned the edges of the clearing again—"has been on the news more times than tonight. And most people go to a hospital when they've been skewered, unless they're running from something worse than a hole in the side."

I forced a half smile as my fight-or-flight reflexes slowly relaxed. "I hoped you'd chalked it up to nostalgia."

"Yeah, lot of good memories here for you, Maya." He snorted and then switched his hold on the knife so it was lying flat in both his palms, pushing it toward us. An offering. "This'll cut anything from rope to animal hide and it's got a pliers, a carabiner, and a can opener on it, too. My father gave it to me just before he died. He built this place, you know. Anyway, maybe it'll help you find your way to his dad. Reckon that's where you're headed."

He flipped all the attachments out and in as he named them, then handed the knife to me.

"Harry." My throat started to close.

"No—" He objected when I tried to give it back and patted my hand awkwardly, like someone tolerating their friend's dog. Or like a solitary man forced out of his isolation by bleeding, self-involved children. "You keep it."

He stared at me for a second and it felt like he was digging the stitches out of my stomach, snapping them one by one and uncovering the clotted mess inside. " 'Be not simply good. Be good for something,' right?"

Turning to shuffle toward the house, he added. "Next time I see you, you better not be covered in blood."

I shook my head at the knife, glowing red in the taillights.

"Blood happens, Harry. I can't make any promises."

———

We drove a mile down the highway, passing my mother's cabin and killing the lights to pull into a curved, paved road on the opposite side of her property. This cabin wasn't a cabin at all. A hulking black building emerged from the woods as we coasted down the driveway, its roof reaching up to swallow the star-filled sky. I'd never seen it from this angle, day or night, but I still remembered the floor to ceiling lakeside windows that looked like gaping eyes when we paddled past. During our summers here, this mansion was owned by a pair of retired doctors, snowbirds who split their time between the Northwoods and the dry burn of Tucson in the winter. I had no idea if they'd left for the year or even if they still owned the place, but the windows were dark. No smoke came from the chimneys. It was as good a place as any to leave Butch's car. Bumping over the narrow path that wound down toward the lake, I parked in the massive shadow of their boathouse, which was roughly the size of Harry's entire cabin.

I glanced up the hill—no movement behind the gaping eyes— then checked the weather on the burner, since it might be the last time we'd have any cell service.

"Clear sky tonight with a low of nineteen degrees. We'll have sun tomorrow morning, then a snowstorm moving in during the afternoon. Low visibility. Good cover."

I had Lucas backtrack to the highway and obscure our tire marks while I checked the supplies. Two changes of thermal clothes rated for subzero temperatures. Tent, sleeping bag, fire starters, water filtration, enough protein bars and trail mix to last us a week, a first aid kit, and a 9mm. I wrapped the gun in an extra shirt and sealed it in a watertight bag. If the canoe tipped, it would be safer there than in my boot. By the time Lucas got back, I'd already strapped on my pack and cinched the waistband tight to alleviate the pull on the stitches. I pointed to his and set out hiking through the moonlit white woods, knowing he would catch up in seconds.

We walked silently along the lakeshore, staying in the shadows of the trees even though not a soul—human or animal—was out on this frigid night. Our breath made clouds in the air and my clouds grew faster, smaller, as we approached the clearing near the shore.

"Have you been here since?" Instinctively, Lucas moved closer to my side.

I shook my head and kept moving, focused only on the snow-dusted shack and the rickety door that shrieked when I tried to open it. Lucas reached in and together we muscled the old wood open and pulled out the canoe.

"How's your side?" Lucas asked as we carried the boat down the rocks toward the water.

"What about it?" I gritted my teeth. Thank God for Kevlar. I doubted I could've held up my end of an aluminum canoe right now.

Wordlessly, he leaned down to break the ice forming at the water's edge. It was only a few millimeters thick, but that could change in a single night. If the water cooled enough, an entire lake could form an ice sheet before sunrise.

I dropped my pack in the canoe and made myself walk back into the dark opening of the boathouse for the life jackets and paddles. They hung in the same place they always had, on hooks along the door. I grabbed them and retreated as quickly as I could, crashing into Lucas. He caught me when I stumbled, but his focus was on something over my shoulder.

"What's that?"

All I saw were shadows. He took the flashlight from me and shined it at the base of one of the studs, where a glint of light sparkled against the rotting wood. I stepped inside and my breath caught as I registered what it was.

"Oh my God."

Scooping it up, I let the pendant dangle from the tarnished, rusting chain. The agate slice. The necklace I'd brought when Derek, Rex, and I had driven to the cabin searching for the mother I hadn't known was dead. Months later, after I'd been released from Congdon and details began mattering again, I realized it had somehow vanished during the attack and I'd never considered returning to search for it—maybe Rex had taken it before he disappeared or maybe it had fallen into the water and washed away. I'd traded the two rocks in my head, an agate lost for an agate found, and refused to let myself look back. But here it was in the rotting boathouse, waiting for me after all these years.

"Was it hers?"

I tried to speak, but nothing came out. Pulling it over my head, I tucked the pendant under my clothes where it made a frozen circle on my chest. I pressed a hand to the spot. "Ready?"

"Maya, I don't know if you've healed enough for this."

"It's this or prison." I gave him a paddle, life jacket, and an impossible choice. "Where do you want me to go?"

He stepped closer and even in the moonlight I could see him struggle. "I know what I'm asking of you, okay, but you've got to believe me. He's not a bad man. Neither of us know what happened that night. We weren't there. And I don't think he was ever able to talk about it with me, but—"

"That's my job." I stepped into the canoe and braced myself. "I help people find their voices."

———

The Boundary Waters. Somewhere in the middle of the lake we crossed the threshold that divided one world from another, where human saturation gave way to one of the last great wildernesses in the country. Everything was covered with a layer of white, snow weighing down the branches of the pines that stood sentinel, the only witnesses to our silent progress. Our oars dipped in time, me in the bow, Lucas in the stern, steering us toward the main portage off this lake, a northward path that fed into another winding body of water. Paddling turned out to be worse than hiking. The twist of muscle in my abdomen screamed every time I pulled the oar and I bit my lip with each stroke, riding the edge of the pain and wishing I'd broken down and taken another pill. While my insides burned, my skin froze wherever it was exposed and even my fingers began numbing through the gloves. It felt like an hour before we reached the portage, and as soon as the canoe nosed the bank, I splashed out, cracking through the ice and looking for a foothold to drag the bow up as far as I could. Lucas was right behind me, and before I could put distance between us his arms encircled me.

"Rest," he whispered in my ear. "Warm up. I can tell you're hurting."

As much as I craved his warmth, it was impossible to let myself take it. Pulling away, I lifted my pack out of the boat and dug through it. "Here. Modern technology to the rescue."

I gave him a set of hand warmers and slipped another pair into my own gloves, glancing at the yawning darkness between the trees. "Packs first and then back for the canoe?"

But Lucas was already putting his pack on backward—over his stomach—and flipping the boat up without any help, balancing the yoke on his shoulders. Grabbing my own pack, I ducked out of the way and turned the flashlight on.

"Too bright." He muttered, and I could hear the hurt from my rebuff slinking into the woods with him. "You can see that a mile away."

So I followed blindly into the black, walking behind his boat-balancing shadow, while he whispered warnings of rocks and roots. As my eyes adjusted I could see spots of ground through the snow, other tracks besides ours, which were too big and too evenly spaced to be anything but human. The Boundary Waters was open year-round and winter campers came for ice fishing and dogsledding, but I couldn't imagine who would be here now, in the transition between seasons when paddling became a dangerous gamble. You could get trapped in the middle of nowhere if a sudden freeze made the lakes unpassable. You could tip your canoe and fall into water with a temperature barely above freezing, water so cold that it sucked you down like Superior, and maybe you would drown or maybe you'd crawl your way out into hypothermia. Either way there was no help waiting for you. There was no 911 here, no phones, no outposts, no emergency services. There were a thousand ways to die in the Boundary Waters, and all of them were alone.

When we reached the next lake and emerged from under the canopy, the moon felt like a spotlight, a hundred times brighter than it had been before. I looked for the tracks again, but they were gone.

We loaded up and pushed out into a smaller channel lined with collapsed drifts of marsh grass. The ice was thicker here in the shallows and I punched at it with the oar, breaking a path into the open water around snow-covered boulders. We veered wildly in some places and not wide enough in others. The canoe scraped the bottom several times and at one point we lodged on a rock shelf, but not hard enough to ground. I shoved us off the shelf with the paddle and we tried another path, then another, breaking our way through by trial and error. It seemed to take forever for the channel to widen again and I wondered if we'd be forced to portage until finally the banks receded, our oars stopped hitting bottom, and we came into a glossy moon mirror of a lake.

This one was smaller and it didn't take us long to paddle to the center, powered by Lucas's long, sure strokes. When we reached the middle, I rested my oar across the gunwales and slipped a hand under my coat, gingerly feeling the edges of the bandage. It took a minute to register that Lucas had stopped paddling, too.

"Look up." Lucas breathed, and I did. Overhead the cloudless sky showcased thousands of glowing and pulsing stars. As our paddle ripples faded off the surface of the water, the pinpoints of light reflected back from below, and it felt like we were floating in the middle of an endless galaxy.

"I missed this."

I'd forgotten how quiet it was, the total silence of the Boundary Waters. It was nothing like living at the mouth of Superior, which consumed everything in its white noise of wind and waves, and I understood why I hadn't been back here, why I'd never come looking for the necklace. It wasn't fear of a dead man. The dead man found me in my dreams no matter where I was. I hadn't returned for the same reason Dad couldn't; we didn't want to have this without her.

I drew a shaky breath as I gazed from horizon to horizon. "Did you know we're made of stardust?"

"Really?"

"Cosmic explosions from before time was time."

She'd told me. It was written in the note she'd left on my nightstand before she'd tucked me in my bed, brushed a salty kiss over my forehead, and locked herself in the bathroom to eat two bottles of aspirin.

We're molecules of living, breathing stardust, Maya, and just like the rocks, we're all different. Some people are strong and beautiful and they can withstand glaciers. Others are weak and brittle, and the best thing we can do is birth a gemstone.

She hadn't signed it with a goodbye or any words of advice or regret. There wasn't even a *Love, Mom* at the bottom. Just a note about stardust, before she tried to turn herself back into it.

"Then why don't we shine?" Lucas asked, pulling me out of my head. I slid my hand up to touch the agate pendant, making sure it was still there before grabbing the oar and setting my jaw against the fire that was going to start raging in my side.

"Maybe we're not far enough away to see it."

We paddled into a larger lake and then portaged in a direction I'd never gone. The trail was a narrow, steep incline and the snow made everything more slippery. I fell twice and hit my head on the back of the canoe once. Just when I was about to break down and ask if we could make camp, Lucas froze on the peak of the hill.

"What is it?"

"Shh." He hoisted the canoe down and propped it on a fallen log, then scanned the perimeter. I held my breath, trying not to make the slightest noise. Finally, he pointed to a spot ahead and to our left.

"There."

He dropped his pack and cut away from the path, his form disappearing in the trees.

"What?" I asked again, and again he shushed me. Sighing, I dropped my pack, too, and picked my way behind him through the standing and fallen trees. Gradually my eyes adjusted and I concentrated on Lucas's feet, watching where his heels landed and putting my boots in the same spots. When we scaled logs, he helped me over and I was too weak to resist. We hiked for at least ten minutes, to the point where I started panicking we'd lose our way back to the canoe. Was he leading me to his father, to their hidden campsite? I'd left the gun in the pack and had no idea how to find my way back to it alone. Then a familiar scent cut through the woods and I lifted my head to see a faint, flickering light eclipsed by Lucas's silhouette. A campfire.

We slowed down and approached cautiously, using the muffling effects of the snow to our advantage.

"—too goddamn early to be breaking camp. You're insane."

"I want to get a jump on today before the storm hits. No chance of finding Blackthorn in a whiteout."

That drew a groan from the other person. I leaned carefully around a tree trunk and tried to count heads at the campsite, which was still a good two hundred feet away. Lucas crept even further up and crouched behind a boulder. I was calculating the risk of trying to join him when a familiar voice spoke up.

"We're not going to find shit until sunrise anyway, which is still an hour away."

The voice belonged to Micah, the U.S. Forest Service ranger who'd volunteered to be part of the Congdon search party, the veteran who had no problem with crazy people. He'd been at all the planning meetings and had kept in contact with Dr. Mehta even after the expedition had fallen through. I could only see one other head beside his, crouched near the fire.

The rangers talked for a few more minutes, discussing routes and lakes. I couldn't tell, though, which Blackthorn they were looking for. Did these two represent the search party Dr. Mehta had assured me was still looking for Josiah? Or had they been alerted of the kidnapping and sent to find and arrest us? As I tried to get a better look at the man tending the fire, Micah stood up and walked straight toward us. I ducked behind the tree as the crunch of snow and pine needles became louder and louder. Holding my breath, pulling my legs in, I pressed myself into the base of the tree trunk. Silence. Then came the sound of a zipper and a thick stream of urine hitting the ground. I closed my eyes and waited until he finished and moved back to the camp. I heard the bang of a pot on the grate just as Lucas appeared at my side.

I touched my ear and pointed at the men, but he pointed in the opposite direction, making a gesture I didn't understand. I shook my head. He pointed away again and leaned in until his mouth grazed my ear.

"Now, before it gets lighter."

Then he drew me to my feet and we moved like shadows into the fading night.

Lucas led us back to the canoe as easily as if we were crossing through my yard to the garage. We didn't speak until we reached the portage trail and stood over our packs.

"We'll make camp here."

"We should get farther away. Head in the opposite direction of where they talked about going."

He moved until he was only inches away and his fingers caught me in the side, pushing enough to make me wince.

"You're not going any further tonight." Then he lifted both packs, one in front and the other on his back, before shouldering the canoe and stepping back onto the trail we'd just made. "Anyway, the safest place to be is the site they're leaving. Get a branch and cover our tracks."

––––––––––

We waited until they packed and left before setting up a few hundred feet away, close enough to catch a glimpse of the icy water but still well hidden, situating the tent behind a giant fallen pine, jeweled with cones. By the time I crawled inside, the hand warmers had given out and my boots were covered in ice from hauling the canoe in and out of lakes. We ate and drank without speaking, then rolled out the sleeping bag.

"Just one?" He raised an eyebrow.

"It's a double. Better for body heat."

His eyes caught mine in the dim flashlight, before skimming down my body.

"Lay down."

"Lucas—"

"Now."

When I did, he pulled my shirt up and redressed the wound. The soiled bandage had bloodstains mixed with a greenish-tinted fluid that had soaked to the edges of the padding. Neither of us commented on it. Silently, he swabbed the stitches with alcohol, found more clean dressing, and bandaged me with ridiculously tender fingers, as if trying to make amends for poking me on the trail. I blinked at the ceiling of the tent, illuminated by the first, fragile morning light as he smoothed tape over my ribs and tugged the shirt back down. Then he slid carefully to my other side and zipped us both into the bag. There was enough room to sleep side by side and that's what I should have done. I should have turned as far away as I could, but I was cold and hurting and too weak to resist the warmth of his body. Instinct took over and we curled into each other, fitting curves into hollows, cushioning bone with flesh. For eight years I'd dreaded going to bed, preferring insomnia to the nightmares and ghosts. I'd never spent the night with a live person before; I'd never felt this foreign surge of comfort or experienced the gift of listening to someone else's heartbeat through their chest, and I knew I didn't deserve it. I didn't deserve anything about Lucas Blackthorn, this boy who'd gone from a panicking, violent kid to someone who lovingly redressed wounds in the arctic dawn, whose lips were brushing over my hair and whose fingers nestled in the dips between my vertebrae.

He should have choked me to death the first day we met, I thought as I drifted into the no-man's-land between consciousness and sleep.

Because I was going to avenge my mother. I was going to orphan him.

27

WOKE UP shaking, turned my head to check for Lucas, and sat bolt upright in the sleeping bag. He was squatting near the tent entrance and rummaging through my pack.

"What are you doing?"

"Getting us something to eat. I wanted to let you sleep a little longer." He didn't move away from the bag.

"The protein bars are on top."

"That's not the only thing in here."

Adrenaline flooded my chest and I tried to keep my voice steady. "What do you mean?"

Turning, he held up a small pot and two bowls of instant udon noodles. His lopsided grin told me he remembered eating them at my house and I stuttered, because it was the exact reaction I'd been hoping for when I packed them a lifetime ago, planning his rescue and the journey to rescue his father. Leaning over to kiss me, he promised to go start the fire and make me some "delicious food." I nodded and forced myself to smile.

The snow started as we finished eating, slurping the last of the broth and heating a fresh batch of filtered water over the dying embers. I was trying to find us on the map, the one I'd taped together at the library, but the snow quickly covered the paper, falling in swirls of obliterating white. Snow was good. Snow meant we'd be harder to track. It also provided a layer of insulation over any lakes that had started to freeze, preventing further ice formation. We added layers, packed up, and hiked back out to a different trail that led us through towering pine shadows, down into a frozen marshlike clearing, and winding over another hill. I started to wonder if we were even on a trail anymore, but Lucas didn't hesitate. Every once in a while, he reached a hand out from under the canoe to skim the trunk of a tree, running his gloves over them like they bore messages in braille. A roaring noise grew louder as we made our way through the white world until Lucas stopped and gestured to an opening in the trees. I looked over the edge of a cliff and barely made out the still-rushing rapids below. Finally, we descended to a winding river where the force of the current kept the water open. As we climbed into the canoe and pushed our way through the frozen weeds, I glanced into the shadows on either bank.

"Are there campsites along here?"

"No, people canoe through here but they don't get out except when they have to portage the rapids."

Which was exactly where the rangers would be looking, in the most remote spots. We knew their route for this morning, but after that they could be anywhere. Maybe the snow didn't matter at all, maybe they used infrared scanners, or even more advanced tracking equipment. We were close, I knew. And the closer we got to Josiah, the more scared I became of being caught before we could reach him, before I could make him pay.

We paddled to another set of still-rushing rapids and portaged up the hill, a fifty-foot climb that felt like five hundred. After we set back in I started getting warm, too warm, the heat burning through my clothes and throbbing into my side. My wound didn't feel any worse, though. I wondered if I should eat again, even though the thought of food suddenly made my stomach turn. Water sounded better, but everything seemed out of reach. The filtration bottle might as well have been at my mother's cabin as in the pack behind me. I took off my hat and unzipped part of my jacket.

My deteriorating state wasn't lost on Lucas. He wanted to pull the canoe over and find a spot to rest, but I pushed us away from every bank he steered us toward. Fumbling blindly in the pack behind me, I grabbed the first aid kit and took another dose of antibiotics and a half pain pill, trying to pacify him and keep him carrying us forward, which was becoming more of an abstract concept. The white in front of us was impenetrable. Boulders and bends in the river appeared like they'd been conjured from the storm itself, obstacles with less and less meaning.

The quote on Dr. Mehta's office wall snaked through my consciousness. *What lies behind us and what lies before us are tiny matters compared to what lies within us.* Something within me had begun to burn.

"Maya, I want you to promise me something." I'd long given up paddling when Lucas's voice floated through the whorl of white.

I waited, not sure if it was really him or something my ill brain was manufacturing.

"Promise me you'll hear him out. Listen to him like you listened to me. That's all I'm asking." A pause, drifting into the wind, bowing the groaning branches of a pine tree over our heads. "Maya?"

Bracing myself on the gunwales, I nodded, hoping he could see me through the whiteout. I didn't notice I was crying until the tears had frozen on my cheeks.

I didn't know how much time passed. There might have been a shooting star. There might have been a whole cascade of comets blasting through the storm, or it could have just been my eyes on fire. I stopped being able to separate the flaming, dizzying flashes in my body from what was happening around me. It wasn't until the canoe grounded, scraping bottom on an ice-covered rock ledge, that I registered the outcropping of giant boulders we had wedged ourselves in between. I blinked and looked back to see Lucas hunched close to my face. His hand felt like an ice pack on my forehead.

"Welcome to my home."

The boulders gave way to woods where Lucas dragged the canoe and hid it under the drooping limbs of a listing pine. I shouldered my pack before he could take it and followed him into the dense trees. There was no trail, no campsites here where the forest seemed impenetrable. I concentrated on Lucas's back, which squeezed through gaps and disappeared in between giant snow-laden branches like magic or a hallucination. He was there and then he wasn't. Heat radiated through my body in waves, adding to the illusion; I could no longer tell what was real. As the pain medicine kicked in, I became clumsier. Needles scraped my clothes and face, combed my matted hair and showered it with flakes. The forest thinned as we moved into an old growth area where the lower branches, deprived of light, had lost all their needles and clawed at us even as the canopy above kept the snow away. Then we descended into a frozen marsh and struggled through quick-sand drifts of dead summer grass buried in white. I wanted to give up, to lay down in the marsh beds and let the cold sink into me, but Lucas pulled me forward. The farther we went, the more excited he became. He pointed out landmarks in a language only he could read. A trio of birch—the three sisters. A branchless trunk rising into the sky—the eagle's nest. And finally, a dead pine partially uprooted and sagging into the wide branches of another—the hugging trees.

We ducked underneath the hugging trees into a shadowed place, old growth on rock bed, and Lucas stopped as his breath made short, quick puffs in the dark.

"There," he whispered.

At first I didn't see it. A rise of rock covered in dead moss and decaying needles blocked the way in front of us, but as Lucas moved forward and I followed him, the perspective suddenly shifted. What appeared to be part of the hill was actually a moss-covered wall, camouflaged so well I wanted to run my hands over it until I found the edges. It arched at least seven feet off the ground, sloping in gradually to a peak where I spotted a glint of metal hiding in the needles—a chimney. A few rocks were scattered around the base and one seemed planted directly into the side of the wall, all overgrown with winter lichen and giving off the impression that this was exactly where the glaciers tossed them ten thousand years ago.

Two boulders flanked the narrow entrance, covered by a flattened piece of bark. Lucas dropped his pack and lifted up the wood to reveal a zipper underneath, a tent inside the hill. He unzipped it and ducked inside. I stumbled forward, squeezing through the rocks with my pack and lowered my head into the void.

"Shut the door." Lucas said from somewhere nearby, and I did, leaving only darkness and strange noises: a rustle of fabric, a scrape of metal, someone fumbling with mechanical objects, and underneath all that, another sound—the unsteady whistle of ragged lungs.

I huddled near the door, waiting, until a flare of light illuminated the tent. Lucas crouched near the chimney in the middle, adjusting the brightness of the lantern. Supplies were stacked along the front wall near me—canisters of beans and dried vegetables, bags of rice, and a hanging rack of tools. I stared at the tip of an ice pick, inches from my face, until a noise from the far side of the room drew my attention. Lucas was bent over a cot, blocking the person lying on it. He unzipped the sleeping bag, unleashing a putrid smell that fell somewhere between unwashed flesh and decaying meat. Gagging, I covered my face with an arm as Lucas whipped away, also fighting for control. His eyes flooded as he coughed. A hand lifted behind him, the fingers bare and skeletal, and grasped Lucas's knee. That was the last thing I saw before my stomach heaved.

Unzipping the tent, I scrambled out from the boulders and as far away as I could before vomiting into the snow and leaves. The pack cracked against my skull and my skin burned hotter than ever as each contraction ripped at the stitches in my side, turning every retch into a sob. When it was finally over I covered the mess with an armful of needles and crawled a safe distance away.

Lucas came out a few minutes later, his face wet with tears.

"Are you okay?"

I'd unhooked the pack and was clutching it like a buoy, panting and still haunted by that deathly hand rising from the shadows. "He's alive."

He nodded and fell to his knees in front of me, covering my hands that were gripping the pack. "He's so much worse. He'd lost weight over the summer, but now he doesn't even look like my father."

Maybe he's not, I wanted to say. Maybe he was never the man you thought him to be. Instead I pulled a hand out from under his and lifted it to his face. He jerked in surprise. "You're burning up."

"Is he lucid?" I pressed. "Does he recognize you?"

Lucas nodded.

"Good. He needs a bath."

I instructed Lucas to go fetch some fresh water while I stayed with his father and started preparing food. Then, together, we could assess his condition and figure out which medicine to try first. He hesitated, not wanting to leave, but finally agreed and said it wouldn't take him long to get to the marsh and back. Inside the tent, the fresh air had cleared the worst of the odor and Lucas tugged me forward to his father's bedside.

Josiah Blackthorn lay on his back. His face was sunken, with the only visible skin stretched pale and gaunt, sandwiched between a dirty hat and beard. The hand that had reached for Lucas earlier dangled off the cot, as if unconnected to any living thing. There was no life in him except for his eyes, which were the same impossible, ghostly blue he'd given to his son and they followed Lucas now, gorging on the sight of him.

"Dad, this is Maya. She's—" He didn't know how to continue.

"I'll stay with you while Lucas gets water." I nodded at both of them and settled myself on the ground.

When the sound of Lucas's footsteps faded away, I turned to the living corpse on the cot. Every trace of the gorgeous, brooding man who'd escaped into the Boundary Waters ten years ago was gone. This was a flesh-covered skeleton, except for two unnatural growths that bulged out of his neck.

"The snow's tapering off and it's not too cold. Would you like some fresh air?"

The blue eyes stared at me. Without waiting for an answer, I pulled the sleeping bag off him and propped him up, threading my arms under his and trying not to breathe through my nose. Dragging him off the cot and out of the tent, I squeezed him through the boulders and in the opposite direction from the marsh. The hugging trees receded into the background of the forest as I jerked his legs over rocks and down inclines. He weighed almost nothing. I could feel the crush of his bones through his jacket and shuddered when, instead of fighting me, his fingers slowly closed over my forearms. On the last drop, I stumbled and fell. Josiah tumbled against a log and I landed a few feet away on a massive boulder, popping at least one of the stitches and crying out in pain.

Holding the bandage and gasping, I waited for Josiah to weakly push himself over and lean against the tree before I remembered my manners.

"I'm Maya Stark, Jane Stark's daughter."

His mouth fell open, but no words came out. This was the culmination of my entire life. Every question I'd been too afraid to ask, every answer I didn't think I deserved to know, every lock I'd learned to pick, every law I'd broken, every patient I'd subdued, every class I'd taken, every palate strengthener, pronunciation exercise, and vocal pattern, every trick and reward, coaxing the nonverbal to speak, bringing words to the wordless, helping person after person because I'd never been able to have the only conversation that mattered.

But now here it was, the moment of fucking truth, and on top of everything I would keep my promise to Lucas, too.

I pulled the gun out of my boot and pointed it at his chest. "Start talking."

28

In the depth of winter I finally learned that there was in me an invincible summer.

—*Albert Camus*

JOSIAH

Leaving Heather Price crumpled on his patio with the money she'd been hunting for, Josiah went back to the truck where Lucas stared ashen-faced out the window. Wrong ad. He'd picked the wrong advertisement, the wrong landlord, probably the wrong life. Throwing the truck into reverse he felt like shit, like the stink of Heather's sickness had rubbed off on him and was making his own son turn away from the smell.

"She was trying to rob us." He explained as they headed back to the entry point.

Lucas kept his face turned toward the woods that quickly closed in around them. "Then why didn't you call the police?"

Josiah wiped a hand over his mouth and checked the rearview mirror. "Because they don't help."

Another mile passed before Lucas broke the silence. "I don't want to leave again. I like it here."

"In Ely?"

"The Boundary Waters."

Lucas didn't speak again for the rest of the drive. Josiah debated the odds of finding a new rental, a short-term lease to get them through the end of the school year and possibly even beyond. He doubted Heather would actually take them to court when she barely seemed able to leave her house to go to work. They could find a bunkhouse to start and then maybe he could buy a trailer or even an old cabin somewhere nearby. He hated the idea of a permanent ceiling, but at least there'd be no more landlords, and the Boundary Waters would be right out their back door.

With that idea in mind, they paddled back out for their spring break vacation, sticking to the bigger lakes that had already thawed, and set up camp on an island melting in the afternoon sunlight. Lucas was reticent while they put up the tent and tarp. He became listless, crawling into his sleeping bag instead of exploring the campsite with his usual energy. He didn't want breakfast the next morning and wouldn't do more than sit at the fire and stare. At first Josiah had chalked it up to witnessing the fight with Heather, but when Lucas's eyes glazed over he figured he'd caught a cold and let him sleep. In the middle of the next night, though, as Josiah was watching his campfire turn to embers, Lucas began screaming. He thrashed at the sides of the tent, pulling the stakes out and clawing at the fabric. Josiah dove inside and wrestled Lucas free, but he wouldn't stop flailing or yelling about bugs. Bugs everywhere, attacking him, except they weren't. It was too early for insects, too cold, but no amount of reason could calm Lucas, whose skin—to Josiah's horror—felt hotter than the charred wood in the firepit.

There was no medicine in their camp and no way out, not when Lucas could thrash over the side of the canoe or capsize the whole thing in his panicking state. It was too dangerous. He held the last remnants of snow to his son's forehead and murmured the same hollow reassurances over and over on a loop, willing the seizures and hallucinations away. When he saw a light flashing over the water, he thought he might be hallucinating, too. Then it drew closer and he made out a lone figure in a canoe.

He shouted over the water and pleaded for help. The light faltered and turned off and again he thought it was a mirage, until finally the bow of a boat slid onto the island's shore.

A small woman bundled in all-weather gear stepped out. Only the top half of her face was visible as she eyed their campsite warily. He explained the situation and asked if she would bring them in. "I can hold him still while you paddle."

After a long pause, where she searched the horizon of trees as if hoping anyone else might come along and volunteer for this job, she finally nodded her head toward the canoe. They loaded the essentials and Josiah strapped a life jacket on Lucas, propping him on his lap in the front, while the woman powered them from the stern, setting off into the night.

They moved slowly, inching through the black. Her strokes were measured and steady and she seemed to know where the shallows and boulders lay even without the flashlight's beam. He didn't inquire what she was doing by herself in the middle of a still-frigid April night. She didn't ask him anything except about Lucas's symptoms, and showed no reaction when Josiah listed them out.

It was almost dawn by the time they reached a small, rock-filled beach where the woman led him to a cabin nestled in the trees. She pointed out a small bedroom, where Josiah laid Lucas's unconscious body that had now begun to shake and told him she thought Lucas had the flu.

"Influenza. My daughter had it once."

Josiah glanced around at the empty cabin. "Was your daughter okay?"

She nodded and turned away. "She is now."

While he wiped Lucas's brow with a cool cloth, she told him the doctors had given her a prescription for Tamiflu. Josiah asked if he could use the phone.

"It's not in service."

Then he asked if he could use her car as soon as business hours began. She nodded and disappeared out the front door. Ten minutes went by, then twenty. After the night he'd endured, he wouldn't have been surprised if she'd simply collapsed into the shadows of the woods. There was something spent about her, as if she'd given away all her vital organs and the frame that was left was fragile, unsupported. Just as the sun cleared the trees, though, she returned with a thermometer and a small manual, a medical reference book they used to look up influenza, its symptoms and treatment. The hallucinations, Josiah hoped, were the product of a fever that the thermometer read to be a hundred and two degrees. Since his breathing was normal and skin didn't have a bluish tinge, he didn't appear to be in immediate danger. He just needed fluids and medicine. The woman didn't have any Tylenol—she didn't seem to own much of anything the more Josiah looked around—but she handed him her car keys.

"Would you go?" He took a step back toward the bedroom. "I'm sorry, I don't want to move him again yet. I'll give you money."

"They won't give me the prescription." She moved to a window, her silhouette ghostly in the half-light of the morning.

"Shit." He didn't want to make Lucas endure a doctor's visit.

"It's okay to leave him here. I'll watch him until you get back."

He pulled his boots on and was halfway out the door before stopping and turning back. "What's your name?"

"Jane," she said and he couldn't tell whether or not she was lying.

He glanced at the bedroom behind her, realizing that for the first time in nine years he was going to leave his son with a total stranger. She dropped her head, shirking his stare and making him hesitate further, but the longer he stood around the longer Lucas went without medicine. He slammed the door and raced to the car.

————

When he got into town, driving seventy in a thirty-mile-an-hour zone, the doctor's office still wasn't open yet so he stopped by the duplex to pick up extra clothes. Two squad cars were waiting in the driveway. Before Josiah could process what was happening, the officers took him down to the station to question him about Heather's disappearance and when he lied and said he hadn't seen her—because who the fuck cared about Heather Price, he needed to get medicine back to his son—they threw him in jail for obstruction of justice. They flashed his record, as if that would scare some bullshit confession out of him, and played a game of bad cop/bad cop that had more to do with him than about finding Heather Price. He'd run into local boys like this all his life, the ones who stared at the same few miles of land so much they thought they owned anyone who dared to walk on it. Cooperating, he described the fight he'd had with Heather, leaving out the part where he'd shoved her into the walls, and asked them to dust his apartment for fingerprints.

"She probably took the money straight to her dealer."

"Heroin?" Sergeant Coombe, the overfed desk cop who seemed to be in charge, chewed on that idea like it had a funny taste he couldn't identify. "We don't have an opioid problem up here."

An opioid problem. Josiah bit back the impulse to ask him if they didn't have "the Internets," either. "Maybe that's why Heather didn't have any friends."

"It's easy preying on a woman with no friends, isn't it?"

He felt a flash of panic, not over Heather—all he'd ever done to Heather was say no, thank you—but about the hollow-eyed woman who paddled alone in the dead of night. He'd left her cabin hours ago and the more time that passed, the less he could remember about her. The color of her hair, the pitch in her voice, the expression on her face when she looked at Lucas: all of it wavered out of his memory, leaving a dark outline that could be inhabited by any manner of person. And Lucas—what would Lucas think when he woke up? If he woke up? The fever might have spiked again. A dozen possibilities competed for the worst-case scenario as Josiah stared at the beige on beige ceiling, crumbled at the corners and hacked up with holes for electrical equipment and video surveillance. He loathed it more with every minute he sat underneath it in handcuffs.

"I've cooperated, haven't I? I've told you everything that happened that day, so there's no grounds to hold me anymore. I'm not hiding anything."

"No, you've been pretty straight with us about giving a missing woman money so she could buy illegal drugs."

"I paid her rent. What she did with the money after that is her business."

Sergeant Coombe flipped a paper over and scanned it. "What about your son?"

Josiah went cold. "What about him?"

"Would he agree with your version of events? Neighbors claim you're two peas in a pod. They never see one of you without the other."

"Lucas has nothing to do with this. Leave him out of it."

"Listen here, Brad Pitt." Sergeant Coombe leaned over the interrogation table. "I'm sure you get away with ordering people around like that in most areas of your life, but I'm the one wearing the badge. I'm the one who's going to find out what happened to Miss Price. And I hope—I really, truly hope—that you had something to do with it, because I would love to see your pretty face behind bars."

"Really?" Josiah mirrored him, leaning in over his cuffed hands. "Because if I were you, I'd hope Miss Price was found alive."

The sergeant slapped Josiah's file on the table. Neither man blinked.

"I know your type. I arrest your type. You might as well say goodbye to that kid of yours because one day you're going to give me a reason. Maybe not today. Maybe not even this case, but if you decide to stick around my town it'll happen. And I guarantee you I'll be there when it does."

They threw him back in the cell to wait out the entire twenty-four hours before they had to either charge or release him, and by the time he got out it was Saturday and all the doctors' offices were closed. He grabbed four boxes of Tylenol, Popsicles, and a wilting rose at the gas station, then raced back to Jane's cabin, hitting the steering wheel and cursing Heather Price the entire way.

"How is he?" He burst through the door and past Jane into the bedroom, where Lucas was alive and sleeping. His skin seemed cooler, but nowhere near normal. Fumbling with the packages, he read the dosing instructions. The adult ones started at age twelve so he switched to the pediatric, but they were based on age and weight. Did he have to know both? Jesus, he couldn't remember the last time he'd weighed his son. "Do you have a scale?"

No answer from the main room.

He walked back to where she sat at the kitchen table, hands in her lap and an empty juice glass in front of her with a wine ring at the bottom. It was nine in the morning. "A scale. Do you have one?"

She shook her head.

"Fine. Whatever. It doesn't matter." He screwed open the bottle and shook out three pills, then went in to wake Lucas, who was weak and disoriented. Josiah fed him the medicine and made him drink as much water as he could before he fell asleep again. Sitting on the edge of the bed, petting Lucas's hair, watching him breathe, Josiah felt like the climber hanging one-handed on the edge of the cliff in the picture on the wall. Lucas was all he had. Lucas was the only thing that mattered. And if he lost his grip on his son, if Heather Price turned up dead and they found a way to blame him for it, there would be no end to his fall.

He'd already had the worst moment of his life, goddamnit.

After a while, when Lucas's breathing seemed to even out, he went into the main room again. Jane hadn't moved from the table. He sighed and sat in the other kitchen chair.

"I'm sorry. I got detained by the police."

She stared at the empty juice glass as if he hadn't spoken, as if he wasn't even there. He looked around, found the wine on the counter, and picked up the dusty bottle that still felt full. "More?"

Shaking her head, she reached out for the cup and rotated it slowly.

"It's a good source of manganese. Red wine. Prevents rust and corrosion. An essential trace mineral, but too much of it will kill you." Her words were jerky, like the thoughts had been pulled at random from dark corners of a disused wardrobe.

"Aren't you going to ask what the police wanted with me?"

She got up and went to the sink. "I thought you'd left him. I didn't think you were coming back."

"That's my son in there. How could I abandon him?"

Rinsing out the glass, she carefully set it next to the sink, bottom up, and watched the drips collect and pool underneath the rim, trapped. "Maybe you thought he'd be better off without you."

"He needs me." Josiah got up and paced to the bedroom doorway, staring at the smooth curves and planes of his son's face, the traces of Sarah in his nose and jaw, the miraculous rise and fall of the quilt over his narrow chest. "Almost as much as I need him."

He retrieved the gas station bag from the bed and paced back to the kitchen, where Jane still leaned into the counter and stared out the window, motionless. He wanted to be outraged that she would even suggest he'd abandoned Lucas, but the fact was he had. He'd left his son for twenty-four hours and if the police had charged him, it would have been even longer; Lucas could have been stuck with this ghostlike woman indefinitely. And Heather Price was still missing. He sighed, not at all sure about what he had to ask next.

"I don't want to take Lucas back to our place right now. Can we stay here a little longer?" He pulled out the half-dead flower and offered her its drooping petals encased in plastic.

She looked past it, into the bag of medicine and melting Popsicles, and told him he could sleep on the couch.

———

Lucas slept most of the day, only rousing when Josiah made him drink fluids and he didn't seem very coherent even then. He needed help to get to the bathroom and fell exhausted into bed afterward, saying his body hurt everywhere. When the fever hit he threw the covers off the bed, only to shrink into a ball and shake uncontrollably from the wave of chills that followed. Josiah kept watch as shadows stretched over the walls, and the only sign of life outside of the bedroom was an occasional rustle that could have been either Jane or a mouse.

After dusk, though, she built a fire at the edge of the lake and he debated leaving her alone, but the hiss and burn of the logs called him, Lucas was sleeping soundly, and the low ceiling of the small room had begun to feel suffocating. She didn't comment when he joined her and sat silently for a while, soaking in the early spring night that hadn't yet given rise to summer's legions of mosquitos. Soon Josiah found himself talking, at first just trying to explain the police situation and Heather Price, but gradually he told her more and more. He told her about shoving Heather, about giving her the money and hoping it would make her go away. He hadn't cared how and he still didn't, wondering aloud how someone could be missing when nobody missed her. Jane listened without reaction. There was something about the way she looked at him, without pity or blame, without lust or dismissal; he might have been speaking to the Boundary Waters itself. He told her about Sarah, about the drifting, all the national parks and wildernesses he and Lucas had seen, and she let him talk, commenting little except to agree that most roofs were ugly, to the very last one people put over their heads.

"I want to be buried out there somewhere." She stared into the black horizon of trees across the water. "To leech into the soil or return to silt at the bottom of a lake. I don't want to end up in a box."

"How about burning? Cremation?" He poked the fire with a stick, sending a torrent of sparks into the air.

"I've been pollution already. I'd rather be useful, for once."

Then slowly she began talking. She told him the history of the BWCA, all the way back to the volcanic rifts and crushing glaciers, and it felt like she was telling him her own story, just as he'd shared his. When he'd asked her name yesterday, she'd faltered and the word seemed foreign on her tongue, but now, describing Ely greenstone and its 2.6 billion–year journey she had an almost desperate confidence, as if she needed to pass on some vital knowledge. She talked about what humans took from the Boundary Waters, from the Knife Lake siltstone ten thousand years ago to the sulfide deposits the mining companies now hunted for their nickel and copper, and she bent further and further forward as she spoke, as though the minerals were being carved from her own core. He'd never met anyone like her. Her inaccessibility didn't repel. Her sad beauty didn't attract. But the longer they sat and added more logs to the fire, the less he worried about Heather Price and the world outside. Here, they became *in*. Everything else was *out*.

When she started to shiver, he moved their log bench closer to the fire and for a while she rested her head on his shoulder. No one had done that, drawn that simple comfort from him, since Sarah had died and he absorbed the long-forgotten feeling, the scent and weight of a woman's head seeking rest. He let his arm drift to the curve of her side, and they sat like that watching flames lick the sky and the lake shimmer in the firelight. At one point he felt a drip of something and saw the front of his jacket was streaked wet. Sarah hadn't been a teary woman. He didn't have any practice comforting one, but he did what felt natural and pressed a kiss into her hair. She accepted it with no response, just like she ignored the cracking branch in the distance that must have signaled some creature finding passage through the night. Josiah looked, but saw only shadows and moonlit wood smoke from the neighboring cabin. Later, after the moon disappeared below the tree line, he broke their strange peace by asking about her daughter again. Everything in her stiffened and, standing abruptly, she left the fire and walked into the house. He watched her go with the uncomfortable thought that the girl was dead. Sighing, he went to get a bucket of lake water and put out the fire, but before he could douse it Jane returned, cradling something in her hands.

"Do you know what this is?"

He stared at it, wondering if it was a trick question. "A rock?"

An echo of a smile crossed her face. Then she turned it to a different angle, illuminating a striped pattern that looked like ripples in a pond. "It's a fortification agate. See how the banding looks like the walls of a fort?"

She kept shifting it in her hands, smoothing her fingers over the stripes and then running them along a rough edge that ended at a point and pressing against it, like she was trying to draw blood.

"Agates are born inside the hollows of basalt and they're stronger than everything around them. They survived the glaciers while the basalt was pulverized. When I found this I was only a sophomore in college, but I knew it meant I was going to have Maya, and she would become everything I'm not."

Jane pressed the rock to her mouth before kneeling and rearranging the stones circling the firepit, nestling the agate into a spot like a diamond in a ring.

"Aren't those valuable?" Josiah asked.

"It's hers," she said, choking up as she patted it into place. "She'll find it."

"She's alive?"

Jane looked up, startled.

"I'm sorry, I just . . . from the way you're acting and being here alone and all, I thought maybe something happened to her."

"She's fine. Now she's fine, now that I'm gone." She turned back to the fire, eyes vacant, and arms hanging limp at her sides. "I was the one who was killing her. Every day, being around me, trying to make me okay, to be okay for both of us. I tried medication, but it made me worse. I did something terrible. And I couldn't bear for her to watch if I did something terrible again. So I left."

"You left your daughter?"

"She's with my husband. She's twelve now. Almost a woman." Then she saw the outrage in Josiah's expression. "It's better this way."

He couldn't sit any longer, couldn't listen to this. "I was going out of my mind in that police station, not knowing if Lucas was okay. I would do anything for him, protect him from any danger."

"What if it was you?" Slowly, she uncurled herself and rose to her feet. "What if the most dangerous thing to your child was you?"

She stared him down and, when he had no reply, glanced up the hill where a single light illuminated the bedroom in which Lucas slept. Then she turned and walked into the shadows, disappearing between the shoreline and the trees. Josiah sat there for another hour, watching the fire die and not understanding anything about the last two days of his life, especially not why he felt compelled to stay and keep watch, putting himself between Jane's empty eyes and his son.

———

The next morning when Josiah woke up, Jane was gone. He fed Lucas Popsicles and made coffee, noticing her car in the driveway. They could take it and leave, but Lucas's eyes were still glassy and dull, and where would they go? He didn't have to be back at work until Monday and as far as the police were concerned, he had a registered permit that said he was camping in the Boundary Waters. He paced through the woods around the cabin and down to the lake, realizing Jane's canoe was gone. Squinting over the open water, blinded by the reflected sun, he wished he could trade places with her, that he and Lucas could paddle out and just keep going, never looking back. It would take strength, he thought, staring at the agate by the firepit, and he had strength. He had will. The dangers in the wilderness were all external, and together he and Lucas could face every one.

That night Lucas ate some canned soup and bread and took a cool bath by himself before going back to bed.

"Where's the lady?" he asked. "The one you were fighting with?"

Josiah frowned at the window, unsure if the sound from the bonfire had carried last night or whether Lucas had experienced another hallucination. Later, after Lucas drifted off to sleep and the sun was setting through the trees, Jane came back. She looked unbalanced, exhausted from paddling and flushed from the wind. Glancing at Josiah as if surprised to still see him there, she dropped into the nearest chair and held her head.

"I'm sorry," he said from across the room. "We can leave tomorrow if you'll give us a ride to my car. It's not too far."

She made a noise he couldn't decipher.

"We'll wash up the sheets before we go. And I can pay you."

At that, she shook her head violently.

"No, really. You helped us and I appreciate it."

Pushing herself up, Jane staggered into Lucas's room. Josiah came to the doorway to see Jane rocking back and forth at the head of the bed, clutching something in her hand.

Crossing to her in two steps, he hissed, "What are you doing?"

She blinked in slow motion and now that he was close to her he could smell the sweet stink of wine rising off her skin. Pulling her out of the room, he half carried her to the steps and shoved her toward them.

"Maya." She reached past Josiah, struggling to go back to Lucas. He grabbed her by the arms and pushed her up the steps.

"That's not Maya. That's my son and we'll be gone the minute you sober up and drive us to our car. Got it?"

She braced herself against the wall, looking like she might vomit, then nodded carefully. "They're different from us. They won't be us."

When she looked up her face was dry, composed, and she transferred something into his hand, the thing she'd been holding. "Some people are strong and beautiful and not even glaciers can destroy them. Others are weak and brittle, and the best thing they can do is birth a gemstone."

"You're not weak, you're drunk," he said, even as she started to tremble and shake.

"Maybe he'll be strong. Like her." Then she stumbled up the stairs to the loft. As the bed creaked, he opened his hand to see a rock covered in crumbles of cold, wet dirt. It was too dark to see what it was.

Josiah slept on the floor next to Lucas's bed that night, listening for any noise, any hint that Jane might come back down and try to approach Lucas again, but the cabin was silent. Later, when he got up to go to the bathroom, he smelled something sour. He checked back in Lucas's room, but the only scent there was sweat and boy and dirty clothes. It wasn't the kitchen sink. It wasn't the garbage. It was stronger at the base of the stairs, and—after a moment of indecision—he climbed up to Jane's bedroom, turned on the light, and immediately wished he hadn't.

She lay faceup, eyes open and blank, crusted vomit spilled over her face, chest, and hair. On the nightstand next to the bed were the three extra packages of Tylenol he'd bought at the gas station, all empty.

He stared in shock for what felt like an hour before the reality sunk in. He was alone in the woods with a dead woman, not two days after being implicated in the disappearance of another woman. They couldn't blame him for this, could they? But he'd bought the Tylenol. His fingerprints were all over the house. Looking around the room, he even found a gun on the floor under the bed, like she'd been afraid for her life. Jesus Christ. He didn't risk touching the gun but went on a frantic search of the rest of the cabin for the missing wine bottle and found it discarded in the trash outside, with remnants of crushed up medicine clinging to the sides. He'd touched that, too, the morning he'd been released from jail. Swearing, he kicked the garbage can, beating the thing again and again until he stopped hearing Sergeant Coombe's voice in his head. *One day you're going to give me a reason.*

Not today. Goddamnit, why couldn't she have waited to kill herself until they were gone? Panting, he walked away from the garbage and looked up, above the tips of the trees into the star-studded sky. His breathing settled down as he stared into the endless night, and then he realized what she wanted him to do. What she'd been asking him when he was too stupid to know it.

Nothing in this world is free, his foster mother had said, and this was the price of their sanctuary.

He lined the car trunk with garbage bags, went back inside and wrapped her body in the soiled sheets, hauled it out over one shoulder, and drove to a place he thought she would have liked. A place under the stars where the rocks were soft and some—he was surprised that he even noticed—shone in the moonlight.

———

"I can tell you where she is." Josiah's voice, ragged and halting, sounded like it was gutting him. For the last half hour, he'd talked without stopping, eating handfuls of snow when his mouth got too dry, closing his eyes when a shudder of pain wracked him, driven to continue by something that had no connection to the gun wavering at his chest.

I'd been ready to pull the trigger, waiting for whatever bullshit he'd invented: excuses, reasons, pleas for sympathy. I had an answer for all of that and I wanted it so badly. I wanted a bad guy to shoot. I was prepared to trade everything for the purity of that rage, even Lucas—beautiful, loving Lucas—but when Josiah repeated her words exactly, as if he'd spent ten years memorizing their last conversation, even vengeance was stripped away from me.

Birthing agates. The same thing she'd written to me before she first tried to kill herself.

"She's not far from the cabin. It's just beyond—"

"No." I jerked the gun at him. "I don't want to know."

He nodded once. Snow had settled on his shoulders and legs, slowly burying him while it skittered away from me as I rocked uncontrollably back and forth, like a screaming baby someone was trying frantically to shush. We faced each other, the gun shaking between us, while I tried to grasp the reality of my mother's death.

After a long pause, he took another handful of snow and said, so low I almost didn't hear it. "Go ahead."

"What?"

"I'd like to be buried here, like her." His eyes moved past me, into the shadows. "In the Boundary Waters."

A branch cracked uphill from us and Lucas shouted my name.

"It's okay." Josiah looked up at his son and forced his skeleton face into a smile. "I wanted to hang on long enough to see you again. To tell you some things about your mother"—he glanced at me—"both your mothers, but I've told Maya now. She knows. And now she's doing this for me."

Lucas dropped to his knees and crawled down the embankment. "No! Give me the gun, Maya. Don't do this. Don't you take my father away."

Tears poured down my face as I looked from Blackthorn to Blackthorn, both beseeching me, one for life, the other for death, each asking for their own impossible ends. I wavered, and the gun fell a fraction of an inch. Josiah's eyes burned as bright as his son's as he made himself lean forward.

"She loved you, Maya. As much as I love Lucas. I think that's why she left."

I broke then, dropping the gun, and fell sobbing onto the frozen, snow-covered rocks.

29

Two years later

WHAT MAKES someone crazy?

It's not a word we're supposed to use. Everything is a disorder, a diagnosis and a treatment plan for some abstract label that's supposed to provide meaning to the hell some of us live every day. Like knowing you're obsessive compulsive will make your hands stop bleeding from being washed too many times. I know it's not right, but there's something addictive about the word. It's visceral. It draws a line and says if you cross this, you're out of the game. You can't be held accountable for the mixed-up chemicals and imbalances in your head. They'll put you somewhere—a home, a hospital, a prison—and you can stare at yourself, or yourselves, while most of the world is happy to let you rot.

My mother couldn't bear the weight of her life and committed suicide.

Josiah Blackthorn was afraid of ceilings and escaped into the wilderness.

Lucas raged against a society he didn't know or want to understand.

I saw my mother in a rock and she told me to cave someone's skull in.

Pick the crazy person. Draw the line. See, it's easy until someone hands you the pen.

The truth is that the people on this side, the so-called sane people, don't have it any better. Feel like crap? Too bad. Not enough money? Don't eat. No one to love you? Boo hoo. On this side of the line you're responsible for everything. One remark can get you fired. One bad day can destroy your life.

I'd walked both sides of the sanity line and when I was prosecuted for the crimes of kidnapping and assault, along with the laundry list of other charges, I was found competent to stand trial. I took responsibility for my bad day and prepared to pay for it with seven years of my life. At the sentencing hearing, reporters from all over the country crowded into the St. Louis County courthouse, overwhelming the bailiffs and irritating the judge. The media listened, impatient, as one by one people got up to testify. The victims had their say—Nurse Valerie soaked up the attention, the orderly I'd kicked in the throat described his injuries—but it was the main victim who everyone came to hear. Lucas took the stand with extreme discomfort. He avoided looking out into the observation area and spoke directly to the judge, telling her in carefully picked words the essentials of what happened, a trail of facts scrubbed of all depth of meaning. He'd tried to escape Congdon a number of times to return to his father. He'd formed an attachment to me, asking me to help him leave, and one night I did. We'd traveled to the Boundary

Waters and found Josiah, who was gravely sick but still alive. At the end of his monotone statement, he paused and made himself turn to the sea of faces.

"I don't understand it here and I'm not stupid; I'm not a savage. My father and I were happy in the Boundary Waters. The only thing we wanted was to be left alone. Maya Stark gave up everything to reunite us." He stopped, swallowed, and faltered on the last words. "More even"—he wouldn't look at me—"than she thought she had."

Afterward Dr. Mehta took the stand, testifying on both Lucas's mental state and my history of abandonment which had made me, in her expert medical opinion and "regrettable hindsight," particularly vulnerable to the Blackthorns' situation. Despite the damage I had wrought to her reputation and professional standing, she asked the judge for leniency.

In the end I was sentenced to twenty-four months and served sixteen. During those sixteen months in the Minnesota women's correctional facility I met a lot of women who should have been at Congdon, women who were probably called crazy, who hadn't gotten the help they needed. Some of them were shrinking into nothing like my mother. Others had blazed into self-destruction like me. One prisoner, an eighteen-year-old taking her last deep inhale between girl and woman, never spoke and I found out through the grapevine she had a stutter. I began sitting with her for meals, teaching her vocal exercises even as she flipped me off and stormed away. It took two weeks for her to tolerate my company and three until she began to try the exercises, under her breath, as though scared to be caught with her mouth moving. After four months she was reading full paragraphs and speaking spontaneously without a repetition and when she asked about me, about my life and what

I'd done to get there, I didn't shut down or distance myself from the conversation. I told her the truth, and she didn't run away. By the time I was released the following spring, she'd become the close friend Dr. Mehta had always encouraged me to have.

Two years after the journey to find Josiah, I don't know which side of the line I inhabit, where in the spectrum of sanity I fall. Lucas and I live in my mother's cabin, the cabin that—according to her will, since she's been declared legally dead—now belongs to me. I can't pass a background check for most jobs, and the local elementary school flat out rejected my volunteer application, but Robert Anderson agreed to hire me for seasonal work at his outfitter store, and that's enough to get us by.

We could've had millions. Agents, book publishers, and even television and movie producers had all approached Lucas, offering more money than crazy people knew what to do with, if he would tell his story. Lucas rejected every one. He's talked about applying for a job with the Forest Service someday, but for now we live quietly and breathe deep. We do yoga while Jasper chases chipmunks in the yard, catch trout so Harry can teach us how to smoke fish, and when we travel to Duluth for therapy we visit my dad, who pats Lucas on the back in his gruff, awkward way and tells him all the ways a ship can be wrecked. Dad never found the *Bannockburn*, and after the grant money ran out, he stopped looking. I think he was ready to let go of the ghosts, but we don't reminisce about the past. Instead, we demolished the kitchen and picked out new cupboards, hardwood with clean lines and soft closing doors. He and Butch drove up to the cabin for the holidays and we ice fished and drank eggnog and on Christmas morning Dad gave me a new chain, shimmering and strong, for the agate pendant. I wear it every day, sometimes over my clothes, sometimes against my heart where I can feel its heavy warmth, and Lucas loves to trace the banding, following the pattern out past the confines of the necklace and drawing the layers into my body. I used my discount at Robert's store to buy a pair of secondhand kayaks, and for the Fourth of July we took a trip to Lake Macbride, where Lucas's parents first met. We paddled with the strange double-bladed oars, using new muscles and sitting closer to the water, a small shift in perspective that seemed to change everything. Slowly we've become more agile. We've learned how to play.

There are still nights, even two years later, when we huddle together in the bedroom under the stairs, our sorrow inseparable from one another, but there are other nights, too, where we find solace on the shores of countless lakes all across the Boundary Waters. All except one.

There's one lake we never return to, the lake whose name we can't even speak, because some things are beyond language, and some pieces of us never left.

That day, the day of revelation in the woods, we brought Josiah back into the burrow and tried to make him comfortable. He refused all of the stolen medicine, even the pain pills, and based on the growths on his neck I didn't think anything short of chemotherapy would make a difference. Lucas didn't want to hear it. He ignored my half-mumbled explanations and his father's eyes that pleaded silently for death. Taking the gun outside, he fired it until it was empty, deafening all three of us and making tears leak into the cracks of Josiah's face. Lucas gathered up all the other potential weapons—hatchets and saws, even fishing lures—and took them somewhere beyond our reach. I didn't ask. I had no questions left in me. We stayed the night, me feverish and fighting a raging infection in one bed, Lucas tending his father in the other. No one slept. Every once in a while, Josiah would whisper something. He told Lucas how he held him as a baby, fitting Lucas's entire head into the curve of his palm. He talked about hiking through giant sequoias and dusty canyons and he told Lucas he was proud of him, and how he knew Lucas would find his own path. They were love letters, goodbye letters, and I tried not to listen because they weren't for me.

Before first light, Josiah surprised both of us by asking to be taken to a doctor. Relieved, Lucas agreed and quickly broke camp. I made tea and crushed a pain pill into it, getting Josiah to drink almost half the cup before he choked and coughed. We turned his cot into a stretcher, bundling and strapping him to it, and then set off toward the canoe. It was slow progress, with Lucas hauling his father through the fresh snow and me burning a trail behind them. I might have been talking, but I couldn't say about what. I only remembered Josiah's face, the pitifully small puffs of air that trickled out of him, and his unblinking eyes, asking me things I didn't want to answer.

When we got back to the canoe, I saw a second boat was also stored under the giant pine. Lucas tied the two together, cut the rope on the stretcher, and lifted Josiah into the bottom of the trailing canoe, propping him against the yoke while I tucked blankets around him.

We set off in the opposite direction from the way we came, Lucas powering the entire caravan while I broke up the layer of ice that had formed overnight. Eventually the river opened up into a wide, island-dotted lake, frozen over at the edges but still navigable. We paddled out to the center and passed an island on which a campsite came into view. Two men stood on the ice next to a packed canoe, clearly preparing to leave. Even from several hundred feet away, I could see it was the Forest Service rangers.

For a moment everything stopped. Lucas quit paddling and the four of us stared at each other across the water, waiting for someone to make a first move. Then the slapping noise of rope hitting water cut through the morning air, and Lucas and I both turned to see Josiah's canoe unmoored and drifting away. He crouched unsteadily, holding the gunwales for support, and in one of his hands was Harry's knife.

Lucas paddled backward, shoving bucketfuls of water with each desperate stroke. Josiah's mouth moved, but I couldn't hear what he was saying. He straightened up, standing precariously as the canoe shuddered and rocked, and lifted a hand to uncover his head. Strands of thin, gray hair fluttered in the breeze, the growths on his neck bulged unnaturally, but it was his smile that overtook that moment, his sublime gratitude as he surveyed everything around him: the dark water, the solemn white pallbearers of the trees, the land that had harbored him and his son, and then—lifting his face—the perfect, endless sky stretching above, that infinite wilderness into forever. He looked back at Lucas one last time with the unmistakable words forming on his lips—*I love you*—then turned away from us, sliced his throat open, and fell into the lake. Lucas leaped from the canoe and began swimming desperately toward him, but by the time he reached the other boat, the lake had already taken Josiah, pulling him down into the shadows, leaving no trace.

Maybe our parents are only ever ideas in our heads, poorly enacted by the people who brought us to life. It's unbearable, what we heap upon them, almost as unbearable as what they see in us. All we can do is hope the bonds tying us together are stronger than those constructs, outlasting our delusions and our failures, maybe even our lives. I talk to my mom in the cabin sometimes. I bring her specimens of minerals and I've begun building her a rock garden with her agate in the center, down by the water's edge where the wildflowers bloom in the summer. Maybe I'm crazy for living in the house where my mother committed suicide, talking to her ghost, and finding her in pieces of basalt littered over the country. Maybe I'm more unstable than the mental health patient I fell in love with. I don't think it matters anymore, which side of the line we walk, now that Lucas and I have decided to try to walk together.

There are some places, though, we can only go alone. Lucas now has permits to enter the Boundary Waters and sometimes he'll disappear for a few days or even a few weeks at a time. The Forest Service rangers took down the Blackthorns' burrow and removed any trace of their habitation, but I don't know if Lucas even returns there when he paddles or snowshoes in. He never tells me when he's leaving. I'll wake up in the morning and his side of the bed will be empty, as if he never existed. I imagine he goes to the lake, the lake we don't paddle through, where something of Josiah maybe still lingers. And I let him leave, accepting every little abandonment as my penance, because there are places I have to endure alone, too.

He'd been so busy breaking camp that morning, packing what we needed and planning the details of our journey, consumed by the hope that his father might be able to recover if we found help fast enough. Neither of us knew when Josiah stole the knife—we'd confirmed the details of the morning to the authorities and to each other—but what I never told anyone was that I saw it later. As we loaded Josiah into the canoe and I tucked the blankets and sleeping bags around his frail body, I caught sight of Harry's gift clutched in Josiah's hand. All the disarming techniques from Congdon flew through my fevered brain and even with an infection storming inside my body I knew I could overpower him, but I didn't. I did nothing. I crouched over him as he jerked the blade under the cover of the blankets and we stared at each other, the sick and the dying, until he gave me a weak nod.

"You take care of each other," he whispered and we both looked at Lucas's back as he tested the connection between the canoes, making sure he could keep his father close and protected. With shaking fingers, I tucked the blanket loosely over the knife he'd concealed, and laid my hand on top of it, blessing it, giving him the permission his son never could.

"Take care of my mom."

He gave me a dark, watery smile, accepting the price of my silence.

ACKNOWLEDGMENTS

Finding Josiah Blackthorn was easy compared to finding my way through this book. I could never have imagined the Blackthorns without hearing the incredible stories of the Lykovs and the Ho Vans, and I will always be grateful to Patty Loew for pointing me in the right direction. Thank you to Angela Mejia for her wonderful knowledge of and love for Duluth. Thank you to Tara and Andrew Griffin for their medical expertise and preference for liver punctures. I'm grateful for my fellow Boundary Waters voyagers, Amy Anderson and Michelle Thorsness, who hang a mean bear bag and understand the importance of wine. Thank you to Virginia, Steve, and Kathleen at the Spirit of the Wilderness outfitters for all their Boundary Waters and Ely wisdom. Thank you, Sean Montgomery, for getting tased and telling me all about it. Thank you to Philip Mejia, who knows the best way to sabotage cars, and to Sergeant Brandon Howard, who knows the best way to take down a suspect.

For their endless support and encouragement, thank you to Tom, Linda, Mya, Liz, Marc, Kristen, Nick, Melonie, Doc, and Godo.

I'm indebted to the research and subject matter authority I found in *Lake Superior Rocks & Minerals* by Bob Lynch and Dan R. Lynch, *A Year in the Wilderness: Bearing Witness in the Boundary Waters* by Amy and Dave Freeman, *Assessment in Speech-Language Pathology* (3rd Ed) by Kenneth G. Shipley and Julie G. McAfee, and Julius F. Wolff Jr.'s *Lake Superior Shipwrecks*. I must also thank the Loft Literary Center, in whose writing studios part of this novel was born.

This book would not have found its way into the world without The Gernert Company and Emily Bestler Books. Thank you to Stephanie Cabot, my incredibly generous and visionary agent, as well as Ellen, Will, Anna, and the whole Gernert team. Thanks are simply not enough for Emily Bestler, who saw past what I was writing and guided this book back to its Northwoods home, and I'm forever grateful for the hard work of Lara, David, and everyone who creates the Emily Bestler Books magic. I would be remiss if I didn't also thank Jane Wood and Therese Keating at Quercus for their invaluable feedback through multiple revisions.

Finally, at the heart of it all is Rory, who said she'd follow me into a house. She'd follow me into the wilderness. Wherever I was, she wanted to be. Rest easy, little girl. We aren't burying any bodies yet.